THE
VISITOR

ALSO BY K.L. SLATER

Safe with Me
Blink
Liar
The Mistake

THE VISITOR

K.L. SLATER

bookouture

Published by Bookouture in 2018

An imprint of StoryFire Ltd.

Carmelite House
50 Victoria Embankment
London EC4Y 0DZ

www.bookouture.com

ISBN: 978-1-78681-375-6
eBook ISBN: 978-1-78681-374-9

This book is a work of fiction. Names, characters, businesses,
organizations, places and events other than those clearly in the
public domain, are either the product of the author's imagination
or are used fictitiously. Any resemblance to actual persons, living or
dead, events or locales is entirely coincidental.

PROLOGUE

In my experience, it starts because you want to be a better you.

You start out by striving to be someone else – the perfect version of you – and then, before you know it, you're acting like someone else altogether.

If you do a really good job, it's amazing how the people around you will start believing in the person who isn't really you.

Once the process has started, it's difficult to back out. It's so much harder to hold your hands up and tell the truth than to just let it play out and see where things go.

After all, you're not doing anything *wrong*. You're just trying to make a better life for yourself... and who can blame you for that?

So, it starts with an opportunity. Meeting the right person is crucial.

I'm lucky. I'm the kind of person who learns from my mistakes.

Sadly, I know only too well where the pitfalls are... I have to live with them every day.

I think I have a pretty good handle on how to meet the right sort of person now, and that's why I chose her.

I started by just watching. And listening. It was innocent enough, at least in the beginning.

Yet things that start well can sometimes start to slide, very slowly, and before you know it, you're out of control. So you must take it easy.

It takes time to build that momentum. Sometimes, you hardly notice it's happening.

You think everything is going well, and then by the time you realise, it's too late. The damage is done.

If people just do what they say they'll do, everything can turn out fine.

But of course, most people do what *they* want to do.

Always selfish. Always far more interested in their own lives.

And before long, the person you've tried to do your best for, put all your trust in… that person will betray you. Just like all the others.

Then you've no choice but to stop them in any way you can.

That's what happened last time, you see. So I made a promise to myself, which I fully intend to keep.

This time, I'll do things differently.

This time, no matter what it costs, I'll do it right.

CHAPTER 1

David

Mr Brown at number 11 is in his front garden again.

This is something of an anomaly for a Tuesday morning, when a) he would usually be at work, and b) he mowed the lawn just two days ago.

I reach for my Rolodex rotary file system. It's an original, a vintage model that I purchased from eBay for a considerable sum. Like my fountain pens and wax seals, it has that certain something that new technology simply lacks. Spreadsheets and databases can't compare with the pungent permanence of real ink or the assurance of thick, textured paper under one's fingertips.

I pull the Rolodex across the table towards me and open it at one of the three yellowed cards I've filed under the letter B.

I select my green fountain pen and make a note that Mr Brown has purchased a new orange Flymo lawnmower. It's one of the less expensive models, the sort that doesn't pick up after itself by collecting the cut grass, but that isn't really surprising. When I scan my earlier entries, I'm reminded that last summer, Mr Brown got rid of his failing fancy gas barbecue and bought a bog-standard coals version.

Also, the rusting wrought-iron bench on the small patio has been replaced with a cheap plastic version. Mrs Brown often sits out there alone and in all weathers, staring for long minutes at the dark cracked concrete under her bare feet.

I completely missed the signs last time, but I don't intend to make the same mistake again.

My attention is brought back to the window.

Mr Brown tugs the mower this way and that, employing a most unsatisfactory method that I feel sure will only serve to churn up the lawn and possibly cause irreparable damage.

I imagine exchanging my slippers for shoes and popping over there to warn him, but as usual, it is only a brief digression. I'm better off staying here, in the safety of my bedroom.

Mr Brown will most likely not appreciate my proffered advice one bit, and besides, how can I tell him I've been observing him from my bedroom window?

A quick viewing through the multi-zooms that Mother gifted me last Christmas – they arrived in a box with the tagline *The World's Most Powerful Binoculars* – confirms Mr Brown's furrowed brow and set jaw. He certainly doesn't look in the best of moods; he looks rather like a man with the weight of the world on his shoulders.

No surprise there.

I replace the cap on the green pen and pick up the red, the colour I've designated to signify an ongoing query in my notes.

MONEY PROBLEMS?

I print the letters neatly, underlining the query for good measure.

I'll need to continue to keep a close eye on Mr Brown for obvious reasons. When people become worried about money, I know only too well how they can swiftly turn to desperate measures.

'David!' Mother calls from the bottom of the stairs. 'Do you want sliced tomatoes in your ham and cheese sandwich, love?'

'Please, Mum.'

I'm about to add that I quite fancy a bag of cheese and onion crisps too, but movement to the bottom left of the window distracts me.

It's Mrs Barrett at number 7, bent almost double and sweeping her back doorstep. Our house, number 9, sits on the curve of the crescent, so when I look down to the left, I'm afforded a view of the whole of Mrs Barrett's yard, including the back door, as I am number 11, the Browns' residence, and a few houses either side.

The house is far too big for her now and must be rather a handful to manage. I thought she might sell up when Mr Barrett died; in fact, I'd already begun to fret who might come to live there if she moved on.

'People react differently when a loved one dies, David,' Mother remarked. 'Some are compelled to escape the memories as soon as they can, while others can't imagine ever leaving them behind.'

It seems Mrs Barrett has turned out to be one of those sorts of people who just stay put until it's their turn to go.

I tap lightly on the glass but she doesn't look up.

Over the last two years, I've done various odd jobs around the house for her, simple things like carrying heavy items upstairs or weeding the borders. I was just about able to manage that, despite the effort it took to leave my room. To her credit, Mrs Barrett has always been so very grateful.

When I started to feel a little better, I got my part-time job and finally plucked up the courage to take the bus every day. Sadly, I found it nigh-on impossible to visit Mrs Barrett several times a week like before, due to time constraints.

I make a mental note to pop next door again sometime soon. Yet as soon as the thought forms in my mind, my breathing turns shallow.

I expect it's because I've had a difficult few weeks. There's no particular reason for me feeling so unsettled, nothing specific I'm able to put my finger on, but then again, there rarely is. It's just the usual stuff, emotions rising up inside and trying to spill out… just when I feel sure I've buried them good and deep.

Mother tries everything to bring me round.

Fancy a walk to the shops with me, David?

Would you mind just taking the bins out?

She means well, of course, but nothing she says can ever get through the impenetrable wall of fear that has installed itself in the forefront of my mind. Just when I think I'm over what happened, it seems to appear again, with a vengeance.

I cope OK with going to work, providing I'm able to follow all the necessary steps in the order I need to. It's the unexpected and the out-of-the-ordinary that brings me out in a cold sweat, and that's what I must strive to avoid.

This is why I know it's so much better to stay home and adhere to my routine, rather than try and offer advice to Mr Brown about his mowing method.

To put things into perspective, I turned forty years old three months ago. I weigh just over fourteen stone and stand a shade above six foot tall.

That considered, it figures that it doesn't look too good to others when you are a strapping man but are afraid of the dark. It doesn't *feel* good when you dare not venture out alone at night.

I learned from my father's fists quite young that real men don't quake, don't cry, don't shake at the thought of leaving the house.

Real men aren't kept awake in the early hours by a raft of terrible memories; they give themselves a shake and simply learn to get over whatever troubles them.

I try my best to keep busy. I try to keep the people around me safe, so they'll never have to feel the fear. And most importantly, I try very hard to stay in the shadows and make sure that nobody else can spot my failings.

It's a life of sorts, but I often wonder if I'll ever move on from here. Living with my mother, doing the same thing day after day. I wonder if anything will ever change.

I don't honestly see how it can.

CHAPTER 2

David

I don't think anything of the banging noise downstairs until I get down and see that Brian Buckley is sitting in my armchair.

Brian is Mother's friend. At least that's what she likes to call him.

He calls out when I appear in the living room doorway.

'Raise the flags, Pat. Dave's out of his bedroom,' he roars, in his broad Barnsley accent.

I ignore him and sit down on the sofa. It's the seat nearest the window and, therefore, the furthest I can physically get away from Brian.

'Here are your sandwiches, love,' Mother says. I'm pleased to see she has given me crisps.

'Thanks, Mum.'

I take the tray and check that the crisps aren't touching the bread. I try to imagine that Brian isn't here and take a sip of tea, placing it down on the coaster by my foot.

'Now then.' Brian's mouth is full of masticated bread. 'What's happening in Dave's world?'

'He's been working all morning, haven't you, love?' Mum chips in.

'Working, eh?' Brian chuckles to himself. 'Working on what, exactly?'

I pop a crisp into my mouth and chew it thoughtfully without replying.

'David?' Mum gives me a nudge.

'I've been collating information.'

'*Collating*, you say?' Brian shakes his head. 'He needs a proper job, Pat. I've told you, I made a lot of contacts in the building trade. Could hardly fail to with forty-five years under my belt, out on site.'

Mother nods. 'You were always such a hard worker, Brian.'

She's known him since school. She was friends with his wife, Carol, before she died two years ago. Mother and I went to the funeral, and when the coffin finally glided through the curtains, Brian threw himself dramatically to the floor, sobbing into the dusty pews.

His grief didn't stop him asking Mother out a week later, though.

'What I'm trying to say, David...' Brian pauses for so long, I'm forced to look up from my plate, 'is that I could probably find you a job on a decent building site, not too far from home.'

Mother blinks.

'That's kind of you, Brian, but... well, I'm not entirely sure our David would do well in that kind of environment.'

'*What* kind of environment? You mean long hours, fresh air and plenty of good strong builder's tea? It might even put some hairs on his chest.' Brian scowls. 'Have you thought about *that*?'

I stare at my plate. I watched a television programme only last week about the new breed of modern man. Apparently he plucks his eyebrows, sticks to a skin-care regime and even waxes his chest hairs. But I decide not to mention this to Brian.

'So.' Brian pushes away his plate. 'Are you going to tell him, Pat, or shall I?'

Mother coughs. She seems to be steeling herself to say something. 'David... Brian and I, we wanted to have a word with you, love.'

I swallow a piece of half-chewed sandwich and watch as her face visibly pales. She looks at Brian, whose own fat cheeks are ruddy with pleasure, and he nods in apparent encouragement.

'The thing is… Brian, well he's…'

'I'm moving in,' Brian says bluntly.

My mouth starts up its chewing action again. With no actual food in there, it feels odd and only serves to increase the fluttering sensation in my chest.

Mother shifts closer to me.

'You know that me and Brian have known each other for a long time now; many years, in fact. I mean, it's not as if we've just met.'

'No need to justify our decision, Pat.' Brian frowns.

But Mother babbles on. 'I mean, obviously we both used to be with someone else, but sadly… Well, it's our time now. And as you know, Brian already spends a lot of time here.'

Too much time.

'No sense at all in paying two lots of rent and council tax,' Brian adds. 'And all the other bills as well.'

If Brian is giving up his one-bedroom rented council flat, then so far as I can tell, he'll be the one largely benefiting from the savings.

I stand up and my plate slides off my knees onto the floor. The remaining bit of uneaten sandwich flops onto the carpet and the crisps flutter down like dry autumn leaves. I feel sick and I can't bring myself to pick them up.

'David? I hope you're not going to take this badly.'

I don't answer her and I don't look at Brian. I just keep walking until I reach the bottom of the stairs.

'David!' I hear Mother plead. 'Can't you at least be a little bit happy for us?'

'Leave him be, Pat,' Brian says as I begin to climb the stairs. 'It doesn't matter what *he* thinks. He's had it far too easy for far too long, and now I'm here, he'd better look sharp. Things are about to get a bit tougher for Mummy's boy.'

Back in my room, I perch on the edge of the bed and rest my head in my hands.

Brian… living *here* with me and Mother? This is surely all my nightmares rolled into one. I can't really imagine it. Can't bear to even think about it.

Yet there is nothing I can do to actually stop it.

I feel a sharp twist inside, as if a thin serrated blade has lodged itself underneath my ribcage. It's twisting and turning, hollowing out my innards.

I wish I had the courage to leave home and get my own place.

A column of blazing heat tunnels its way up through the middle of my torso. But this time it's not because Brian is moving in.

I spend a lot of hours lying on this bed, dreaming of a future I'm sure I'll never touch.

I often imagine myself on some sort of adventure. Walking the Great Wall of China with like-minded people, or perhaps taking photographs of New York from the very top of the Empire State Building. Maybe the odd selfie or two with someone special.

Of course they are just dreams, and afterwards they always seem too adventurous and completely out of my grasp. Yet these are not fantasy worlds; they are places that ordinary people successfully visit all the time. That tells me it can be done.

Other times, I think about getting a different job. Perhaps in a busy office in Nottingham city centre. I enjoy my current part-time job, but this would make more use of my organisational skills and my natural aptitude with numbers.

I'd spend my lunch hour chatting with colleagues or taking a brisk walk around Market Square for the fresh air. Then, at the end of the working day, I'd make my way home on the tram to my nice neat little flat in a leafy suburb. My very own calm oasis, just outside the city.

Lots of people have this kind of life. They're always complaining about it, too; I've heard customers at the shop, people on the bus… nobody seems happy with their lot.

Brian moving in wouldn't matter if I had my own place.

I know only too well that if I was to seriously formulate any real plans, well, that's when my heart would start up like a frenzied jackhammer, and before long I'd get that awful feeling… like I'm about to throw up at any second.

I'm a prisoner in my own head. Worse still, on days like today, it feels like nothing will ever change and I'll be trapped here forever.

The heat inside is for myself. Sometimes I wish I could just self-combust.

CHAPTER 3

David

Mother shakes me out of my melancholy.

'Fancy a cup of tea and a biscuit, love?' Her voice floats upstairs.

I don't answer. If I stay quiet, she'll go away; she always does.

At that moment, I hear a scraping noise outside. I move over to the window and press my face close to the glass to get the right angle.

I can see a young woman down there. In Mrs Barrett's yard.

She potters around, staying close to the back door, which makes it quite difficult to see her from my current position. I twist the handle and push the side window slightly ajar.

I take a step back, in case she suddenly looks up at the glass, but then relax a little when I see she seems fully absorbed in her task. She's stuffing clothes, or something similar, into a large black garbage bag.

Mother and I have lived adjacent to Mrs Barrett for more years than I care to mention. To my knowledge, she doesn't have any adult children, and in all the years I've known her, she has never so much as had guests to stay over for a night or two.

Keeping slightly back from the glass, I focus in on the visitor. I am pleasantly surprised.

It is unusual, these days, to find a young woman with a preference for plain, modest clothing and minimal make-up. She is of slim build, with shoulder-length brown hair, and seems purposeful, with a pleasing economy of movement. I can't help noticing she has dainty hands, which appear to like keeping busy.

At least that's the impression she gives as I watch her through my binoculars.

So far, I've only seen her from behind and in profile. It proves difficult to study all her features in detail when her hair keeps falling over her face like a dark caramel-coloured curtain.

Something about her reminds me of someone.

Quite unexpectedly, she straightens up, pushes flat palms into the bottom of her back and shakes the hair from her face. A pert nose, full lips and astonishingly dark eyes and brows reveal themselves.

Using the back of her hand, she briskly wipes her forehead and looks down the long, narrow yard. She sighs, her small breasts rising and falling beneath a silky biscuit-coloured blouse.

I swallow hard and lower the binoculars, stepping back into the room until I'm well away from the window.

I take a couple of deep breaths and close my eyes.

I don't have to feel bad about this, I tell myself calmly. I'm doing absolutely nothing wrong.

I lay down the binoculars and walk slowly downstairs.

Strains of a televised football match emanate from the lounge as I enter the kitchen. Mother stands washing dishes at the sink.

'Ah, there you are, David.' She lifts out her sud-covered fingers for a moment or two and looks at me, her sharp, avian eyes narrowing at my expression. 'Are you feeling all right?'

'Yes, I'm fine,' I say faintly.

'I called up earlier and asked if you'd like a cup of tea. I've bought your favourite arrowroot biscuits from—'

'Have you spoken to Mrs Barrett lately?' I cut in.

'Mrs Barrett? I'm afraid not.' She turns back to the sink. 'I really ought to pop round there at some point. Perhaps you might come with me, David.' And then her hands stop moving in the sink and she turns round again to face me. 'Why do you ask?'

'It looks like she might have a visitor. She hasn't got any grown-up children, has she?'

To avoid Mother's incisive glare I pick up Brian's tabloid newspaper from the counter and stare blindly at the front page.

Mother coughs.

'No. No, she hasn't got any family, though I don't think it was through choice. She once told me it was a regret of hers but something she had just learned to accept.'

'It might be her niece, then,' I offer.

'The visitor is a girl?'

'A young woman.' I nod. 'Quite a bit younger than me by the looks of it.'

'I see.' Mother swallows hard. 'There's... not going to be a problem, is there, David?'

I feel a rush of heat in my face but I say nothing.

'It wouldn't do for her to think you've been...'

'I was looking out of my window and she came outside, into the yard,' I say quickly. 'I was already looking. I didn't...'

'That's all right, then.' Mother is relieved. She pulls her hands out of the sink and flicks off the soapy bubbles. 'Well, perhaps Mrs Barrett's taken in a lodger. That house is far too much for her to manage now.'

'Yes. Perhaps that's it.' I step back into the gloom of the hallway. 'I thought I might go round there now and ask Mrs Barrett if she needs any help... ask her if there are any odd jobs that need doing. It's been a while.'

Mother opens her mouth as if to comment, but then closes it again.

*

In the event, I don't go to Mrs Barrett's house. Instead, I go back up to my bedroom and stand at the edge of the window.

It's important to consider the situation logically.

I don't know who this person, this visitor of Mrs Barrett's, might be. I can hardly go blustering round there offering my help. I don't want to make a fool of myself.

Besides, I'm wearing my old checked slippers and my comfy cardie with the worn cuffs and missing buttons.

First impressions are very important; everyone knows that.

The young woman is no longer in the yard, but the bag full of clothing is still out there, gaping open like an abandoned coal sack. I hope this means she'll be coming outside again before too long. Wind and rain are forecast for this evening, so if she leaves it there, the contents will doubtless get wet and scattered all over the yard.

While I wait for her to reappear, I pluck out a blank card from the Rolodex and fiddle with the settings on my camera.

About ten minutes later, my patience is rewarded when the young woman appears and proceeds to tie up the bag, before walking halfway down the yard to the bin and dumping it in there.

She's wearing a brown wool cardigan now, which she pulls closed across her body as she returns to the house. She doesn't pause, doesn't look around, and within seconds, she is back inside. I hear the door close behind her.

Although I'm a little disappointed, it doesn't matter. I have what I wanted.

Using my powerful zoom lens, I've managed to get some nicely detailed images with the camera.

I flip out the small memory card and pop it into the side of my laptop. While it loads, I pull out the old grey suitcase from under my bed and begin to search through the photographs.

CHAPTER 4

Holly

Holly Newman stood at the window of Mrs Barrett's kitchen and filled the kettle for the umpteenth time since she'd arrived.

It felt so strange, being in the area again. Especially since nothing seemed to have changed around here at all in over ten years.

Take this very crescent, for instance. The mostly detached houses, built in the sixties, stood proudly on their modest plots. Small front gardens led to longer, narrow yards at the back.

Aside from the odd neat porch, and the ostentatious white Grecian pillars that the people at the end had added, the facades were unchanged.

Holly used to pass by here on her way home from school when she travelled to college each day. The third house in still had a front garden full of gaudy and, Holly had always thought, rather sinister-looking gnomes.

National newspaper headlines constantly screamed of local corner shops shutting down in favour of the sprawling superstores that seemed to be springing up everywhere, but here, at the top of Baker Crescent, it was a different story.

Fred Crawley the butcher, Mr Timpson the greengrocer, and Mr and Mrs Khan's general store, complete with its small integral post office, all stood in a line. Immovable as ever.

Holly had been just eighteen years old when she'd left the area for the bright lights of Manchester and the 'amazing opportunity' she'd been persuaded to chase. What she'd give now to rewind *that* decision.

She sighed and flicked the switch on the kettle, listening to the faint hiss of the element.

In effect, she was right back where she'd started. But she refused to think of it like that. Being back here now signified something else: that she'd drawn a line under everything that had gone before. Everything she had endured.

Holly had left behind the people she prayed she'd never have to see face to face again… all but one, anyway. She yearned to see him, the love of her life, more than anyone, but she had no choice but to bide her time.

She had emerged from hell itself and was ready to start again. And this time, she would make it work.

There was no definite plan as yet, but she could feel the determination drumming at her very core.

She cast her mind back to twelve years earlier, when she'd left school. Wollaton Secondary Modern – they'd changed the name now – was only about half a mile away from here. She had achieved moderate grades, which was a wonder, considering.

The thing that loomed largest in her memory was the enormous relief she'd felt as she'd walked out of those crummy peeling iron gates for the last time. It had been a welcome change from the crushing sense of dread she'd suffered every single morning of her schooldays. The prospect of the long, miserable day that stretched ahead of her.

On her last day, she'd watched with amusement as the squealing knots of girls in her year cried, hugging each other, lamenting the end of their time together.

Strains of their shallow promises had reached her ears as she drew closer. How they were all going to *stay in touch*, how they would *always be friends* no matter where in the world they ended up. And of course, they'd already planned to meet soon to catch up.

Life wasn't like that. Holly knew.

People soon forgot you. They often said good things would happen that never did.

There existed a parallel universe to the soaps and feel-good programmes on television. An everyday reality where bills didn't get paid, electricity was cut off and kids went to bed hungry most nights, hoping against hope that nobody would come into their bedroom to hurt them.

Lots of the girls who had been breaking their hearts out in the school yard had come from indulgent homes. They had enjoyed being the apple of the eye of parents who were still married.

It had been a state school, so not many of them knew real wealth. But Holly recognised that those girls had been rich in other things. The belief of parents and teachers that they could and would do well in life. Food in the cupboards at home. A clean, fashionable uniform that wasn't third-hand or frayed at the hem.

Those girls had been able to believe their own hype so completely because they'd been shielded from reality. They hadn't known yet just how shitty life could be.

Holly had never seen any of them hanging around the small park across from the school. This was the place where she'd usually sit at the end of each day, after the library closed. Sometimes she'd stay there for hours, until it was impossible to delay going home.

But on that last day, the library had been closing early to mark the end of the summer term, and the park was flooded with rampaging, drunken students trying to prolong their student days.

She decided she'd just have to keep out of Uncle Keith's way until her aunt got back from her cleaning job.

Nobody had asked Holly to sign their shirt or blouse as she shuffled slowly towards the exit, making her way alone through the excited throng of people. If they'd asked, she'd have refused anyway. It was all so two-faced. Half of the hugging girls she'd walked past had done nothing but bicker behind each other's backs over the past year.

They thought they were sad to be leaving their friends and teachers, but Holly had known that really they were grieving the end of their little empires. They had been secretly gutted that they'd no longer be in a place where they were empowered to bully those they perceived to be different to them. Where they'd been able to make people's lives – people like Holly – an utter misery.

She'd smiled to herself as she reached the gates and allowed herself a moment or two to look back at the building and the other leavers.

Good luck to them in their mind-numbing jobs, which were the only option they'd be able to secure without any qualifications. Hopefully they would find themselves at the other end of the scale. *They'd* be the ones who didn't fit in and were at the mercy of the people in control.

Karma was a marvellous thing, Holly had thought.

'Hey! Wait up.'

She'd turned at the sound of a voice calling behind her.

It had been Markus, of course. There was no one else.

'You don't want to wait for me? That is OK,' he grinned as he pushed through the crowd towards her. 'I will catch up with you anyway.'

Markus spoke excellent English but had still retained a discernible trace of his native German accent. He knew what it meant to be an outsider here too.

They had been in the same maths and history groups during the last two years of school and had gravitated to sitting together against the never-ending spit balls thrown from the back of the classroom.

Holly had suffered because she wasn't with the in-crowd and Markus because he was German, gay and fostered. 'I am what is commonly known as *a triple threat*,' he'd joke.

Now he looked around the school yard.

'You and I, we are the only ones alone here, it seems.' He indicated the thick rope of celebrating students that snaked around the quadrangle without ever seeming to near the exit gates.

'Oh, I'm used to it now.' Holly shrugged.

'Ah, but you see, now we are not so alone. We are together. Which is better, yes?'

She nodded and smiled at him. 'Suppose so, yeah.'

'What exciting life awaits you, Holly, when you walk through these iron gates of hell one last time?'

'Oh, you know,' she said airily. 'Film star, supermodel, brain surgeon… haven't really decided yet.'

He nudged her. 'Come on!'

'I've honestly got no idea.' She grinned. 'I just want to get as far away from this place as I possibly can, and soon. But I have to find somewhere to go first. A new home, new start. Easier said than done, isn't it? In the meantime, I'm going to college to get some secretarial skills under my belt.'

'Well, *I* am going to make some money,' he said, all at once serious. 'Lots of money.'

'Oh yeah, doing what?'

'Hmm, this is just one small detail I've yet to decide.' He shrugged. 'See you around then, I guess?'

She'd left his question unanswered as together they walked out of the gates, finally leaving behind the all-consuming misery that had been secondary school.

Although Holly hadn't known it then, far from escaping the torture of the classroom, she had just taken her first step on a journey that would lead her to a far worse fate.

CHAPTER 5

Holly

Holly was to sleep in the second bedroom of Mrs Barrett's three-bedroomed house, but it was still a good size. There was a double divan bed in there, and a rather dated mahogany wardrobe and cumbersome chest of drawers, but still, there was plenty of room for one person. Mrs Barrett said that in all the years she and her late husband had lived in the house, the second bedroom had barely been slept in.

Upon her arrival, Holly had lugged up a couple of medium-sized packing boxes, a rucksack and a small, scuffed case containing all her worldly goods, but she hadn't got round to unpacking any of it yet.

It wasn't much to show for the ten years she'd been away, supposedly making a bright, sparkly future for herself. The mere thought of some of the stuff she'd had to face made her want to drown her sorrows in the litre bottle of wine currently buried under her meagre collection of mismatched underwear.

Yet for now, her past problems were being overshadowed by her present-day predicament.

Overdue credit card bills, an unsatisfied county court judgement and a stack of unopened communications from a long list of creditors was just for starters.

Her only saving grace was that it was a well-known fact that it took credit and collection agencies a while to catch up with people when they moved house. And hopefully, she'd managed to make it doubly difficult for them.

There was also the problem of how she would ever find Geraldine again, now she was eighty miles away from Manchester. If it nearly killed her in the process, she would find a way to do it. And when the moment came, she would reclaim what was rightfully hers.

Holly squeezed her eyes closed against the menacing thoughts that threatened her new positive state of mind. Dr Freeman had warned her, trained her to spot bad thoughts and nip them in the bud before they could drag her down again.

The last eighteen months, in particular, had been a very difficult time. This period had included her very darkest hours. Times when she had quite honestly been a mere whisker away from ending it all.

It had been a chance remark from a fellow patient that had changed all that. Her words, over a shared cup of coffee, had been: 'Don't you just wish you could rewind it all and start over again?'

That simple question had somehow struck a chord with Holly and forged a way through the darkness where all the therapists and doctors could not. After that, she had never taken her eye off the faint light at the end of the tunnel as it grew steadily stronger, day by painful day.

On a brighter note, since making the final decision to come back to Nottingham, she had invested hundreds of hours planning and visualising – had taken on board everything the numerous self-help books she'd read had suggested – in order to give herself the best chance of succeeding in getting her life back on track.

Only then, when she felt grounded and secure again, would she be ready to do whatever was necessary to retrieve what was rightly hers.

The kettle clicked and she made the tea, feeling both determined and resolved that she would never let anything or anyone use or ruin her again.

She carried the tea through to the front room on a small decorative tray.

'Thank you, dear.' Cora Barrett reached eagerly for the china cup and saucer, her third of the afternoon. 'Do you know, I feel quite spoiled. You're an angel. Truly.'

Holly smiled, sitting down on the sofa, cradling her own small mug. '*You're* the angel, Mrs Barrett, for letting me stay here for a while. For giving me the benefit of the doubt.'

'How many times do I have to tell you… it's Cora!' the woman gently scolded. 'If we are to be good friends, then I have to insist that you call me by my first name.'

'Point taken.' Holly smiled. 'I'm very grateful to you, *Cora*, is what I wanted to say.'

'Absolutely nothing to be grateful for,' Cora said firmly. 'Our meeting outside the post office was pure serendipity; in my book, it was a clear sign that you coming here was meant to be. It was perfectly obvious to me that you were a nice girl.'

Holly winced at her kind words, doubting that was the case at all.

It had been just over a week ago. Holly had been back in Nottingham for a matter of hours and had been trying to cash a cheque at the post office inside the Khans' corner shop, but they'd insisted she hadn't got the correct ID required for the transaction.

'But I haven't got a passport or a driving licence! It's only for twenty pounds, for God's sake,' Holly had pleaded. 'And I really, really need the cash.'

Customers behind her in the queue had shuffled and muttered. When she turned around to glare at them, she saw an odd mixture of pity and judgement in their expressions.

But the sour-faced old hag behind the counter wouldn't budge an inch and a humiliated Holly had been forced to walk past the short queue to the door.

Outside, she'd leaned against the wall sobbing, the strength in her legs and resolve in her heart finally dissolving. To her, it had felt like the end of the world.

That was when she'd felt a firm hand on her shoulder and heard a concerned voice.

'It can't be that bad, dear, surely?' She had opened her eyes to see an elegant older lady studying her inquisitively. 'Fancy a nice cup of tea in the café?'

Despite her embarrassment, Holly had nodded and followed Cora to the small café at the end of the road. As they'd entered, the smell of freshly baked scones and fragrant brewed coffee instantly soothed her frayed nerves.

They had chatted over lattes for what seemed like hours, and Holly ended up telling Cora rather more about her problems than she'd initially intended. Once she started, she found she simply couldn't stop. The relief had been enormous.

And now here she was, a guest in Cora's home. Markus used to swear by harnessing the law of attraction to manifest one's dreams, and finally, after ten long years, it seemed to Holly she might just have the hang of it.

'It's such a treat to have a nicely mannered young woman for company. I had the measure of you instantly that day, and finding out you grew up near here was the icing on the cake. Your good nature shone through, my dear.' Cora looked towards the pale spring light that filtered softly in through the living room window. 'Since Harold passed, it's easy for me to go a day or so… sometimes longer, without speaking to another soul.'

'I'm sorry,' Holly said quietly. 'That must be awful.'

'Now, now, ignore me. We really mustn't fall into the doldrums.' Cora sat up a little straighter, her cup rattling in its saucer.

'I might appear to be a defenceless old bat, but I can look after myself, you know. The way I see it, I've no choice but to do so. You'll never catch me moping around for long, and despite the tough time you've been through, I suggest you avoid it too.'

That was what she'd chosen to tell Cora: she'd been to Manchester and had a very *tough time*. Cora had reacted kindly, sympathised completely. If she'd known what had really happened, Holly knew she wouldn't have slept at night.

'I agree. I've no intention of moping around,' Holly told her. 'In fact, I've been thinking that I might pop into town tomorrow and register with a couple of employment agencies. I've searched online and there doesn't seem to be much going in the permanent job market at the moment, but with a bit of luck, I might be able to pick up a temporary position.'

'That's what I like to see,' Cora said approvingly. 'A young person who is willing to put themselves out there and look for opportunities. That's what I kept telling my friend Pat next door.'

'Your friend was looking for work?'

'Oh no,' Cora laughed. 'It was her son, David. You see, something very… unpleasant happened to him a couple of years ago that affected him so badly he can't bear to go out after dark, even now. I kept telling his mother at the time that he should get himself out there and find the opportunities for himself. They never just drop into your lap.'

'Sounds awful.' Holly took another sip of her tea.

'Oh, it was. He was out of work for some time, but I'm pleased to say he's all sorted now. It's a shame he has to put up with that horrible man, Brian. His mother's *friend*, you see.' Her lips pursed in disapproval. 'David dislikes him intensely and I admit, he's a very difficult man to warm to.' She paused a moment. 'I've known David since he was a small boy and I'm used to his ways now. He's a little bit… how should I put it…'

'Different?' Holly offered.

'*Different!* Cora repeated. 'That's it exactly, a very good word to describe David. But he's a kind person. He's done bits for me around the house, stuff I would've found very difficult to manage on my own.'

'Well, I'm here to help you now too.'

Cora nodded and smiled. 'Quite. And when you're ready, dear, you can take the new towels up to your bedroom and start to make yourself comfy. I think we're going to get along very well indeed.'

Holly beamed. 'Thanks again, Cora. I'll try not to be under your feet here for *too* long.'

'No need for that, dear, you've already thanked me a hundred times, and there's no rush to leave at all. You're welcome to stay for as long as you like. In fact, I sincerely hope you will.'

CHAPTER 6

Holly

After what seemed like an age, Holly made her bid to finally escape Cora's chatter.

She felt unkind thinking such a thing, but she couldn't simply sit around drinking tea and listening to Cora's life story day after day, as tempting as Cora obviously thought it was. It was time to face the contents of her meagre cases.

'I'd better go upstairs and get the unpacking out of the way,' she said, edging towards the door.

'That's a good idea.' Cora placed her cup and saucer on the coffee table and shuffled to the edge of her seat. 'I'll come up and help you.'

'No!' Holly said it too quickly, and Cora looked rather taken aback. 'What I mean is, it's very kind of you, Mrs Barr... *Cora*, but I won't have you wearing yourself out on my account.'

Cora opened her mouth to protest, but Holly shook her head.

'Honestly, I'd feel much better if you just stayed down here and enjoyed your tea. I'll be back before you know it and you can finish telling me about your lovely wedding day.'

'Fair enough, dear,' Cora said, placated. 'I admit that if I do too much, I probably *will* suffer with my lower back all evening.'

Upstairs in her room, Holly sighed and sank down onto the bed. There was no harm in taking just five minutes first to enjoy a bit of peace and quiet before she started on the onerous task that lay ahead.

It felt almost like she'd gone deaf, escaping Cora's endless litany about how she'd met her late husband, Harold, and then the riveting run-up to him proposing on Tower Bridge in London. The worrying thing was that Cora was only up to her early twenties in the timeline of her life. Goodness knows how many more hours of reminiscing it would take to bring Holly up to the present day.

Holly silently scolded herself. A thoughtful person wouldn't entertain such mocking thoughts. It wouldn't do her any harm to lend a friendly ear to a lonely lady who'd taken pity on her.

Poor Cora had obviously been starved of contact with other people since Harold's death and had stored up all her happy memories, having no one to share them with. It was clear that now Holly had arrived, the floodgates had been opened and they were all simply spilling out.

Was it *really* too much to ask of herself to take a more compassionate view?

If Holly wanted to stay here in Cora's home – and there was no doubt at all in her mind that she did – she would just have to learn to put up with her new friend's constant chatter and focus instead on being thankful for her kindness and hospitality.

Holly stared trance-like at the large picture window. A cool, stark brightness lit up the glass, although the inside of the room was still quite dark. It was mid March and the sun, in its higher position in the sky, seemed to be trying to stoke up a little heat and cheer but wasn't quite managing to sustain it.

When Holly closed her eyes, she could still see the glaring square of the window emblazoned on the dark canvas of her mind's eye, like the moment a camera flashes and captures a photograph.

The side window was slightly ajar, and a faint breeze crept in, tickling the surface of Holly's skin like a lingering shadow. It was too cool in here, and now rather draughty, too. She glanced around the room and noted there was no radiator.

Cora had already told her that she and her late husband had lived in the house all their married life and, like lots of elderly people, had never got around to installing central heating. Holly could understand that decision if money was scarce, but somehow she didn't think that was a problem for Cora Barrett.

She made a mental note to ask if there was a small heater she could use to warm up the room for an hour before she came to bed.

She sat up and shifted to the edge of the mattress. Maybe the cold was a blessing in disguise. If it had been warm and cosy in here, she could probably have come up with a hundred great excuses to put off the dreaded task of unpacking.

Her motley collection of luggage hunkered down against the opposite wall, almost daring her to gather the courage to begin. In an impulsive burst of action, she sprang across and grasped the straps of the ragged canvas rucksack that had accompanied her to half a dozen music festivals over the years.

She squeezed her eyes closed and then opened them again, ordering the memories back in their box. Now was not the time.

Thinking about music festivals was safe ground, but before she knew it, she'd be trying to work out how she could have made better decisions and stopped the whole horrendous business from happening.

Sadly, it just wasn't possible to wipe out the mistakes of the past. All she could do now was set things straight, however long that might take.

She would find a way to build a better future.

CHAPTER 7

Holly

As Holly tugged at the buckles of the rucksack, a small pile of trainers and shoes spilled out over the floor.

She paired them up and arranged them neatly on the bottom of the fusty-smelling old wardrobe.

Next, she took a deep breath and pulled the suitcase across. Layers of folded tops, cardigans, jeans and sweaters were revealed when she unzipped it and peeled back the canvas top.

She'd already dumped some of the clothing she'd brought with her in a bin bag out in Cora's back yard. The clothes had been old, but that wasn't the reason she'd discarded them. It had been because of the memories attached to them.

Day after dragging day, week after long week spent hidden away from the outside world at the clinic. The same pair of old black leggings and baggy grey sweater, worn like a second skin that had the power to protect her.

She bent down and began to unload the contents of her sparse wardrobe. Most of this stuff now bagged around her shoulders and bottom and gaped at the waist, but it hadn't always been like that. She could remember a time when her hip bones were undetectable beneath a padding of fat.

Her fingers quivered slightly in nervous anticipation at what lay beneath the garments.

She took her time, hanging the two pairs of trousers over the heavy wooden coat hangers that Mrs Barrett had kindly left for her use.

She laid her worn knitwear more carefully than required in the chest of drawers lined with faded floral paper that perhaps had once been scented. Now all she could smell was the distinctive unpleasant odour of camphor.

As she removed the garments, one by one, the horror of what lay beneath began to reveal itself.

Lots of envelopes, in different colours, shapes and sizes. Some opened, with their rucked contents shoved hastily back in, but most unopened, as if they had just slid through the letter box that morning.

Holly hastily gathered them together in an untidy pile, purposely refusing to look at them directly but side-glancing just enough to shuffle them into something that resembled a vague order.

She took out the brown folder that she'd filled with paperwork before she left Manchester. Reaching for an empty plastic carrier bag that had held the sandwich and drink she had purchased when she'd alighted from the train, she crammed all the envelopes and paperwork inside and tied a knot in the top, then stuffed the bag unceremoniously under the bed.

Her breathing felt rapid and shallow now and her hands were shaking a little as she remembered hiding from debt collectors as they hammered on the door of her tiny flat.

She leaned on the narrow windowsill and pressed her face close to the glass, feeling the now welcome chill of moving air against her cheek.

All the houses here on the crescent had sizeable gardens, most of them long and narrow. Mrs Barrett's seemed a little shorter than the others because of a dense cluster of mature bushes and trees at the bottom that gobbled up about a quarter of its length.

The gardens that flanked it were different, she noticed. The one on the right had a manicured lawn, a few bushes at the bottom and neat empty borders – no flowers. The one on the left featured a rather scruffy, patchy lawn. Its main purpose appeared to be to house a plastic slide and swing set and a paintbox-blue playhouse that was set on a patchwork of faded coloured slabs.

In fact, all the gardens were different from one another, each fitting a purpose for the family that lived there. There was a kind of order even to the shabbier yards. Holly supposed that without order, everything fell apart, and it was definitely time for her to impose some in her own life.

But she couldn't bear to open those letters yet, nor look through all the paperwork, which she knew would be laden with legal threats. Some part of her realised that she couldn't hide here forever, of course; it was unavoidable that judgement day would finally arrive.

For others, as well as herself.

By that time, she'd be fully prepared and ready to face the worst. She'd learned the hard way that it was far better to plough through life than to just let it happen to you.

It had been over a year after that last day at school that she'd set eyes on Markus again.

As she'd rushed to catch the bus to her secretarial course at college, a deep voice had called her name from across the road. The small queue of people in front of her had shuffled in anticipation, and she'd glanced the other way to see the bus approaching.

'Holly!'

She'd stopped walking and turned to see who had called to her, and Markus had waved.

The rumble of the bus behind her grew louder, but she ignored it. She liked Markus and they were well overdue for a catch-up. She'd managed to get to know a couple of girls at college who were also on her course, but they were just acquaintances rather than friends.

She had waited until Markus crossed the road. He seemed so much taller and broader than when she'd last set eyes on him. He wore his floppy fringe swept back now, and she thought how it suited him.

He'd dodged the traffic and taken a final leap onto the pavement, folding her into his muscular arms.

He seemed so pleased to see her, she found it quite disarming.

'It's been too long, Holly.' He was grinning. 'I want to know all about the exciting life you have been leading since leaving school.'

'Hmm.' Holly had twisted one side of her mouth up. 'Well, that should take all of about five seconds.'

'Same old dry sense of humour.' He'd squeezed her arm.

'What about you?' she'd ventured. 'Have you made your first million yet? Found Mr Right?'

'Ha! Let's just say I'm well on my way to both.' He'd glanced down the street towards the shops at the bottom. 'Do you have time for a coffee before you go? I have an opportunity to tell you about… You never know, you might be interested. Unless you're happy with your wonderful life now?'

'Yeah, right,' she'd muttered.

About to turn down his offer, she'd paused to think. She'd already missed the start of her first session at college, as the next bus wasn't due for twenty minutes. It was only Health and Safety anyway. Boring old Miss Newton droning on about office rules.

'I can spare an hour.' She had shrugged. 'But I'll have to share your drink, 'cos I've got no cash on me.'

'That's no problem, consider it my treat.' Markus had beamed, clearly delighted that she'd accepted his invitation.

CHAPTER 8

Holly

Holly stood up and walked over to the opposite side of the room.

She pushed one of the packing boxes with her foot. It shifted easily towards the bed, over the dreadful brown-and-orange-patterned carpet that had somehow managed to completely suck out any illusion of space in the room.

Sitting on the edge of the mattress again, she tore off the strips of masking tape and unfolded the flaps of the box.

Her hand froze as she stared at the first item.

The silver-framed photograph of Evan lay face up. Her eyes immediately prickled, turning the sun-kissed brown hair, the freckles and the pert nose that melted her heart into a soft blur.

She reached for it and held it against her chest, resting her chin on the top of the filigree frame while her tears fell unchecked.

Was he missing her the way she missed him?

She should have wrapped the photograph in a towel or something, packed it safely at the bottom of the box. But she remembered now that his picture had been the one thing she'd wanted to keep looking at right until the last moment before she left.

She could hardly bear to look at it, and yet she had found it impossible to set aside. He was the reason she would make a future here, so they could be together again.

She squeezed the hard metal frame closer to her, feeling the bite of sharp corners that dug into her soft flesh.

She applied more pressure. Wincing at the unforgiving metal and wishing for a moment that she could tear those responsible to pieces with it, but knowing full well that even that wouldn't go an inch towards repairing the harm they had done to her. To him. To their relationship.

She promised herself there and then that if ever she began to feel doubt or allowed the bad thoughts to take a hold, she'd look at that photograph, because it would give her the strength to carry on and the confidence that one day she and Evan could be together again.

She wouldn't allow anything to get in the way of that.

Ten years earlier, her aunt and uncle had tried to clip her wings when, after speaking to Markus, she'd decided to leave Nottingham for Manchester.

Of course, on reflection, she now very much wished she'd gone for another option, but hindsight was the perfect science when applied to anyone's life. And she'd never regretted getting away from the two of *them* at last, especially Uncle Keith.

'What do you mean, you're leaving home?' Aunt Susan had gasped, her mouth falling open as she stood in the doorway of Holly's poky bedroom. 'You can't go just like that. What about your college course?'

'I can, and I *am* going,' Holly had said simply, stuffing random pieces of clothing into a holdall. 'College was only a stopgap until I found a way of getting out of this dump.'

Her heartbeat had quickened when she'd heard the familiar sounds of her uncle labouring upstairs. Aunt Susan had looked back and shaken her head at the great lump when he finally reached the doorway.

'She's going, Keith! Leaving… after all we've done for her.'

'Is that your way of thanking us for taking you in?' he'd rasped, still out of breath from the short climb. 'When your useless mother drank herself to death, you were headed straight for the children's home… You've a short memory. You were glad enough to accept our hospitality then, weren't you, you little tart?'

'I've nothing to say to you.' Holly had glared at him and then softened her voice to address her aunt. 'Look, I'm sorry, Aunt Susan, but I need to get out of this place, get away from Nottingham. I've been offered the chance to make a fresh start in Manchester with my friend, and—'

'Manchester?' Keith had scoffed. 'What's Manchester got that you can't find here?'

'Well it hasn't got *you*, for starters,' she'd retorted.

'Holly! Don't you dare speak to him like—'

Holly had raised her hand. 'Save it, Aunt Susan. Don't make me go there.'

'Go where?' Keith had bristled, his flabby cheeks wobbling, magnifying the already outraged expression on his face. 'If you've something to say, then bloody well say it. I've nothing to hide.'

Holly had shaken her head and reached for her toiletries bag, tucking it inside an old grey rucksack.

'Holly, you're not being fair,' Susan had pressed her. 'It was an easy decision for me, you're my own flesh and blood, but Keith didn't have to take you in. He was so good about it, and now this…' she'd nodded to Holly's bags, '*this* is how you repay him?'

Holly had stopped packing at that point and looked up.

'Your husband is a slimy, creepy excuse for a man, Aunt Susan.'

'You little…' Keith had stepped forward, incoherent with indignation, but Holly had raised her voice above his garbled complaints.

'He walks in on me when I'm undressing before bed. He makes lewd comments about my knickers on the clothes dryer and he pushes up against me whenever he walks past me in the hallway.'

'She's a lying little bitch, Susan,' Keith had hissed, his face paling.

'Oh yes, and he watches porn DVDs in the living room when you're at work.' Holly had slipped on her denim jacket and grabbed both her bags. 'So don't tell me I'm lucky, because I can't wait to get away from the dirty pervert. I'm just sorry you've always chosen to turn a blind eye to it all, Aunt Susan.'

Both speechless, they'd parted at the doorway as Holly pushed through.

'Thanks,' she'd called as she bounded downstairs, glancing back at their incredulous faces. 'For nothing.'

Keith had started shouting then, but she hardly heard any of his insults as she darted out of the front door, leaving it wide open as a final act of defiance.

Freedom! The air had felt fresher, the ground firmer beneath her feet.

'Manchester, here I come,' she sang operatically in the street, and laughed out loud as she drew a frown from a passing dog walker.

When she'd arrived at the bus station, Markus had been waiting for her, looking just as bright and relieved as she was to be leaving. Together they'd boarded the coach and he had opened a miniature bottle of vodka, with which they'd toasted the city they were leaving behind.

'Bye, Nottingham, I won't be back.' Holly had taken a swig of the vodka, coughing as it bit the back of her throat. 'Onwards and upwards.'

'Onwards and upwards,' Markus had agreed as he finished the tiny measure.

And now, ten years later, here she was. Back in Nottingham again.

She had come full circle and managed to do it in the worst way possible.

CHAPTER 9

David

I push my plastic snack box, which Mother has packed to the brim with fruit and treats, into my small grey rucksack and leave the house.

After closing the door behind me, I stand for five seconds or so surveying the street. All seems quiet and safe, so I brace myself and set off down the short path to the wooden gate that leads out directly onto the pavement.

The bus stop is just a seven-minute walk from the house, and as I stride briskly up Baker Crescent towards the main road, I draw in a lungful of freezing air, relishing the burn of the late frost on the back of my throat.

As I pass the Browns' residence, I wonder if either of them is watching me from behind the curtains.

I once saw a news special about sniper killers in America. How their high-powered rifles can pick people off even from a fair distance away.

If someone shoots me in the back of the head now, there's nobody around to witness it. No Good Samaritan to call an ambulance. Theoretically, the killer could get away scot-free.

I pick up my pace but I don't run. I won't give *him* the satisfaction of thinking I'm in the least bit spooked.

Even though spring is just around the corner, this unusually cold weather always serves to remind me of Guy Fawkes Night. The scent of the bonfires from early November seems to linger in the early chill.

I detest the various bonfire celebrations that pepper the district at that time of year. The big organised event at nearby Wollaton Hall always brings hordes of families to the area.

It's not that I mind people having fun. In fact, I've often wondered what it might feel like to attend such an event, to stand in the open air with one's friends and watch the staggering light displays that split the sky. To enjoy a hot toddy, be relaxed and at ease… instead of watching the fireworks as I usually do from behind glass, alone at my bedroom window.

It always amazes me how readily people embrace these events, feeling comfortable and knowing exactly how to act. The very thought of it brings me out in a cold sweat.

Last year, I actually got as far as pulling on my quilted jacket and wellington boots. In the end, however, I couldn't quite muster the courage to go through with it.

'Get going, man,' Brian bellowed as I dithered at the door. 'You might find yourself a young filly, have some fun. You're not going to get any how's-your-father stuck up in that bedroom, that's for sure.'

The last thing I wanted was to *pick up a woman*, to use another of Brian's unfortunate phrases. After everything that had happened, I couldn't imagine ever having the confidence to do so again.

I shrugged off my outdoor clothing and marched back upstairs, leaving Brian's crude remarks hanging in the air behind me.

It was just the thought of all those anonymous bodies surrounding me, pushing up close. Personal space didn't exist when you were in the middle of a crowd, did it?

Theoretically, anyone could slip their hand into your pocket and relieve you of your wallet. A swift punch to the head could floor you, and you could end up trampled before the people around you even noticed you'd gone down.

In a crowd like that, people could watch you quite easily. Without you even realising it.

I glance behind me now, pulling my thin scarf up around my mouth.

At least work gets me out of the house each morning, and sometimes, whilst I'm there, I can even forget the past completely... for a while, at least.

The fact that Kellington's is so conveniently situated close to home was one of the reasons I was persuaded to apply for the job in the first place.

Granted, *part-time car park attendant* didn't sound the most exciting of career moves at the time, but when Mother read out the details of the vacancy from the local newspaper – ten months ago now – it instantly appealed to me.

I knew the exact location of this rather grand shop, with its small private car park to the rear. The successful candidate would be managing the parking space and, by the sounds of it, working quite autonomously for the daily four-hour morning shifts.

Set back from the busy thoroughfare of Huntingdon Street in the centre of town, the car park can be accessed by vehicle only from a quiet, unobtrusive side street.

Of course, that doesn't stop some drivers trying it on. A stone's throw away from Nottingham's most popular shopping mall, the Victoria Centre, it remains a desirable and convenient space for harassed shoppers who don't fancy negotiating the jammed, expensive multistorey car parks nearby.

I've noticed there's a big emphasis on being a *team player* in the jobs market, something that's overrated if you ask me. I used to work in a busy printing and lithography office in Lenton, fetching and carrying for the more important members of staff there, who took great delight in having fun at my expense. Banter, they liked to call it.

There's a lot to be said for relying on your own initiative and getting on with a job with the minimum of fuss.

My resolve to work at Kellington's was cemented the day I was called for interview, when I set eyes on the small external kiosk with windows that looks as if it's been tacked on to the side of the store.

The existing attendant, a rotund, seemingly jolly man, nodded to me from his swivel chair as I cautiously made my way to the back entrance, as per the interview letter. I couldn't help noticing that from this spot, the attendant had an unimpeded view of the entire car park.

I watched as a car reversed out of a nearby space. The attendant punctiliously recorded its departure on the impressive list of handwritten car registrations in front of him.

And it occurred to me, at that very moment, that life at Kellington's might not be so bad.

If I was successful in securing the post, it would be just one step on from sitting at my bedroom window in my current security role.

By the time I entered the premises and was welcomed into the managing director's office, I'd managed to slow down my breathing and unclench my fists a little.

I often find pleasure in thinking back over the significance of that day.

You see, by that time, I'd actually started to believe I might never leave the house again.

The prescribed medication had helped, and on better days, I'd take the odd trip out to the shops with Mother. This was a big improvement on the raw panic that had flooded me after… well, after it had happened.

But that day at Kellington's, realising I might have found a place where I could feel integrated and useful again, it felt as if a tiny extinguished flame had started to burn once again in my chest.

Don't get me wrong, I know only too well that life is full of disappointments, and I remember thinking as I entered the store that I had a good way to go before I could claim to have found my niche there.

I reach the bus stop in no time and check my stance, ensuring my shoulders are pushed back and both feet are planted firmly on the ground. I read somewhere that looking confident is paramount to disguising fear and discomfort when one is out in public.

There is nobody else waiting, and the digital display informs me that the bus is still four minutes away. So I allow myself to indulge in a little more memory-mining.

Mr Kellington himself and his assistant manager, Josh Peterson, interviewed me together. This confirmed my view that, far from being an inconsequential position in the company, the job I was applying for was in fact rather highly valued.

After cursory introductions, Mr Kellington asked why I thought I'd be suited to the role on offer, and I surprised myself by availing him of my Neighbourhood Watch monitoring processes.

The Rolodex, the detailed notes and observation techniques, and even my penchant for employing traditional administration methods where possible, rather than utilising modern technology, were all mentioned.

I decided, at the last minute, to leave out my frequent use of binoculars and zoom-lens camera.

'Well, you certainly seem suited to the job,' Mr Peterson said, the corners of his mouth twitching. 'Not sure I'd want to live next door to you, though. Do the other residents know that you're a—'

Mr Kellington cleared his throat.

'You seem, let's say, very... observant, David,' he remarked drily. 'Just the kind of person we're looking for. You also strike me as a man who takes his duties very seriously.'

On my mother's advice, I had taken glowing references with me. There was one from her friend Beatrice, who worked as a nurse at the city's respected Queen's Medical Centre. The other had been provided by Christine Abbott, the team leader of Wollaton's Neighbourhood Watch scheme.

'These are excellent,' Mr Kellington confirmed. 'Although I always rely more on my gut feeling about a candidate than on what strangers might say. Hasn't let me down yet.'

The following week, I started my new job.

I'd never seen Mother so proud, although I couldn't help noticing that while she continually boasted to friends and neighbours that I now worked for Kellington's, she made no mention of my job title.

Although it's tough in the winter months to work outdoors in the biting cold, and even in snow flurries on occasion, the small convector heater in the kiosk – which I prefer to refer to as my office – ensures that frostbite is kept safely at bay. It's a joke I like to call on in the cold weather, with our regular customers.

I sit there, warm as toast, with the large window in front of me, looking out on to the car park and the sliding glass hatch at the side that opens directly into the store's foyer and allows me to speak to staff and customers. Everything organised and to hand, just as I like it.

And of course, I can't deny that I both enjoy and take great pride in my job.

I think I can safely say that the bad time is finally behind me. And long may it stay that way.

CHAPTER 10

Holly

With the unpacking mostly done, Holly reluctantly admitted that she couldn't string it out upstairs much longer. It was time to go down again.

'Get a grip,' she muttered out loud as she felt the familiar resistance inside flare up. She hated that Geraldine's voice piped up in her head so frequently, especially since, infuriatingly, she'd often been right: sometimes Holly was her own worst enemy.

Cora now had a solution for her chronic loneliness and Holly had found a much-needed home and, hopefully, a stable base from which to begin rebuilding her life.

There was just one last thing to do.

At the bottom of the suitcase lay a laptop. It had been Geraldine's, and Holly had managed to sneak it out of the house without her even missing it, such was the wealth of possessions the other woman had.

She took the lead and plugged it into the wall socket at the side of her bed. The battery was completely flat but should be fully charged by the time she came up to bed later.

When she got downstairs, Cora was still sitting in her armchair by the window, leafing listlessly through a magazine.

'There you are, dear. I was beginning to fear you'd got lost up there.' She laid the magazine on the arm of her chair. 'Now, where was I? Ah yes, our wedding day.'

Holly sighed inwardly but managed to raise a smile.

'That's right,' she said, perching on the end of the sofa. 'March 1966.'

'I remember it as if it were yesterday…' Cora's eyes glazed over; she had immersed herself in the past so completely that the odd grunt and affirmative nod from Holly was all that was required to give the impression that she was listening.

She stared in fascination as Cora's soft, drooping features grew steadily more animated, more alive.

Rather than feeling guilty, Holly felt this was what Cora wanted from her. Simply another human being to sit and witness her life lived so far. To listen without interruption whilst she brought her memories out to polish again.

It was heartening and understandable.

Holly began to relax a little, caught up in the rhythmic waves of sound as Cora told her story.

She closed her eyes, allowing a slight smile to play on her lips as if she were visualising the eighteenth-century church and the hand-made Nottingham lace that had trimmed nineteen-year-old Cora's ivory wedding gown.

A rap at the back door made her sit up sharply, her eyes springing open.

Cora frowned slightly.

'Who can that be?' She glanced at the heavy wooden clock on the mantelpiece. 'Too early for Mr Brown.'

Apparently Mr Brown only lived a couple of doors away. Holly recalled Cora telling her he'd been taking care of the heavier garden duties for the last few months.

'Shall I see who it is?'

'It's all right, dear, I'll go.' Cora sighed and clambered awkwardly out of her chair.

Holly eased herself back down onto the sofa, her heart pounding at roughly twice its usual speed at the interruption.

What if it was…?

She shook her head to dispel the unhelpful thoughts. It was important to keep up with this more positive frame of mind; it was going to do her no good at all to fret over impossibilities. She was safe here.

She *was* safe, because nobody could possibly know of her whereabouts.

The back door opened and she relaxed as she recognised the bright tones of mutual greetings. The visitor was obviously someone Cora was pleased to see.

'Come through, dear,' Holly heard her say as the back door thudded shut. 'It's been far too long.'

'Yes, it has, and I'm sorry about that,' a woman said, her voice drawing closer. 'I was going to pop round this week anyway, and then David said he'd seen a young woman – oh, hello!'

Holly guessed that the woman standing in front of her was in her early sixties. She had mid-brown hair that was shot through with grey at her temples, and her entire outfit also consisted of varying shades of brown.

'This is Holly, my visitor,' Cora said without hesitation. 'She's staying with me for a while. Holly, this is Pat. She lives next door.'

'Hello.' Holly stood up.

Pat reached cautiously for her outstretched hand as though she was about to pet a dog whose intentions were ambiguous.

'Hello… Holly,' she said softly. 'I'm very pleased to meet you. My son – David – he's spotted you in the yard once or twice, so I thought I'd pop round and introduce myself.'

'Oh, I haven't seen anyone else in the other gardens,' Holly remarked.

'No, he saw you from upstairs.' Pat's cheeks flushed a little. 'He… spends a lot of time working in his bedroom.'

There was a beat of silence until Cora jumped straight into her tea duties.

'No, no, I'll make the tea,' Holly insisted, glad to get out of the room. 'Give you two a chance to catch up.'

She stepped outside the door and pulled it to, but not fully closed, behind her.

The two women's voices dropped lower, but she was able to catch certain phrases, like 'poor girl' and 'lovely to have some company'. Then she heard Pat's concerned voice: 'We're going to have to watch David.'

Holly forced herself to loosen her jaw and walked into the kitchen.

She wasn't quite sure whether she wanted to meet this David person or not.

It reminded her of the day she'd left Nottingham with Markus. She hadn't got a clue what kind of people they'd meet in Manchester; it was a leap of faith. Markus had already spent some time there, but he'd only been there long enough to make tentative contacts.

It had been a milestone because it was the moment all her plans and intentions had finally turned into hard action. Both terrifying and exhilarating at the same time.

CHAPTER 11

Holly

The coach journey to Manchester had been something of a nightmare. It had taken four long hours in total, as they'd had to make a change at Leeds.

The second they boarded and found their seats, Holly's heart sank. She'd imagined a pleasant, rather exciting trip, but already seated behind them was a young family with a screaming baby and a boy of about six years old who Markus insisted was the image of the child, Damien, from the horror movie *The Omen*.

The boy did indeed prove to be a little demon, persisting in kicking Holly's seat for what felt like the entire duration of the journey.

'Sorry, love,' his ineffective, harassed mother kept leaning forward and saying to Holly in between half-hearted attempts to chastise the little monster.

In front of them sat two teenagers who'd brought two enormous bags of McDonald's takeaway onto the coach with them. Holly could almost feel the saturated fat settling into the pores of her skin as the entire oxygen supply seemed to quickly convert to burger and chips fumes.

Infuriatingly, virtually as soon as they'd finished the vodka and the coach had pulled away, Markus promptly fell fast asleep despite the commotion that surrounded them.

On reflection, Holly realised, too late, that his suggestion that she travel to Manchester with him had come so quickly that she hadn't stopped to properly consider the implications.

She had precisely fifty pounds folded away in the pocket of her rucksack, and another thirty-five pounds in the bank. That amounted to all her worldly goods and available funds.

'Don't worry.' Markus had shrugged when she'd confided in him. 'You'll get a job in no time. My friend, he has many contacts.'

She wondered afterwards why she'd allowed him to be so vague about the 'wonderful opportunity' he'd talked about when they'd initially gone for coffee. He'd told her all sorts of stories about the money he'd made working for 'the boss', as he liked to call his mystery contact in Manchester.

'He's a very private man,' he had explained, wiping frothed milk from his top lip with the back of his hand. 'And he likes to explain opportunities to people himself, rather than you taking my word for it.'

His word for *what*, exactly? Holly had wondered.

'It's nothing dodgy, is it?' Eventually she'd sought reassurance. 'I'm not interested in getting involved in anything illegal or—'

Markus had held his hands up.

'It's nothing like that. The boss has had me travelling around the north-east, learning the trade in his clubs and pubs. It'll probably be something different for you... if he thinks you've got potential, that is.'

'Potential for what?'

'Stop reading things into what I'm saying.' He'd laughed and waved her away. 'I've told you, it's nothing dodgy.'

She'd felt a curl of discomfort in her gut, but ignored it. Things had got much worse at home lately, and this opening had come at just the right time.

Aunt Susan seemed to be working longer hours, which left Holly stuck in the house alone with creepy Keith. At college, she'd fallen into the same pattern she'd previously had at school, going straight to the library at the end of each day. But Aunt Susan didn't get home from her cleaning job now until nine, and the college library closed at six.

It was a constant dilemma, and that was why, when Markus had invited her to go to Manchester, she'd found herself accepting, even though the arrangements were vague. It also meant leaving her college course halfway through.

Still, the pull to get away had been stronger than the sum amount of her concerns.

As they'd sat waiting for the coach to depart, she'd continued to press Markus for more details about his boss and the amazing opportunity he'd found himself chasing.

He'd relayed tales of hopping from club to club, gaining hospitality managerial experience, mixing with VIP customers, with champagne on tap.

He'd looked at her earnestly. 'My opportunity is probably different to what yours will turn out to be. I don't have many details, Holly, but you know, you only get places in life by taking risks. So you should think of it as an adventure.'

They'd sat in silence for a short time before he turned to her again.

'I've never asked you about your past. I know we were on friendly terms at school, but we don't really know each other, and now… here we are leaving town together.'

'What do you want to know?' Holly had shrugged, thinking she didn't know anything about his background either but wasn't that curious. As far as she was concerned, she was more than happy to leave the past behind.

'I don't know. I suppose… did your parents have any diseases?'

Holly burst out laughing, and Markus joined in.

'What kind of a question is that?'

'OK, don't answer that,' he grinned. 'I do not ask the best questions, for sure.'

He'd said she would only get places in life by taking risks, but she wanted to ask him what kind of risks he was referring to. Yet he already looked half asleep, so in the end, she didn't bother trying to reason with him.

She remembered thinking that she couldn't summon a word in the English language for the way she was feeling right at that moment. It was a sensation that hovered ominously between fear and excitement, dread and anticipation.

Once the coach had begun to move and her aunt and uncle's two-bed terrace was a good few miles behind her, another feeling began to brew in her stomach. But there were fewer feel-good vibes attached to this one.

She was unable to kick the feeling that *risky* was how all this suddenly felt. A young woman like herself, venturing into the unknown with no guarantees and no safety net.

As Markus snored softly beside her, all the cautionary tales that had been recounted in her old school assemblies began to emerge from a dark, dusty place in her mind.

Sex slaves, prostitution, violence on city streets... She'd thought at the time that all this stuff had gone over her head, that such concerns would never apply to her. But it was now apparent that her brain had carefully filed all the unsavoury details away and was choosing now as a good time to revisit it all.

Holly ferreted in her pocket for her headphones and turned on her music in a futile attempt to blast away the unwelcome musings. She looked down at her iPod and was reminded that Aunt Susan had bought it for her eighteenth birthday, only a few months earlier.

She felt a stab of remorse then, wondering if maybe she'd been a bit hard on her aunt before she left the house.

Holly was forced to admit that, despite her weak will when it came to her husband, her aunt had a good heart. After all, she hadn't *had* to take her niece in and give her a roof over her head.

She had been estranged from Holly's mother, Julie, for several years before Julie's untimely death.

It wasn't Aunt Susan's fault her husband was a perv. They'd married very young, as evidenced by the single photograph on the mantelpiece. Keith had actually been skinnier than her aunt in those days, but he'd still had the same creepy eyes.

But Aunt Susan had let him get away with his crude comments. She had always found a reason to leave the room as he sat openly ogling Holly's legs in the early days, when she'd still, naïvely, worn a short skirt in his presence.

No, she concluded, as she stared out of the coach window into the failing light. She shouldn't feel bad. Aunt Susan *had* known what Keith was like and had clearly made the decision to put up with it.

That had been *her* choice, no one else's. She shouldn't have expected Holly to do the same.

CHAPTER 12

Holly

Holly grasped the handle of Cora's back door and pushed down, but the door was locked.

As she ferreted in her handbag for the spare keys Cora had given her, she found herself hoping beyond reasonable hope that the older woman was out.

Although Cora had evidently become accustomed to spending long stretches in the house without seeing another soul, she'd also told Holly that every few days she forced herself to head into town. She'd stop at the coffee shop on the corner, she said, and then pick up a few bags of shopping before grabbing a cab home.

Holly supposed that today must be one of those days.

She twisted the key in the lock and stepped inside. As she'd hoped, the house was silent. She could even hear the loud tick of the grandfather clock in the hallway, Cora's pride and joy that had been passed down by her mother's side of the family.

She closed the door behind her and dumped her bag and keys on the kitchen counter. There, she found a note from Cora.

Popped to supermarket. Back soon x

She felt her shoulders relax a little, and the thumping headache that had developed on the bus journey back from town receded just a touch.

After surviving virtually a full day of Cora's incessant reminiscing the day before, Holly had thought that she might actually
scream if she had to accompany her on one more minute's
meandering down ruddy memory lane.

If she was a decent person, she probably wouldn't entertain
such unkind thoughts. But you couldn't stop thoughts dead just
because they were selfish, could you? If anything, if you didn't
acknowledge them, they'd probably grow stronger.

Holly was overjoyed that Cora had taken her in so readily, but
that didn't mean she had to sacrifice her sanity every single minute
of the day from here on in. Or maybe it did. She wasn't really in
a position to be fussy right now.

She poured herself a small glass of orange juice and sat at the
scuffed wooden table for a few minutes, allowing the silence
around her to trickle soothingly into her bruised ears.

There had been so much noise in town today. Holly had done
the rounds of three busy recruitment agencies with their mostly
indifferent staff. Her suspicions had been correct. There really
weren't that many decent job vacancies around currently, certainly
not for unskilled staff or with training provided.

Once she had explained in the first two appointments that
she didn't possess a university degree or hold a sheaf of impressive
qualifications in her non-existent portfolio, she saw their already
sparse enthusiasm fade away before her eyes.

It had taken all her resolve not to give up.

When she had entered the third and final agency, Office
Cherubs, she was met at the door by a woman with dry brown
hair, over-tanned skin and rabbit-like teeth.

'I'm Karen, recruitment consultant,' she said, extending a hand
together with her self-important title. 'You must be Holly?'

Holly smiled and nodded, relieved that she wasn't going to be
treated as a pariah this time. She felt hot after rushing across town
to get to the building at exactly two p.m., her appointment time.

Karen led her to a quiet corner in the large open-plan office. Various people sat at desks dotted here and there, but nobody showed any interest in her.

Holly sat down and gratefully accepted the glass of water offered to her. She felt dead on her feet.

They had an informal chat and she was relieved that the woman seemed to accept her brief account of work experience without too many searching questions.

'I think you'd be perfect for a vacancy we've just had in literally fifteen minutes ago,' Karen said brightly. 'Sales assistant for an upmarket shop in the centre of town. I could send you over for interview first thing tomorrow if you can email me your references before we close up today. How's that sound?'

'Sounds great,' Holly nodded, trying to ignore the voice in her head that was starting to panic a little. 'I can email them when I get home, if that's OK?'

'Perfect!' Karen beamed, pushing over a pen and some papers. 'Now, if you can just fill in this application form, I'll print off the job description and person spec. They're paying above minimum wage, so I expect this vacancy will prove popular when it goes online in the morning. Must be your lucky day, walking in just as we got it through!'

Holly had managed to complete the application form without too much bother and left soon after, assuring Karen she'd be emailing the references and ID documents.

'I'll call you later with the time of your interview and details of where to go,' Karen had replied. 'Here's my card.'

On the bus home, Holly had fretted about whether her paperwork would stand up to scrutiny. The last thing she wanted was anyone raking up trouble for her.

If Geraldine found out where she was, she'd have to up sticks and leave again. Holly would face her when the time was right and not before, otherwise she would have no chance of triumphing.

On the spur of the moment, she'd got off the bus a few stops earlier and walked to the street where she'd lived with Aunt Susan.

She'd already decided she wouldn't just brazenly walk up to the house and knock on the door. She didn't want to risk finding Keith home alone or Aunt Susan telling her they'd washed their hands of her.

She'd never received reply to the note she'd sent to her aunt and she'd taken that to mean she wanted nothing more to do with her niece. But now she realised that the chances were, Patricia had never even posted it. The last thing they'd have wanted, with hindsight, was her to keep in touch with relatives who might realise what was happening and convince her to leave Medlock Hall.

No. It was best if she just kept watch, visited a few times. She might get lucky and bump into her aunt. It was bound to happen if she kept coming here.

She had turned the corner and froze.

The terraced houses had now completely gone and in their place stood a sprawling block of offices.

As she had stood there aghast, a woman emerged from the offices.

'Excuse me!' Holly had crossed the narrow road. 'Can you tell me when these offices were built? I've just returned to the area and I remember there used to be houses here.'

'That's right, we've been here... let's see... about seven years now. Our business was one of the first to move in here.'

Holly had thanked her and watched as the woman went on her way.

In that moment and despite her aunt's faults, she had felt so completely and utterly alone.

Once she had finished her juice, Holly walked into the living room and looked around at Cora's drab, dated furnishing.

It was a decent-sized room and it would be improved no end by getting rid of the heavy lace nets that swamped the window and swapping the gloomy fabrics for bright modern prints.

If Cora would give her a free hand to make improvements, Holly knew she could work wonders in here, but she didn't intend to broach the subject.

Cora Barrett was a woman most definitely set in her ways, and she had very rigid ideas of how things should be. Holly felt sure that in Cora's eyes, the room looked perfect.

She glanced up at the Artexed ceiling and the tarnished brass candle chandelier above her head. Living here was like being beamed back to the fifties.

However, the house itself was impressive and Baker Crescent was considered one of the better roads in the area. In the future, with younger owners, Holly had no doubt the accommodation would be transformed. One day, the dusty old museum she stood in now would be just a vague memory.

She sighed and took hold of her thoughts again. Old patterns of depressive thinking weren't going to help her put the whole awful mess behind her, of that she felt certain.

She peeked through the window, but thankfully there was no sign of Cora returning from the shops yet.

Without even really considering what she should do next, Holly padded upstairs and stood outside the front bedroom, Cora's room.

The plain, glossed white door was closed, so she gave it a firm push. As it began to open, it caught on the carpet underneath, so she kept pushing.

The room smelled a little fusty, as if it hadn't actually been used for some time.

It was over-filled with heavy walnut furniture that crowded it out and gave the otherwise sizeable space a claustrophobic feel.

The dusty burgundy velvet curtains were half closed, and Holly snapped on the light to save her squinting unnecessarily into the gloom.

She walked over to the chest of drawers that stood by the window. The top was a sea of framed photographs, many of them featuring a gloriously young and vibrant Cora with various people, but mostly with Harold, whom Holly recognised from their wedding photograph on the mantelpiece downstairs.

She picked one of the photos up and studied it. Cora stood clutching the hand of a young girl with ribbons in her hair on Blackpool seafront. Cora was smiling but the child looked surly.

The photograph was black and white, but Holly could imagine the dull grey colour of the foaming sea behind them and the dirty beige sand on which a group of hapless donkeys stood, waiting forlornly for their next riders.

She replaced the photograph and didn't bother inspecting the others. She felt fed up enough as it was without studying those long-ago scenes. It was nice to see Cora looking happy in most of them, but when Holly compared that glowing girl with the wrinkled woman she had become, she felt even worse about her own future.

How was it possible that years could flit by so quickly, robbing people of their happiest times?

She felt the keen passing of her own life, the division between the girl she had been before and the woman she had turned into.

Effectively she was betraying Cora's trust by sneaking in here. That wasn't the person she wanted to be.

She asked herself the question: would she want someone snooping through her room and rifling through her personal items? *Most definitely not*, came the uninvited reply.

Yet something in her demanded she take the opportunity to look around. That way, she had less chance of being fooled as she had been before. She might get a measure of who the real Cora was.

In the past, she had fallen far too easily into believing that people were who they said they were. It was a mistake that had cost her dearly; that might have already ruined her future and robbed her of the love of her life.

And she couldn't quite believe that the old lady really had nobody in her life. No children of her own and therefore no grandchildren; not even any elderly friends to go and play bingo with, or whatever it was that old people liked to do these days.

It was quite sad, yet she couldn't help thinking that Cora and Harold had obviously kept themselves purposely isolated all these years, and now Harold was long gone and Cora found herself alone.

Maybe she wasn't quite the frail old lady she liked to pretend to be... People could surprise you.

Holly inched open the drawers one by one. After nearly asphyxiating herself with the smell of mothballs, she came across a large, tattered brown envelope in the last but one drawer from the bottom.

She slid it out and peeked inside. More photographs and a few papers. She was about to replace it when something caught her eye at the top of one of the letters.

Her heart lurched when she read the lines beneath.

It seemed that she'd been right. Cora had a secret of her own.

CHAPTER 13

Cora

As Cora moved slowly up and down the supermarket aisles wondering what Holly might like for tea, she felt she had turned a corner in what had become a mundane, uneventful existence.

Holly had left the house earlier to go into town and find herself a job, apparently. Although Cora had assured her there was no rush to pay rent or anything of that sort, at least for a few weeks, Holly had been insistent. It was rather a shame, just when they were getting to know each other; and Cora thought of her very much as a *visitor*, rather than a temporary lodger.

She selected a two-pint carton of semi-skimmed milk and laid it in the rickety trolley with a wonky wheel that she was having trouble pushing in a straight line.

Still, who'd have thought things could turn around so completely in a single afternoon, and so out of the blue like that?

Cora had been standing at the end of a short queue in the post office, waiting to purchase a book of stamps. That had been her sole reason for leaving the house that day, as she only sorted out the bank business twice a week. She'd needed to post a couple of cheques for bills and realised she'd run out of stamps.

She didn't like all this online banking business, nor the thought of direct debit payments that gave the energy companies cash before she'd even received the full quarter's service.

What was the world coming to? What had happened to paying the correct amount for a service actually received and used? Harold had always refused to give out his bank details to companies.

'Blighters can take what they like once I grant them access to my funds,' he would roar upon receiving a letter informing him he could save money by paying in regular monthly instalments.

My funds. He'd always referred to it as *his* money, and she'd had to ask for every penny she needed.

She'd never in a million years have been able to take a person like Holly in if Harold had still been around. Even completely bed-bound – as he was for the best part of a year before he died – he'd have caused a big fuss if Cora had brought someone in need back home, even if it was to stay with them just temporarily.

He'd even forbidden Cora from giving loose change to that poor homeless chap and his dog who sat on the corner of the high street in all weathers, for goodness' sake. Harold had always maintained that 'homelessness is a lifestyle choice'. What utter nonsense.

Sadly, against her better judgement, Cora had allowed him to get away with his dictatorial manner for all of their married life, and it was only really once he'd gone that her anger had surfaced. She had finally realised the impact his bigoted attitudes had had on her own life. Nobody had ever wanted to befriend them; people preferred to stay away.

It had to be said that when Harold died, there had been a welcome new sense of freedom that Cora had never experienced before.

Harold had cleverly always insisted he only imposed certain measures and precautions to keep her safe.

'You're too gullible to be out on your own, love,' he'd say. 'I'll come with you, make sure nobody tries anything on.'

As a young, newly married woman, Cora had initially been flattered, but of course it soon dawned on her that her husband was controlling her for his own selfish reasons. He wanted to ensure she was there just for him; he didn't want to share her with anyone else: friends, acquaintances, even children. Harold had never wanted children.

As usual, a wave of sadness came with the realisation of so many lost opportunities.

The mood gripped her until she reached for the rich butter biscuits that Harold would certainly have forbidden her to buy because of the extortionate cost. She placed two packets carefully in the trolley and allowed herself a smug grin.

Sometimes she was too hard on herself, she knew that. It wasn't at all easy, in those days, to escape a difficult marriage. With no job and no friends, Cora had felt paralysed to do anything about her circumstances. It had simply been easier to put up and shut up.

She knew a lot of women hid their true feelings for one reason or another.

Take Holly. She seemed a nice enough young woman, but Cora wasn't fooled by the happy-go-lucky character she seemed fond of displaying on the surface. You didn't live as many years as Cora had without garnering a sense of people, and she was absolutely certain that there was more to her young visitor than met the eye.

She'd thought as much that day when she'd abandoned the post office queue and gone to speak to the sobbing undernourished waif who seemed utterly inconsolable that she wasn't able to get her twenty pounds from the counter.

Even though some customers had shown their disapproval, and others their pity, Cora had sensed there was a determined young woman underneath the frail exterior who was in need of neither.

She would be loath to admit it to anyone else, but as she had been trying to comfort Holly, the thought had occurred to her that without Harold around to dictate her actions, she might view this wretched young person as a sort of personal project.

She could offer assistance and help guide her to a more fulfilling life, while bagging herself a companion in the process.

After all, wasn't that what ladies used to do in times gone by? They'd advertise and pay for a female companion so they didn't have to put up with the achingly long hours of loneliness that Cora herself had suffered with no prospect of respite.

The Victorians got a lot of things right, and they set great stock by order and routine, just like Cora herself.

It had occurred to her that day that this could be a match made in heaven. It was all a matter of striking the right balance to break through the generation gap.

She had begun by regaling Holly with interesting stories about her life. Holly had seemed genuinely interested and this had encouraged Cora to continue.

She'd asked her visitor a couple of pointed questions about her own past, and it hadn't escaped her notice that each time, Holly had cleverly – or so she thought – refrained from answering by luring Cora back into her own reminiscing.

But she was in no rush. She could wait.

When Holly was prepared to open up a bit and trust her with her personal history, then Cora would tell her the truth.

That was, the truth about what Harold was really like.

Not the *other* truth.

She didn't intend telling anyone about that until she'd made up her mind exactly what to do.

CHAPTER 14

Holly

'This is Pat's son, the nice young man I told you about who lives next door.' Cora beamed as she looked alternately between Holly and the tall, serious-looking man called David – not really that *young* at all – who now stood in front of her.

He had dark brown hair desperately in need of a cut. He was pale, as if he might never have had a tan at all, and wore wire-rimmed spectacles that did him no favours unless he was actively trying to look like a geek. On top of all that, he was fidgety.

'Hello, I'm Holly.' She extended her hand. 'Cora's told me a lot about you.'

David pressed his palm to his thigh for a moment or two before grasping Holly's hand. His fingers felt unpleasantly hot.

'David Lewis.' He introduced himself abruptly.

It seemed as if he were forcing himself to stand there when his feet were perilously close to running out of the house, away from her enquiring eyes.

When he finally released her hand, Holly fought the urge to wipe it on her jeans.

'It was so nice to see your mother yesterday, David,' Cora remarked. 'She said you'd spotted Holly out in the yard and wondered who on earth she could be.'

'I wasn't… I mean, I just happened to look down from my window and…'

'Don't worry, I didn't think you'd been spying on me,' Holly quipped.

Both she and Cora laughed, but David's face remained impassive, a deep, mortified bloom creeping into his cheeks.

Holly was instantly reminded of Evan's cheeks. They'd flush just the same if practically anyone at all, apart from Holly, spoke to him. She felt a little squeeze in her heart.

'It's so nice of you to come around and say hello, David,' she said, speaking a little more softly. 'I don't know anyone around here yet, so I do appreciate it.'

David shifted on the spot, his cheeks continuing to glow. His eyes darted to her face, but he looked away again before she could offer him a reassuring smile.

After a beat of silence, he cleared his throat. 'Mrs Barrett, if you have any jobs you'd like doing while I'm here, it would be a pleasure to help you in any way I can.'

He spoke in a rapid, formal manner, as if he were reading the words from an invisible prompt.

Cora clutched at her chest, her mouth forming a perfect O. 'David, what a gentleman you are. Isn't he, Holly?'

'Yes,' Holly agreed. 'He certainly is.'

She watched as David found a sudden fascination with a fleck on his sleeve.

'Actually, if you don't mind, David,' Cora said, 'I could do with a chair bringing downstairs. It's the one in the corner of Holly's room. It really would be quite heavy for us girls to try and shift on our own.'

Holly grinned. She'd already got used to Cora's everyday sexism. 'I'll make us all a drink, then.'

As she walked towards the kitchen, she became aware that David had followed her into the small hallway. He faltered at the bottom of the stairs.

'Is it all right... I mean, to go into your room?' His voice sounded scratchy in his throat and Holly watched as his fingers twisted against themselves.

'It's fine, David. I'm in the back bedroom, the one on the left,' she said easily. 'Cora insisted I take the room overlooking the garden. Now I feel like I've pinched her bed!'

'Nonsense,' Cora called from the other side of the door. 'Since I've been on my own, I've slept in both rooms, depending how the mood takes me. I'm quite happy with the front bedroom for now.'

'You just can't tell some people, can you?' Holly whispered, gently nudging David and grinning.

His arm jerked away from her as if she'd given him an electric shock.

'Sorry, I didn't mean to...'

But before she could finish her sentence, David had bounded up the stairs.

CHAPTER 15

David

Upstairs, I stand frozen in the doorway of the back bedroom like an idiot.

Next to the window is the wooden dining chair that Mrs Barrett asked me to bring up here just a few months after her husband died.

Harold Barrett was a small, wiry man with a tight mouth and mean eyes.

In his fitter years he was a keen gardener, always preferring plants and the vegetable patch at the bottom of the yard to spending any time with the meek boy who watched him digging for hours from over next-door's fence.

I remember waiting until he turned his back to shake the soil from a clutch of spindly carrots or similar, and then I'd seize my moment to dash into the house to see Mrs Barrett.

She used to bake a lot in those days, and there would always be something nice for me in one of her tins to have with a glass of juice.

'Is he here again?' Harold would grunt when he shuffled in from the garden, and Mrs Barrett would always answer him curtly whilst smiling at me, her mouth stretched almost too wide for her face.

'Yes, he is here again, and I for one am pleased to see him. Even if nobody else is.'

Harold's eyes would harden like little brown nuts and he'd shake his head and walk away without saying another word.

Despite Mrs Barrett's assurances that I was most welcome, my guts would feel like mush inside. Her face said one thing, her words another... I felt uncomfortable but didn't know why.

It was a feeling I'd learn to get used to with other people over the coming years.

When Harold died, I asked Mrs Barrett why she was moving the chair.

'Well, I'll be eating alone now, you see,' she said, her dull eyes staring at the wall. 'I've no use for two chairs any longer.'

That's why I initially made the effort to pop round a bit more; for a chat, at least. To try to make Mrs Barrett's brown eyes sparkle again. But nothing really worked. Still, I suppose it felt a bit like I was paying her back for all those times she'd been a friend to me during my difficult younger years when Father was trying to make me into the brusque, macho son he'd have much preferred.

Yet something about seeing her alone, getting older with the empty years stretching out in front of her, made my scalp tighten, and I found myself less and less keen to come around here.

But now that her new visitor – Holly – is here, the atmosphere in the house feels altogether different.

In a way, I'm glad the chair is coming downstairs again. It shows Mrs Barrett has someone to sit down with again.

It occurs to me that to get to the chair, I'll have to walk past the end of the bed. I take a step inside the door and then see that there are garments strewn across the quilt, including a bra that looks as if it has been cast off with some urgency.

I'd never openly admit it, of course, but I've never actually touched a bra or even seen one up close except in a shop. You can't linger in department stores to look at stuff like that, not when you're a single man of a certain age, anyhow.

I've never been able to work out how, when the other customers and assistants don't know you personally and can't possibly know if you're married or have a girlfriend, they somehow seem to know with an unspoken certainty that you have no business being near women's underwear.

People look at me like I'm some kind of creep; a *weirdo*, one woman hissed as she brushed by me at the three-pairs-for-two knicker island in Debenhams.

I'm just curious, that's all. I mean, there's nothing sinister in wanting to have a look, is there? Although it's probably that sort of curiosity that got me into so much trouble last time.

I've seen Mother's bras, of course, hanging on the washing line like great rigid white bowls. They're an engineering miracle.

The flimsy bra on the bed is the colour of unfurled spring leaves, and the modest cups are smothered in layers of delicate lace that look as if they might shred under one's fingers.

I slip my finger inside my collar to loosen it slightly.

'David, is everything OK?'

I visibly jump and spin round to find Holly at the top of the stairs.

'Oh! Yes, I…'

'The chair's right there, look. In the corner.'

She squeezes past me. Her body feels warm against my arm and I press myself back into the door frame, my entire face burning like a candle.

She doesn't notice, just strides across the room. Using her foot, she pushes away an open suitcase that lies in front of the chair.

'Sorry about the mess.' She sweeps her hand around the room. 'I confess I've only just started unpacking. Shameful, really.'

There's a large framed photograph on the bed. The light from the window is shining directly on to it, so I take a step nearer and tilt my head to get a better look. I see a male face with pale hair and dark eyes.

She follows my eyes and snatches up the picture.

'You can get to the chair now,' she says tightly. 'I think Cora might be waiting for it downstairs.'

I nod and walk past her, stooping to pick up the chair. I hesitate at a rustling noise behind me.

I glance sideways and watch as she gently wraps the photograph in tissue paper and places it in the top drawer of the chest.

She covers it with a folded sweater and then closes the drawer with a muffled thud that somehow seems to have an air of finality about it.

CHAPTER 16

Cora

Cora sat in her armchair by the window with a nice fresh cup of tea and a slice of toast and marmalade, cut in two neat halves.

Holly was a good girl. She'd seemed so grateful for the modest meal Cora had served up last night. A salmon fillet and vegetable medley – nothing special, and yet her young visitor's eyes had lit up as she declared she hadn't eaten anything as posh as salmon for an age.

What a treat it had been for Cora to sit with another person again and chat about this and that without the pressure of saying the right thing or tripping herself up in some way, as had been the case with Harold before his illness moved him permanently upstairs.

As the cancer took a firmer grip, his temper had worsened. Far from showing appreciation for his wife's constant care and attention, he had grown increasingly critical.

'This steak is overdone,' he would bark. Or, 'Same old boring sandwiches again. Can't you come up with something new?'

But one day, it was as though someone else entirely took over Cora's body, and she could only sit back and watch.

Harold had picked up a sandwich and peeled back the top slice of the dainty triangle to look beneath. When he saw the thick-sliced ham and tomato underneath with a thin spread of mayonnaise just as he liked it, he huffed disparagingly and dropped it back on the plate like a piece of dirt.

Cora had stood up quite calmly and whipped the plate from under his nose. She'd picked up his mug of tea from the bedside table and simply walked from the room with a serene look on her face, turning back only to pull the door closed behind her with a hooked foot.

Harold had bellowed insults for what seemed like hours.

Cora had taken her own sandwich and tea into the lounge, closed the door and put *Antiques Roadshow* on with the volume turned up at least twice as loud as Harold ordinarily allowed it.

The faint rumble of his bellowing eventually grew dim and then stopped. When Cora crept up over an hour later, he had fallen fast asleep, still sitting up in bed.

She left him as he was and slept on the sofa.

The next morning when she took up his breakfast, the incident wasn't mentioned by either of them, but Cora noticed he never complained about his meals again. Her only regret was that she hadn't done it years ago.

Over tea, Holly had been excited about a job she had applied for at one of the agencies in town. It was working in retail at some posh department store, apparently.

Cora knew of a few such shops in the city but had never set foot in any of them. Harold had always baulked at the price of goods in the more stylish window displays and moved her hastily on.

Vaguely it occurred to her that she might know someone who worked in such a shop, but the information, though it danced tantalisingly close to her consciousness, did not come quite close enough for her to grab it.

She hadn't told anyone, not even Dr Geeson, but in recent months she'd noticed this sort of thing happening more and more. It was the same sensation as trying to grasp the contents of a dream upon waking. The harder she tried, the more it evaded her.

On occasion, she could recall a vague sense of something she had once known or been told, but the detail was a devil to recover and Cora had reached the conclusion that it was far easier to give up than to feel continually frustrated that she could only grasp a thread of it.

Of course, there was no denying she was getting older, but she was far from over the hill. A bit of forgetfulness she could handle, but the trouble was, the newspapers and magazines seemed to be full of articles on dementia: how you could tell if you had it, what you could do to avoid it... Far from being helpful, Cora found it all rather a worry.

Holly's voice broke into her troubled musings.

'The agency just emailed my details over to the store. I've an interview at ten thirty in the morning!' she told Cora excitedly. 'It's just a retail assistant position, not great money, but I've checked and I can easily get there on the bus. I never thought I'd be given an opportunity within days of arriving here.'

'And this is a full-time position?' Cora said, her voice brittle.

She wasn't really interested in Holly's job and felt quite peeved that her new companion had already found something else to do with time that could have been spent listening to Cora's interesting stories.

Holly had seemed so fascinated by them when she'd first arrived, but now, this wretched interview was suddenly all she wanted to discuss.

'Yes, full-time Monday to Saturday, with a day off in the week.' She thought for a moment, a runner bean speared mid-air on her fork. 'Oh yes, and once I'm up to speed, I could request two Saturdays a month off if I want them.'

'As I've said before, you needn't rush into anything on my account.' Cora sniffed. 'You don't want to take some dead-end, low-paid job just for the sake of it, do you now?'

Holly's face dropped, but Cora couldn't help herself.

'You know, I could probably lend you a bit of money to tide you over, if you needed it.'

'Thank you, Cora,' Holly said, laying down her cutlery. 'That's really kind of you, but I wouldn't dream of putting on you like that. If I get the job, I'll even be able to pay you some rent.'

'Nonsense, I wouldn't have offered unless I meant it. And I think of you as my guest or a visitor, not a tenant.'

Holly paused, keen to make herself properly understood.

'It's not just the money, Cora. It's about starting a new life here in Nottingham. Perhaps I could make a few friends at work and go to the cinema or the bowling alley... just normal stuff that people of my age do, you know?'

Cora stood up and picked up her plate.

'Oh, are you finished already?' Holly exclaimed, watching her face. 'You've only eaten half your meal, I hope I didn't—'

'I'm just not hungry any more,' Cora said curtly. 'I think I'm going to have a little lie-down.'

CHAPTER 17

Holly

That night, Holly fell fast asleep as soon as her head hit the pillow, but then, in the early hours, she woke and tossed and turned for what seemed like forever.

At some point she dropped off again, and quite deeply, because the alarm trilling out at seven thirty woke her with a start.

A warm feeling flooded her solar plexus, followed by a fluttering in her stomach when she remembered her interview today. Three hours and she'd be there... This could be the start of solving her problems and making a fresh start. Far earlier than she'd expected.

She pushed her feet into her old slippers and grabbed a worn, bobbled cardigan from the bottom of the bed.

She looked down and saw the laptop, the amber light on the front now turned to green, indicating it was fully charged. She'd thought about it a few times, this important portal to finding and contacting Evan, but she hadn't really felt strong enough to deal with what she might find.

Today, though, felt like a good day, a lucky day. She promised herself she'd take a quick look later. She couldn't afford to crush her spirit, but she had to try every avenue out there.

She owed it to herself, and to Evan, to be vigilant.

And if she got the job today, one of the first things she'd already decided she'd treat herself to was a fluffy white dressing gown like the one Geraldine had worn. Well, not *exactly* like that one, of course – Holly could never afford a Ralph Lauren robe – but it would be something just as soft and comfortable.

It seemed a bizarre and indulgent thought to have, but it would signify something powerful to her. She'd learned from the past that the value of staying upbeat was immeasurable.

That would be, of course, if she had enough left over after starting to make inroads into the mountain of debt she'd incurred over the past year.

The payday loans, overdrafts and credit cards had all been used not to buy fancy clothes and make-up or fabulous restaurant meals, but to pay for her various methods of trying to find Geraldine and Evan.

A private investigator, cabs, train fares, online searches and, finally, the documentation she'd needed to collate to come back to her home town… it had added up surprisingly quickly.

The fluttering sensation moved up to Holly's throat.

She'd lain awake in the early hours, but for once, it hadn't been the debt that was unsettling her. She'd been fretting that she'd upset Cora in some way. She couldn't fathom exactly how; she was just judging it on Cora's grim expression and the way she had snatched up her unfinished plate so suddenly.

They'd been having a perfectly nice conversation and Cora had made a real effort to prepare a nice tea. Then, out of the blue, a strange look had come over her face and she'd simply stood up and left Holly sitting at the table to finish her meal alone.

Perhaps the older woman was getting a little confused. Holly had noticed the other day that the tea canister had been put back in the fridge and the fresh milk in the cupboard.

She'd decided not to mention it. Cora was in her seventies and Holly didn't want to make her feel uncomfortable. After all, no harm had been done; she'd probably just got a lot on her mind.

Holly decided she'd go downstairs now and make Cora a cup of tea. Perhaps they'd have breakfast together and put last night behind them.

She could only try.

Two hours later, Holly boarded the bus for the twenty-minute ride into town.

She'd given herself an hour to get to the interview, but still she couldn't get rid of the uneasy churning in her stomach. She knew herself well enough to determine that the best thing she could do to avoid the steel grip of anxiety was get into town early and walk off the nervous feeling once she arrived.

She paid her fare and took a seat, already feeling calmer now that she was on her way and wouldn't be late for her interview.

As the bus trundled away, she turned to catch a glimpse of Baker Crescent.

It was odd to see that the curtains were closed again at Cora's bedroom window. The door to that room had been ajar this morning and Holly had glanced in to see a neatly made bed and drawn curtains. Cora had already been up and pottering around downstairs.

Holly wondered if she'd had gone back to bed, although she had her pegged as a bit of a stickler for rising early and getting things done.

She thought about the contents of the letter she'd found in Cora's bedroom and smiled.

She wasn't sure how, but maybe the closed curtains had something to do with *that*. There was no rush to find out; time would tell. The last thing Holly wanted to do was make Cora aware she knew her secret. She would no doubt be annoyed, and quite rightly.

Before she'd left the house, Holly had made tea and toast as planned and Cora had seemed her usual bright self again, so she'd decided not to mention last night's little misunderstanding – if that was what it was.

She hadn't mentioned this morning's interview either; she got the feeling Cora was somehow irked about her news. But as she'd left the house, Cora had called goodbye and wished her luck. It had been a relief.

As the bus inched its way through the traffic, Holly stared out of the smeared, cloudy glass at the park beyond.

Despite being on the threshold of spring, the air still had a spiteful nip to it. At least the sun was out now, brightening the young pale green leaves on the bushes that surrounded the park's gaudy children's play area.

Holly too felt brighter, as if some of the weight had already been lifted from her shoulders. It was a welcome feeling, one that had been absent from her life for too long.

It was only a matter of time before Geraldine caught up with her. That was why it was imperative for Holly to go on the offensive, take her by surprise. Getting in first was the only real chance she had of setting things straight.

The bus slowed down again, groaning like a great beast as it eventually stopped and let two people off.

A group of older boys who looked like they ought to still be at school boarded the bus. They sniggered and leered at the other passengers in that way teenagers sometimes did when they thought they knew everything there was to know about life; that nothing could touch them.

They stormed past Holly's seat cackling and sniping at each other like a pack of dogs.

She looked out of the window and waited for them to pass.

She could sense the dark thoughts crowding in at the periphery of her positive attitude like jackals. Just waiting for a chance to bite.

She took a deep breath and closed her eyes for a second or two.

Everything is going well. Everything is going to be fine.

She wouldn't let her past define her any more… Today was all about her future, and she would push aside anyone who tried to stop her in her tracks.

She had to do it for herself, and this time ensure she made a much better job of it.

CHAPTER 18

Holly

As soon as the memory drifted closer, she got the familiar sick feeling in the pit of her stomach.

Ordinarily she'd push it away as hard as she could, back in its box and snap the lid shut. But today, she felt so good she thought she might just risk allowing herself a few minutes to think about what had happened.

To move on, she knew she had to revisit the past in an effort to construct an organised timeline that might help her now she was feeling better.

Markus had reassured her more than once during the coach trip to Manchester that he had already organised temporary accommodation for the two of them.

'Where?' she'd asked. 'A hotel or an apartment?'

He had laughed. 'Take a chill pill, Holly.' He'd shaken his head. 'I had you down as a little more of a maverick rather than the worrying, nervous type.'

'I'm not worrying *or* nervous,' she'd lied. 'I'm just asking, is all.'

He had smiled and closed his eyes again. 'Trust me. Everything will be fine.'

The cold rain had lashed their faces as they'd alighted from the coach at Manchester bus station. Reversing beeps and vehicle headlights had lit up the darkness and showered them with a blaze of artificial brightness that Holly had found herself turning away from.

Markus had brought a holdall and a rucksack, the same as Holly had, and they'd waited in turn behind the other passengers, ready to pull their bags from the under-vehicle luggage stowage.

A scruffy-looking man in his twenties had been waiting for them as they walked into the foyer. Markus had introduced him simply as Tyrone. He'd nodded towards Holly without looking at her and then handed Markus a hand-scrawled note with some directions, and what looked to Holly like timings.

'Everything's on there,' he'd said, his eyes darting around the station. 'You've got my number, yeah?'

'Yes,' Markus had agreed, and glanced at his watch. 'We are supposed to meet Karla here… five minutes ago, actually.'

'I know nothing about that, man,' Tyrone had mumbled. 'See you back here at eight in the morning, yeah?'

'Fine,' Markus had said confidently. 'Thank you.'

When Tyrone had disappeared, Holly grasped Markus's arm. 'Where's this woman who's supposed to be meeting us? What if she doesn't turn up… where will we stay?'

'Holly, Holly!' he'd drawled. 'Relax. She will show, I promise.'

She did show. Half an hour late.

It was after eleven at night and the coach arrivals seemed to have slowed to nothing. Apart from a steward in a high-vis jacket, it appeared that Holly and Markus were the only two people still waiting.

Suddenly a tall, impoverished-looking young woman in jeans and high heels, with stringy black hair, had appeared out of nowhere and walked quickly towards them.

'Is that her?' Holly had asked, hardly able to keep the hope out of her voice.

'I don't know.' Markus had shrugged. 'I have never met her.'

An uneasy feeling had gripped Holly's stomach yet again, but the woman was closer now, so she'd had to keep her thoughts to herself.

'Markus?' the woman had said in a broad Manchester accent. Her face was plastered with greasy-looking make-up, her eyes heavily painted with eyeliner, but her dry, chapped lips had been left with no colour.

'Yes, and this is my friend Holly.' Markus had smiled but the woman didn't return it. 'You are Karla, I presume?'

'Yeah.' She'd checked her watch. 'Look, I need to be somewhere else in twenty minutes, so we'd best grab a cab.'

'Where are we staying?' Markus had asked once they'd shoved their luggage in the boot of the cab and were on their way. 'Is it an apartment, or a house?'

Karla had turned around in the front passenger seat and looked back at him like he'd fallen from the sky.

'Dunno, mate. I just do as I'm told.' A smirk had played around the corners of her dry mouth as she'd added playfully, 'Might be a five-bed mansion in Altrincham for all I know.'

It turned out *not* to be a mansion in an affluent area of Manchester.

The cab had turned suddenly from the brightly lit main road and progressed slowly down a warren of dingy side streets. Holly had spotted dubious-looking groups of hooded characters clustered together in the dense shadows.

She'd gripped Markus's upper arm and squeezed to signify her nervousness, but he had stared out of his own window and hadn't reacted when she hissed, 'I thought your friend had a decent place for us to stay?'

When the cab finally came to a standstill, Markus paid him in cash.

'It's that one, with the broken glass.' Karla had pointed to the most run-down house in the middle of a terrace of five. 'See you around, yeah?'

Without answering her, Holly had pushed the door of the cab shut and the heavy black vehicle had pulled away.

'Markus, I don't want to stay—'

'Holly, please,' he'd said sharply, his feet scuffing on the wet pavement. 'We just need to get through the next couple of days, that's all. Unless you've got money for a swanky hotel, that is.'

When he snapped, it unnerved her. She'd never known Markus anything other than smiling, joking, reassuring in his manner. Maybe he was also feeling unsure about how safe his arrangements were. Earlier, he'd certainly implied that everything had been taken care of satisfactorily.

'This will all be behind you if you impress my friend,' he said simply.

She'd waited, but as usual, no further details were forthcoming. She was getting sick and tired of hearing about this mystery *friend* who apparently held their future in his palm.

Markus had rapped twice at the peeling front door with the boarded-up panel, but there had been no reply. He'd shrugged at her and then turned the handle and pushed… and the door had creaked open, catching on the rucked-up carpet inside.

Holly had followed him into the house, having decided she really had no choice but to front it out. That was definitely what Markus was doing. He might appear confident, but she'd noticed his tense jaw and the odd exaggerated blink.

She'd just have to look at it as the start of her new adventure, she told herself for the umpteenth time.

As Markus closed the door behind them, a figure had appeared in the doorway of what Holly presumed would be the front room in a normal, functioning household.

It was at that precise moment, when she'd looked into the man's lifeless eyes, that she had realised this first night was probably going to be a far worse experience than she had previously imagined.

CHAPTER 19

David

I watch as the driver of the silver BMW parks up at the top of the car park, behind the assistant manager's outsized Range Rover.

I've seen this underhanded strategy many times since I started the job. Some folks think that if they park as far away from my office as possible and use a larger vehicle as cover, I won't notice they are parking illegally.

Barely blinking, I train my eyes on the spot, and within a matter of seconds I catch a glimpse of the driver disappearing up the near-invisible alleyway in the top corner.

It's a little-known short cut through which one is able to double back onto the main street and the shopping mall beyond.

I smile in satisfaction as my eyes drop to the clipboard.

I already have his full registration number, recorded a mere second or two after he entered the car park. I pick up the phone and speed-dial Bob at Clamp 'Em, a company we use that's located a mere stone's throw from the store.

'Be there in a jiffy, David,' Bob says brightly. 'We'll give him a nice two-hundred-quid surprise for when he gets back from his shopping trip, eh?'

I sigh with contentment and lean back in my padded chair.

Job satisfaction is a fine thing. The outside world is a different matter altogether, but here, in my office, I am king.

My word is law, as that arrogant Beamer driver is about to discover.

I grab my high-vis jacket and quickly lock up the office. I've probably got five minutes at the most before Bob arrives with his specialist clamping equipment.

He's got the offending vehicle's registration number and he can get on with the job without me, but if I'm honest, I don't want to miss all the fun.

I use the shop's back entrance and bump into Cath, the receptionist.

'I'm after Mr Kellington, Cath,' I say briskly, one arm tangling up in my jacket as I try to get it on. 'I've some important information for him.'

Cath's mouth seems to fight a smirk, but I'm probably imagining it. There's nothing funny about a parking violation. 'He's upstairs, David, just about to interview for the sales assistant vacancy. You might catch him if you hurry.'

I race upstairs up to the small suite of management offices.

Mr Kellington likes to be aware of everything that happens on the premises. I know he'll appreciate me taking the time to inform him about today's rogue driver.

I probably initiate about four or five clamps a month, and Mr Kellington once informed me that this figure was *double* the number carried out under the previous parking assistant's watch.

'Our last attendant didn't quite have your... shall we say, *enthusiasm*, for punishing offenders,' he'd said, smiling at me in that funny way he sometimes did when I handed him my weekly parking violations report. 'He always warned them first, you see.'

I've no time for that sort of softly-softly approach, particularly when drivers pass a large black-and-white sign on the way in:

CUSTOMER PARKING ONLY. OFFENDERS WILL BE CLAMPED.

If that's not a clear enough warning, I don't know what is.

As I near the top of the stairs, I spot Mr Kellington and Josh speaking to a smartly dressed young lady. Josh sweeps an open arm to steer her into the meeting room.

I'm just on the brink of calling out, to catch them before they disappear into the office, when, entirely of their own accord, my feet suddenly stop dead.

From a distance, I didn't register the significance of the shoulder-length light brown hair, nor the dark, brooding eyes and sensible flat shoes.

But when she turns to thank Josh for holding the door, I realise exactly who she is.

It's the girl from next door.

Mrs Barrett's visitor.

CHAPTER 20

There are lots of things I don't recall very clearly, but I remember watching her. In the café.

It didn't take me long to work out that when she could, she sat in the same place.

Once she was busy chatting, it wasn't too difficult to squeeze in at one of the tables just around the corner. The ones that are usually free because they're tight for space… but also conveniently out of her line of sight.

Just a friendly suggestion: she should learn to speak a little more quietly.

I learned a lot about her just by listening, even before we actually met.

She gave me the idea; she made me want to get to know her better.

She'd do well to remember that.

She can't see me from down here, has no clue that I have a bird's-eye view of her every move. She spends most of her time in the living room or the kitchen, and occasionally she comes out into the yard.

It hasn't taken me long to establish her routine. I know that if I can get around the back of the house, stand under the cover of an oak tree that shades the unmade path that runs across into open fields, I can watch her in the bedroom, too.

She always puts on the light and then closes the thin bedroom curtains. Sometimes she stands there for a few moments, illuminated by the stark light behind her, staring out into the darkness. It seems as if she knows I'm here, watching. I often feel like she's reaching out to me, wanting me to show my face.

Of course, I never do. For now, it's best she hasn't got a clue that I'm getting to know her, watching her live her uneventful life.

There's no need for her to know my intentions at this point. She'll become aware of them soon enough.

CHAPTER 21

Holly

The day after her interview, Holly started the new job.

On her arrival at the main entrance, she was impressed that Mr Kellington himself had taken the time to give her a tour of the large three-storey premises.

Afterwards, he spoke to her for a good thirty minutes in his office, availing her of the family history behind the company and the ethos that he said made Kellington's different.

'We're a business like any other,' he began, lifting his chin and tweaking his black-and-white-spotted bow tie. 'But our customer service must never be sacrificed in favour of the balance sheet. As my father told me when I started here fifty years ago as an apprentice: the customer always comes first at Kellington's.'

Holly nodded in all the right places, but as Mr Kellington continued, she started to understand.

'When a customer approaches you, we don't click the stopwatch here, Holly. If they want to talk about the holiday they've just returned from in the Caribbean, then listen. Maybe tell them it's a place you've always wanted to go, or talk about your own holiday experiences to build some rapport.'

Fat chance of that, Holly thought. She hadn't taken a holiday in years.

'Get to know the products inside out so you can best advise the customer on what they need. They might not know themself, and you can help them make the necessary decisions. And the most important thing of all,' Mr Kellington added, 'is to remember there's no hard sell here. You will receive a good commission structure for all goods sold, but we want our customers to return, not to feel they've been pressured or fleeced.'

Holly immediately thought about her last job before leaving Manchester. It had been in a vast, impersonal call centre, selling life insurance. The manager had told her to say literally anything to get the customers to buy, particularly during December, when family took priority over telesales products and any spare cash was spent on presents.

'Scare them with the facts,' he'd said. 'Ask them what good all their gifts will do if their family get lumbered with crippling funeral costs.'

'That seems a bit mean,' Holly had countered. 'To be talking about death, I mean, at Christmas.'

The manager had laughed at her naïvety. 'It's a fact of life, love! Try googling celebs who've died on Christmas Day; you'll be surprised how many there are. Rattling off a few well-known names who've carked it soon brings it home to the customer that these things can happen to anyone. Get their bank details and get them off the phone quick as you can, so you can sign up the next one.'

She'd lasted almost three weeks there, until a recently widowed lady had broken down when Holly had used the 'Christmas death' sales line. She'd decided there and then that she couldn't do it any more.

So when Mr Kellington outlined the exact opposite policy at the store, Holly smiled appreciatively and nodded.

'As my father once said to me, people buy from people,' he stressed. 'And I would add that they especially buy from people that they trust and like.'

She left the MD's office not only feeling that she knew practically every last sales tip that Mr Kellington's father had ever uttered, but also with a sense that there was a chance she might make a real difference here, and be good at it too.

That wasn't something she'd been used to in her previous call-centre roles, where new staff were viewed as constant, transient fodder.

It would've been easy to take everything Mr Kellington had said with a pinch of salt and concentrate on maximising her own sales – she'd been very pleasantly surprised at the excellent commission structure – but Holly decided to follow his advice.

He might appear a touch eccentric, wandering around the shop floor with the little notebook he scribbled in constantly, and his striking bow ties – a different design for each day, apparently – but clearly he knew his stuff. And she could tell that his store was a personal passion rather than simply a means of earning as much money as possible.

The assistant manager, Josh Peterson, was particularly helpful. He sort of took Holly under his wing, giving her bits of useful inside information, like Mr Kellington's bizarre bow ties. He also pointed out Emily Beech, the top saleswoman in the company.

The store showrooms were split into three levels. Bedrooms downstairs, lavish home accessories and staff offices upstairs, and on the ground floor, which was to be Holly's base, lounge and dining furniture and also lighting.

Holly would be one of four sales assistants working the ground floor, and Emily Beech was another.

Josh lowered his voice, even though Emily was busy with customers over the other side of the showroom.

'She's only worked here for a year, but between you and me, with commission, her salary has just exceeded thirty grand. That's considerably more than any of the other sales staff. Jeez, it's not that far off my own pay.'

Holly's eyes widened. She thought of what a salary like that could do for her in terms of paying off her debt and achieving the fresh start she craved so badly… Everything suddenly felt so much more achievable.

When the recruitment consultant had flagged up this job, Holly had expected a standard retail assistant post, paying the minimum wage. She'd imagined it would entail nothing more strenuous than giving customers a bit of information about the products and then pointing them in the direction of the cash till.

Now Josh was telling her that her modest £13K basic salary could be inflated to massive proportions. If she did the job right.

When Josh returned to his office and the customers had left, Holly walked over to Emily Beech.

The shop was quieter now, possibly as it was almost lunchtime, and Emily was standing near the expansive front window, checking her phone.

As Holly made her nervous approach, she registered Emily's well-cut navy trouser suit and crisp white blouse. She couldn't help wondering how this elegant woman managed to stand all day in the towering black patent stilettos that encased her feet.

A sleek butter-blonde bob hovered, razor sharp, over Emily's shoulders, framing a perfectly made-up but curiously expressionless face.

Holly suddenly became painfully aware of her own dull complexion. The lank hair that she'd tucked impatiently behind her ears to keep it off her face until she could muster the enthusiasm to wash and style it; her bitten, unvarnished nails.

Now, she wished she'd made more of an effort before leaving the house that morning, not that she'd have looked much different. There was only so much you could do with dry, overdyed hair and dowdy, ill-fitting clothes.

It was difficult to be motivated when there was so much that needed attention. But Holly reminded herself that if she could earn a salary remotely near Emily's, then she too would be able to invest in a new wardrobe and a good haircut.

She felt like a penguin waddling across the shop in her scuffed flat shoes, but she forced herself to go through with it. Josh had mentioned that all the sales assistants were on the same level; Emily had no seniority over Holly.

She wasn't going to change her life by running away from an opportunity to get on the right side of someone who could teach her a lot, even if that meant sucking up to her a bit. It simply had to be done.

She stretched her mouth into something she hoped resembled a friendly smile.

'Hi, I'm Holly! Pleased to meet you.' She extended a hand. 'I'm really looking forward to getting stuck into the job. Josh was telling me you're a great saleswoman.'

'The *best* saleswoman, I think you'll find,' Emily said coolly, without looking up from her phone. Slowly, indifferent eyes drifted over Holly, but her proffered hand was ignored. 'Let's hope you're a bit tougher than the last one we had here. She ran off crying after a couple of weeks. Pathetic.'

'Oh!' Holly swallowed, taken aback. 'I didn't know that. Anyway, maybe we can have a chat over coffee or something. I'd welcome any tips you could give me.'

'I don't socialise at work if I can help it,' Emily said airily. 'I'm here to make money, not friends.'

'I just wondered if you'd have time to talk a bit about how you close your sales. I've heard that's the tricky bit, and—'

'Sorry. I take it you've heard the phrase *time is money*?' Emily cut her off, striding away on her spiked heels. 'See you around,' she called over her shoulder.

For the rest of the day, Holly purposely stayed in the background, well away from Emily's barbed comments. She floated around the periphery of the large showroom, making notes on the furnishings and exchanging pleasantries with customers.

However, behind her useful naïve facade, she was learning fast.

She might appear a little shy and uncertain, wandering here and there without any real purpose. In fact she was a woman on a mission, discreetly shadowing her colleague.

Emily might refuse to have a conversation with her, but she couldn't stop Holly watching and learning.

As far as Holly was concerned, securing this job had been a gift that ultimately could help her find Evan quicker.

She'd already decided that she wouldn't be dissuaded by someone like Emily Beech.

CHAPTER 22

Holly

By her third day on the job, Holly had stopped her aimless drifting and dared to venture a little closer to Emily as she interacted with customers.

She noticed that her colleague saved her energies for a certain type of shopper. One might say the more *discerning* customer. She usually made three or four sales each day – furniture and accessories of varying costs. But there was nothing remotely pricey enough to explain the sky-high commission that Josh had claimed she was earning.

The majority of customers who shopped here held a certain fascination for Holly. They weren't exactly the sort born with a silver spoon in their mouths – many seemed to be self-made business people – but some of them weren't far off.

They complained loudly about getting stuck in traffic on the way to their exclusive health club, or bemoaned the fact that they'd have to rush to make their restaurant reservation at lunchtime.

Holly got the distinct impression that none of them had known a particularly hard life, although, to be fair, you could never be sure. Still, she'd have bet good money that not one of them had left home in search of a better life, escaping the misery of being poor and a virtual outcast.

But Holly herself had a lot to be thankful for, and she vowed to keep reminding herself of that. If she was ever in any doubt, all she had to do was conjure up the dread and fear she'd felt that first night in the Manchester hellhole.

That always served to put things into perspective.

The emaciated man who had appeared in the living room doorway at the dilapidated house had looked as if he'd just woken up.

'Who are you?' he'd croaked.

'We were told to come here,' Markus had replied nervously. 'Just for a couple of nights. We—'

'Got any stuff for me?'

'What? No! No, sorry.' Markus had patted his pockets and held up his empty hands to show he had no drugs.

The man's bony features had hardened when he saw there would be no benefit to him. He'd turned to leave.

'Where shall we crash, man?' Markus had called after him.

'Anywhere you can,' he'd muttered, and shuffled back into the front room.

Markus had moved to the doorway and Holly had stayed behind him, peering over his shoulder.

The room had been gloomy, the heavy curtains almost closed. There had been a sour, rotten smell pervading the place and Holly had clamped her hand over her nose and mouth.

Groans emanated from the darkest corners and she saw vague writhing, tortured shapes.

'We can't stay here,' she had hissed, stumbling back into the hall and pulling in a big breath of the slightly less polluted air.

'We've no choice, Holly,' Markus had told her firmly. 'Wait here and I'll have a scout around.'

Holly had huddled close to the front door, next to their luggage.

She'd felt a welcome trickle of cool fresh air through the broken glass behind her. Her stomach had felt raw with nerves and she'd thought she might need the loo soon, shuddering at the thought of the bathroom arrangements in a place like this.

The house had been shrouded in a curious silence, punctured only by moaning from the doomed figures she'd spotted in the room next door. She dreaded to imagine the pain those people were experiencing to be making such harrowing noises. They certainly weren't sounds that arose from pleasure of any sort.

Goodness knows what danger she and Markus might be in here, and the risk of picking up some nasty disease had to be pretty high.

Why had Markus given her the distinct impression that his boss would be taking care of them when *this* was the true reality of what awaited?

At that moment, Markus had returned from upstairs, his face grim.

'There are people everywhere, and every room is like that one.' He'd shuddered, nodding to the room next to them. 'There's a free corner in one of the bedrooms. We should grab that now, I think. We can sleep in shifts to keep our belongings safe.'

'Never mind keeping the luggage safe; we need to keep ourselves safe,' Holly had countered. 'I'd rather sleep in a local park than here.'

She'd felt close to tears and he'd slid his arm around her shoulders.

'Come on, we can do this, Holly. It's raining and freezing out there. I'll make sure it's just the one night, OK? At sunrise tomorrow we'll leave.'

A wave of tiredness and hopelessness had rolled over her. What was the point in fighting? They were here now, so it was a case of just getting through to the morning.

'We will look back soon and laugh at this, I promise.' Markus had winked at her. 'Tomorrow we will move on to our new life.'

'Where's your boss?' she'd pleaded. 'I thought he had everything in hand.'

'Tomorrow, you'll see.' Markus had shrugged.

That night had been ten years ago now, and despite Markus's assurances, she still wasn't looking back and laughing.

A clear, cultured voice flooded the showroom via the store tannoy system. Cath, the receptionist, was trying to chase down Mr Kellington.

Grateful for the interruption to her disturbing memories, Holly set about neatening the elaborately carved chairs nestled around the bespoke Italian dining room set.

She ought to be counting her blessings. Finding a place to live with Mrs Barrett and securing a decent job that had the financial potential to kick-start her recovery plans was something to celebrate.

But as usual, whenever she ought to be enjoying a rare moment of contentment, the troubling memories always found a way of elbowing their way in and ruining everything all over again.

She resolved to put a stop to it. She would give everything to this job and be a success.

That was by far the best way for her to begin the healing process, and to ensure that she and Evan would be together again. She felt it in every fibre of her being.

CHAPTER 23

Cora

When Cora got home from town, she went straight upstairs.

She took a cursory look in Holly's bedroom. Everything seemed to be in order in there. The girl was quite neat and tidy, which was a relief.

Cora had read in the newspaper recently that young people from Holly's generation had been largely spoiled by over-generous parents and consequently were barely self-sufficient. It was probably an unfair generalisation.

Holly hadn't said much about her early family life, but she had made one or two vague comments that had led Cora to believe she hadn't been particularly cosseted, nor indeed nurtured appropriately, as one might expect.

Cora walked over to the window, and that was when she saw the flashing green light on the floor. A laptop.

She'd popped her head round the door yesterday evening to bid Holly goodnight and the girl had been sitting up in bed tapping away on it. Nothing unusual about that, but she'd had the most dreadful scowl on her face and Cora could have sworn her eyes looked moist.

She'd slammed the lid shut and smiled over-brightly, bidding Cora goodnight as if nothing was wrong. Which, of course, usually indicated that something was.

Last year, Cora had attended a free ten-week computing course at the local library. It had covered basic IT skills and had been billed as suiting 'silver surfers', which she had found a silly and irritating term.

Surprisingly, she'd taken to it like a duck to water. Their tutor, Anna, had shown them how to compose a letter, write and send emails, and negotiate the internet.

It had been a revelation to Cora: whole department stores and supermarkets to browse at the click of a button!

She had fully intended buying a computer to use at home after the course, and Anna had offered to help her select and purchase a suitable model. But then the tutor had moved away to care for a sick relative, and Cora's new-found computing enthusiasm had seemed to disappear with her.

She stared at the laptop. She could open it right now and, provided it hadn't got one of those password locks on it, have a little practise before her skills became too rusty. She'd been thinking of getting a lightweight coat for the spring, and it would be useful to look around online to save her walking all round town in search of one.

She felt sure Holly wouldn't mind.

Cora glanced at her watch then and realised the time had quite run away from her. It would have to wait for another day after all.

She walked out of the room and across the small landing. Picking up her bulging handbag, she went into her own bedroom and closed the door behind her, setting to work immediately.

Huffing and puffing, she eventually managed to get everything sorted, and only had the bed to make and the curtains to open when she heard a tap on the bedroom door.

'Hang on,' she managed, perching on the edge of the bed to get her breath back and calm her heart rate down.

Was this how it felt, she wondered, when a heart attack struck? At her age, you often got to wondering how you'd go, how exactly it would happen.

Cora's preference was for quick and painless... but that was everyone's wish. Last year, an old man had been vocal in the greengrocer's and that had set her thinking.

'Not to drag on for months but to give me long enough to put my affairs in order,' he'd declared, obviously having given it a lot of thought.

He had a point, Cora admitted. It occurred to her that should she pop her clogs right now, this minute, nothing at all would be *sorted*.

She knew it was something that needed addressing without delay, and she fully intended to take action. She just needed a little more time to finalise her thoughts and speak to David.

Holly called out her name.

Cora hadn't heard the back kitchen door open and close, or footsteps on the stairs. It was frightening really; she should lock up in future before getting sorted up here.

'Cora? Are you all right in there?' Holly called again, this time in a concerned voice.

'I'm fine, dear,' she said. 'I'm just getting my breath back. Come in.'

The door opened and Holly peered round it cautiously. Her eyes darted this way and that as she squinted a little in the gloom.

'You've got the curtains closed,' she said, stating the obvious.

'Yes, I've just had a little lie-down.' Cora shifted uncomfortably under Holly's stare. It was glaringly obvious, what with being a little out of breath and ruddy-cheeked, that she hadn't been resting.

Whatever, Cora told herself. She didn't have to provide an explanation to Holly. This was *her* house, *her* bedroom and *her* business.

Nobody else needed to be involved. Yet.

Holly, God bless her, seemed to sense Cora's reluctance to chat and went back downstairs to make them a drink.

Cora finished her tasks in the bedroom and went downstairs herself.

'David came around this afternoon,' she told Holly after thanking her for the tea. 'He says he's seen you at work.'

'Kellington's?'

'The very same.' Cora looked pleased. 'Didn't I tell you? He works there as a parking attendant.'

'No, you didn't say.' Holly frowned. 'I haven't seen him there.'

'Well, he's stationed outside mostly, I think.' Cora chuckled to herself. 'To hear him talk, he's got more responsibilities than Mr Kellington himself.'

'He seems very fond of you, though, David,' Holly said. 'I'm glad you've got someone close by to look after you a bit... after your husband passed, I mean.'

'Oh yes, David has been coming round here since he could walk.' Cora smiled and gazed into the middle distance. 'Harold had been ill for some time. The day I went upstairs and found him cold and still, David was the one who calmed me down, phoned the ambulance. He stayed with me until the next day, slept right there on the sofa.'

'That was kind of him,' Holly said softly.

'Yes.' Cora smiled at her. 'The mark of a true friend.'

CHAPTER 24

Holly

At lunchtime, Holly took her salad and a tatty paperback up to the top floor. There was a pleasant roof terrace area there where customers and staff could get coffee.

She found a table next to the large windows that overlooked the cityscape, then opened the plastic container and poked unexcitedly with her fork at the spinach leaves and flaked tuna she'd cobbled together that morning. Not the most appetising meal, but it was still a while until her first payday, and watching the pennies was mandatory.

She opened her book at the folded-over corner, resolving to buy a bookmark when she saw a nice one. Anyone who valued books knew that bending page corners wasn't the done thing.

It seemed that everything she touched held a memory just waiting to spring free. Take this book, for instance, *A Kestrel for a Knave* by Barry Hines. It was the only book she owned, the only one she'd kept from her school days.

She remembered sitting night after night in the furthest corner from the door in the library with this book. For a short time she'd been able to lose herself in its pages, forget how shitty her life had become.

Ironic, she thought now, that what she'd considered a bad life back then had actually turned out to be the *better* times.

Regardless, the book still had the power to hold her entranced and, munching on a few tasteless spinach leaves, she began to read. Within moments the story pulled her in and she was there with Billy Casper in the school assembly, holding his breath when the boy coughed and invoked the wrath of the headteacher, Mr Gryce…

'Hello, Holly.'

Surprised, she looked up at the sound of the hesitant voice.

'Oh, hello, David!' She placed the book face down on the table and laid down her fork. 'Cora only just told me you worked here. Apparently you spotted me the other day?'

'I didn't know it was you. I wasn't following you around or anything, I just had to tell Mr Kellington something important and Cath, the receptionist, said I might catch him as he was about to interview someone for the new job, and then I realised…'

He stopped to draw breath, his face growing redder by the second.

'And then you realised it was me,' Holly provided.

'Yes,' he said. 'I realised the person being interviewed was you. Mrs Barrett's… visitor.'

He shifted from foot to foot, staring at the book on the table but saying nothing more.

'Small world, isn't it?' She smiled. 'Join me if you like.'

His face flushed further still.

'I… I can't,' he said. 'I'm just getting a coffee to take back to my office. But thank you. Thanks for asking me to sit here with you.'

'Hey, it's no big deal.' She shrugged and picked up her fork again.

David didn't move.

'I've worked here for ten months and nobody's ever asked me to sit with them. In here.'

'Oh!' Holly paused before continuing. 'Well, you're always welcome to join me, maybe when you have a longer break.'

'I don't take breaks as a rule.'

'Why not? You're entitled, you know.'

'There are drivers around here who'd take advantage.'

'Parking up outside, you mean?'

'Violating the rules,' David said gravely. 'There are a handful of regular offenders who'd love to get one up on me.'

'I see.' Holly jabbed at her salad with the fork. She was getting a little tired of the stilted conversation. 'Well, don't let me stop you then.'

'Billy Casper,' he remarked.

'What? Oh yes.' She patted the book. 'Good old Billy Casper.'

'I've read it,' he said. 'It's rather sad at the end.'

'Yes, it is,' she agreed. 'But I think there's hope there too. Wouldn't you agree?'

He thought for a moment. She waited for his opinion on the story, but it didn't come.

'I'll get my coffee then,' was all he said. 'Goodbye, Holly.'

'See you around, David.'

She smiled to herself as he moved away without replying. He was an odd one, for sure, but it took all sorts and she was used to taking a chance on people. It was often the people who appeared most normal that you had to watch.

Ten years ago, she'd really had no choice in the matter. She'd had to trust Markus and agree to his plan to stay for one night in that hellhole of a house.

But at the time it had certainly felt like she'd made a mistake putting her faith in him, as they'd lugged their cases and rucksacks upstairs.

They'd had to squat down in a filthy corner in the upstairs front bedroom. It had stunk in there too, of unwashed bodies and worse. As her eyes had adjusted to the near darkness, Holly had spotted a foul-smelling bucket under the window, spotlighted every time a car drove down the street.

She'd clutched a handkerchief to her mouth and nose and drawn her knees up under her chin. She could smell, very faintly, Aunt Susan's perfume on the lace-edged hankie. She recalled her aunt giving it to her when Holly had got upset one night over her mother's death.

Those times had been rare. Holly hadn't enjoyed a close relationship with her mother.

Since Holly had been about ten years old, alcohol had been Julie's number one priority. With the worsening drink problem, the little girl had never known what was coming next.

There were sometimes strange men in the house, in the bedroom with Julie. Little Holly had stood at the door and listened to the giggles and moans of pleasure, and wondered why her mother had instructed her to stay downstairs in the cold living room on her own.

Other times, Julie had been very ill and Holly had had no choice but to mop up diarrhoea and vomit all night long.

Consequently she had always felt happier and more secure when she'd been on her own. Still, she'd often grieved her skewed view of the mother–daughter relationship.

She'd overhear the girls at school talking about enjoying a shopping day or going out for lunch with their mothers, and it stung. Holly had never known how that felt.

Aunt Susan had been sympathetic on the rare occasions Holly had got upset in front of her, and now, as she sat clutching the scrap of lace-edged cotton to her face, she felt a pang of loss at the thought of having left her aunt so abruptly.

She only allowed herself a moment of such sentimental indulgence, though, swiftly reminding herself that she shouldn't get sucked in to reinventing her time with her aunt and uncle as a cosy family atmosphere.

The reality was that during the daytime, she'd been as miserable as sin at school, at the mercy of the mean girls there, but she'd still felt more at home – and certainly safer – in the school library and even the park than she had in the house alone with creepy Keith.

When her aunt finally got home from work in the evenings, Holly had to pretend everything was fine, because it was painfully clear that Susan would always refuse to contemplate that her husband could possibly be anything but decent.

Tomorrow, she reminded herself, a fresh new start would await her.

Beside her, Markus let out a soft snore. She'd decided not to bother waking him in an hour's time, as they'd agreed. She'd realised there was no way she could manage even a second of shut-eye in this godforsaken place, and there was no sense in them both staying awake all night.

If Markus got some rest, Holly had reasoned, he'd hopefully rise refreshed and ready to sort out some alternative arrangements for their accommodation tomorrow evening.

She was yet to find out exactly what her new opportunity might be, but whatever she was offered, she'd already decided she had to take it.

She honestly didn't care what she would be doing, so long as it was legal and she made some money. She longed to get some independence back.

Back then, that had seemed to be the most important thing.

CHAPTER 25

Holly

After lunch, a wealthy-looking middle-aged couple entered the store. Holly watched in amazement as Emily sprang into action like a newly wound clockwork toy.

She sashayed across the shop, her arms extended before her as though greeting dear long-lost friends.

'Mr and Mrs Fenwick,' she announced dramatically, sweeping by salesman Ben Dixon, who for a moment or two had looked in danger of getting to the customers before her. 'It's been far too long!'

Quickly tiring of watching a newly energised Emily air-kissing her customers and assuring them how well they looked, Holly opened the large cardboard box in front of her and carefully peeled away the masses of bubble wrap to reveal an exquisite black glass Lalique vase.

She gently fingered the tiny, almost translucent pale pink glass flowers that dotted the lip of the vase and then cascaded down one shoulder. It was truly one of the most beautiful things she'd ever seen.

'And how's dear Willem doing at boarding school?' Holly tuned back in to Emily's impressive performance as she gently dusted off the vase. 'They're so lucky to have him, little genius that he is. You must be *so* proud.'

Holly allowed herself a small cynical smile, noting that her endlessly irritated colleague could convincingly morph into Miss Personality when the mood took her.

It also didn't escape Holly's notice that the whole time Emily was oohing and aahing at the digital photographs of the Fenwicks' *amazing* break in Milan on Mrs Fenwick's phone, she was steadily leading them, inch by inch, towards the front of the shop, where the brand-new range of gold-plated feather boa lamps had been displayed.

Without noticing her ploy, the Fenwicks followed, continuing to loudly gush over every detail of their fabulous lives since their last visit to the store.

Holly even felt a grudging respect for Emily. Whatever she might think of her as a colleague, there was no doubt at all that she was extremely good at her job.

She carefully placed the vase on the special marble pedestal stand that Josh had brought over to display it at its best. She swallowed hard when she saw the tiny white price sticker that would be concealed by its base.

Two thousand pounds. For what amounted to a fancy piece of *glass*, for goodness' sake! Yes, it was beyond beautiful, but it occurred to her that in the real world, that amount would cover some people's rent or mortgage payments for months.

Following Josh's earlier instructions, she clicked the silky black security rope in place in front of the pedestal. They used it purely for show, to discourage customers from getting too close to the most fragile pieces.

'Now, I've something special to share with you.' Emily's voice dropped lower, but fortunately Holly was well within eavesdropping range. 'As soon as I saw these divine lamps, I thought of you. I shouldn't really tell you this, but…' she glanced around, apparently to ensure nobody else was listening, 'we only have the two lamps in. They're limited-edition stock direct from the exclusive Haus of Rome, and as you can imagine, they're like gold dust to source.'

Holly noted Emily's meaningful pause before her killer finish.

'They're retailing at twelve hundred each, or as a special deal, I can do the pair for just two thousand pounds.'

The extortionate price tag elicited a snort from Mr Fenwick, but his wife remained entranced by the convincing sales patter.

'However, there's good news,' Emily continued smoothly. 'I've had special clearance from Mr Kellington himself to offer them to you, my best clients, for a mere eighteen hundred the pair.' She flashed an excited smile, as if she could barely believe the bargain she'd been able to extend to them.

'I don't know,' Mr Fenwick said doubtfully. 'Perhaps we'll have a look around before we make a decision and—'

Emily cut in as if he'd never spoken.

'I immediately thought of you because I know how much Mrs Fenwick loves her black-and-gold colour scheme in the lounge. I can almost picture them there myself.'

'You're so right, Emily!' Mrs Fenwick clapped her hands together and turned to her husband. 'Oh darling, they'd go so perfectly in there.'

'We already own more fancy lamps than you can shake a stick at,' her husband growled. 'The house'll be in danger of resembling Blackpool illuminations soon.'

'But I could take out those Tiffany-style lamps we've had for a while and put the new ones in their place.'

'I don't know, Amanda. These lamps are very expensive, and—'

'Look, I'm probably going to get in trouble for doing this,' Emily confided. 'But what if I could do them for sixteen hundred the pair? They're so exclusive, they're probably the only two in the whole of the East Midlands right now. I'd *hate* you to miss out.'

There was a beat or two of tense silence.

'You know, darling, I just don't think I can go home without them,' Mrs Fenwick simpered, leaning in to her husband. 'And sixteen hundred... well, it's a bargain.'

'Oh, go on then.' He rolled his eyes and sighed dramatically. 'You two just tie me up in knots every time I come in here.'

Emily and Mrs Fenwick embraced and giggled together conspiratorially like schoolgirls.

Holly smiled to herself as she carried the surplus packaging from the vase into the back office. Emily didn't have a clue that this afternoon she'd kindly provided her with a masterclass in how to sell the most expensive items.

She pushed the box and bubble wrap into the waste materials corner of the small room, ready for collection by the warehouse staff.

When she turned to leave, a handwritten list on the desk caught her attention.

It was a breakdown of bottom-line sales prices for all the items currently on display in the store. Josh had shown her a similar list on her first day.

'You can check here how far you can discount the more expensive items to give our regular customers the best deal,' he'd explained.

Holly shook her head in disbelief when she read the top line: *Haus of Rome feather boa lamps – £1,250 the pair.*

The Fenwicks had just paid £350 over the odds for their lamps, and yet they'd been made to feel they'd been given a very special one-off deal to reward their loyalty to Kellington's.

Emily had added a very nice fifteen per cent boost – at the higher price – to her commission total for the month.

The following day, Holly witnessed her colleague using exactly the same method on different customers when she sold a pricey mirrored coffee table for twenty per cent higher than the back-room list price.

You had to hand it to her. She knew exactly how to sell to Kellington's wealthiest customers, each time securing herself a very generous bonus in the process.

They all thought they were her special VIP clients, receiving a preferential service from Kellington's top saleswoman, but of course, the last laugh was always on them, as they fell for Emily's flattery hook, line and sinker.

Holly got the distinct feeling that when it came to boosting her own salary, there was much to be learned from her colleague.

Emily appeared to have an instinctive sense of what made people tick.

CHAPTER 26

Holly

On arriving home from work each day, Holly walked down the side of the house and used the back door, which led directly into the kitchen.

It was a large room, with mismatched, dated units. No work island or breakfast bar; just a small wooden table in the centre of the room that now, thanks to David, had two chairs pulled up to it.

'Hello?' she called out to Cora, as was her habit upon stepping into the house. 'Oh!'

She stopped and closed the door softly behind her. Cora sat at the table with a man who looked to be in his mid forties. There were two mugs on the table, and some paperwork.

Cora looked up and smiled.

'Holly, this is Mr Brown. He lives two doors down; it's the house with the green front door and the mature weeping willow in the garden.'

'You make it sound very grand, Cora.' Mr Brown grinned. 'Hello, Holly.'

'Hello,' Holly said shyly.

He was a good-looking man in an outdoors type of way, with a ruddy complexion and light-brown hair. He wore a checked shirt and khaki combats that somehow held the suggestion of toned muscle lying below them.

He stood up and inspected his hand before extending it to her. 'Just checking I'm not covered in soil. It's the gardener's curse.'

They smiled at each other and Holly felt Cora's eyes on her.

'Mr Brown is here to do the garden,' Cora said from behind him.

'My name's Nick, by the way.' He sat back down. 'Mr Brown makes me sound a bit like a bank manager.'

Holly laughed.

'Well, I wouldn't presume to introduce you so informally on your first meeting with my visitor, Nicholas,' Cora said with a tight smile. 'One has to at least try and preserve a few manners these days, wouldn't you agree?'

It hadn't escaped Holly's notice that Cora always introduced *her* to other people by her first name.

'I was just showing Cora a few sketches of some plans for the garden,' Nick said, turning a couple of sheets around on the tabletop so Holly could see.

'It all seems very modern,' Holly said, surprised that Cora approved of such a lack of traditional features. 'Decking and a pond. Lovely.'

'Nicholas is very talented.' Cora beamed.

'You're making me blush now.' He glanced at the wall clock. 'Oh well, I'd better get on. Thanks for the tea and the chat, Cora.'

'Any time, Nicholas.' Cora smiled. 'You know that.'

'Are you starting it soon… the landscaping work?' Holly asked.

'Oh no, we're still at the planning stage,' Nick said. 'I'm just here to mow the lawns today.'

'I'll take another look at the sketches and let you know which one I prefer next week,' Cora said, gathering up the paperwork. She looked at Holly. 'I've just a few bits to finish off upstairs and then we can have tea together, dear.'

After the long day at work on her feet, Holly's heart sank at the thought of another long night ahead filled with Cora's endless nostalgia. She hadn't been sleeping that well, so felt doubly exhausted.

Last night she'd sat up in bed for ages, sifting through what felt like thousands of Facebook profiles, trying and failing to find the right ones.

She seemed to be able to drop off to sleep no problem, but then regrets and unresolved pain from her past tended to resurface with a vengeance in the early hours and savage her with the ferocity of a terrier until dawn finally broke.

Nick went outside and Holly heard Cora's heavy footfall ascending the stairs. Still clutching her handbag, and with her shoes and short rain mac on, she stood at the kitchen window and watched as Nick wrestled Cora's antiquated mower out of the shed.

He'd slipped off his fleecy checked shirt and now worked in a pale green T-shirt. As he pulled the mower out, his back muscles rippled under the thin fabric. When he turned, his toned biceps grew taut.

To her horror, he looked up sharply and grinned at her.

She took a step back, but it was too late. He knew she'd been watching him.

He beckoned to her, and as it would be rude to ignore him, she opened the door and stepped down onto the paved patio area.

Her attention was diverted when a ruddy-faced man leaned over David's side of the fence.

'Alright love? Just wanted to say hello, with you being new and all that. I'm Brian.'

He leaned his forearms over the fence and she saw that they were heavily tattooed.

'Hello,' she said tentatively. 'I'm Holly. Pleased to meet you.'

'On your own, are you?'

'Sorry?'

'Moved in here on your own? No boyfriend or anything.'

Her flesh crawled.

'Oh, yes… sorry, I just have to have a word with…' she pointed to Nick and fortunately, he turned off the mower and came over.

A few long strides and he was next to her and the man drifted back up the garden.

'How are you finding it then, life on Baker Crescent?' Nick said.

'I… well, everyone seems very nice,' she stammered, willing the heat in her face to do one. 'Cora has been very good to me.'

'Hmm. She can be an eccentric old bat at times. Goes on a bit with her stories, but I'm very fond of her.' He nodded. 'Have you had the misfortune of meeting your other neighbours yet?'

He nodded to the house next door.

'You mean David? Yes, we've met.'

He watched her steadily but didn't comment. She felt he somehow wanted more from her, and so she began babbling to allay her embarrassment.

'I met his mum, Pat, briefly too. They seem very nice. In fact, I'm working at Kellington's in town, where David is a parking attendant.'

'*Watch him,*' Nick hissed.

'Sorry?' She swallowed.

'David.' He kept his voice low. 'Watch him. That's all I'm saying.'

She felt a flush rise from her neck. 'I… I'm not sure what…'

'Some people pretend to be one thing when really they're something else altogether… if you get my drift.'

'I'm not sure I do,' she said slowly. 'Do I need to be worried?'

Nick opened his mouth to speak, but the words caught in his throat. His eyes slid sideways, focusing on the small window behind her.

Holly twisted round to see Cora standing in the doorway with her arms folded.

Wordlessly Nick turned and scurried back down the garden.

Nick had kept his voice low, so she doubted Cora had overheard what he had said.

Holly knew that the older woman thought a lot of David. She might not like to hear Nick's strange warning.

Holly waited for her to say something but Cora simply turned away and began chopping salad.

Holly stepped back inside the kitchen just as someone knocked frantically at the door.

CHAPTER 27

David

I sit at my bedroom window for what seems like hours, going over everything Holly said at work earlier. Mother calls it fretting.

'It does you no good at all, David,' she always says when she senses I'm in the grip of it. 'Just let go of whatever's worrying you. It's no use churning it over and over in your mind.'

But setting aside troubling thoughts is far easier said than done. Nobody knows that better than me. Mother might call it fretting, but this time it feels a bit more than that.

For the last two years I have embraced my eventless life, my boring routine. That's not to say I've sometimes wished for a little more variety in my days, but Mother and I, we were managing just fine.

Now, with Holly appearing next door – a good thing – and Brian moving in with us – most definitely a bad thing – it feels like the ground beneath me is suddenly not as rock solid.

Holly kindly invited me to join her for coffee in the terrace café at work. My anxiety was rooted in the fact that I might have inadvertently snubbed her.

Join me if you like. That was what she said, and now I can't remember for the life of me what my response was.

As usual, I started ranting on about nothing, with the nerves and all. I think I said I couldn't spare the time away from my desk.

That wasn't really the reason. I was too worried to sit down and start a conversation with her. I felt nervous of long silences; afraid we'd have nothing to talk about.

Yet now I'm home and can look back in a calmer frame of mind, I realise it wouldn't have done any harm just to sit down and chat for a few minutes.

We might have talked about the book she was reading, or the weather… or a hundred and one other things, come to that.

I wonder how I appeared to her. Nervous and unfriendly? Or perhaps just a bit off.

That's the thing about being different. It's so hard to know how to act in order to appear… well… normal, I suppose.

Growing up, I was told so many times by adults – teachers, Mrs Barrett, and Mother herself – to *just be yourself*. They meant well, but I knew even back then that *myself* was the last thing I needed to be. At least if I wanted to try and fit in at school.

Being myself meant never joining in with popular activities, always sitting on my own on school trips, not laughing at the jokes everyone else found hilarious, choosing the library instead of playing footie on the field. That was me, after all.

Things got more complicated as I grew older and entered the world of work. After A levels, I managed to get an apprenticeship at a small textiles factory.

Here there were no teachers to supervise, no responsible adults to watch out for the kids who were perceived as different. The worst bullies on the shop floor were the management. It was the same story at the printing firm, too.

I soon learned that *being myself* was the worst possible way to endear myself to colleagues. Yet I just couldn't pull off how to behave normally, how to fit in like the others.

Just like the kids at school, colleagues grasped within minutes that I wasn't like them.

No matter how often I sniggered at jokes I didn't get, or put myself through the agony and discomfort of drinks after work, they still weren't fooled.

There was a seamless continuation from my school days. The sly grins, the subtle nudges and the same clandestine whispered conversations that broke up the instant I entered the room.

I've learned the hard way that people who don't fit the social norm, for whatever reason, are damned if they do and damned if they don't. Simple as.

And that's why, earlier today, I didn't try to be the person Holly might have expected in the café. That's why I just acted normally... normal for *me*.

She probably thought me a bit stand-offish, and that's what bothers me now. Because I didn't mean to be. I really, really didn't want to come over like that.

She couldn't have been left with a positive impression, but there's nothing I can do about it now.

Or is there?

I decide, on the spur of the moment, to pop round to Mrs Barrett's on the pretence of checking the water pressure, which we sometimes have problems with around here.

I change into my jeans and trainers and a rather nice blue sweater that Mother says brings out my eyes, which I always think sounds a bit of a sinister thing to say.

The dragging sense of dread has given way to a lighter step, a sense that things might yet be salvaged.

As I reach forward to turn off my computer monitor, I happen to glance down into next door's yard.

My hand freezes on the monitor button and I wince at the sharp pain as I unwittingly bite down on my tongue.

Once I realise what's happening, I race downstairs and rush past Mother, ignoring her astonished expression.

Once outside, I instinctively know not to go anywhere near *him*, but I must warn Holly. I wonder if Mrs Barrett knows what's happening out in her garden.

Even though I know she doesn't use it much, I bang on the front door, and when there is no answer, I ring the doorbell. Still no answer. With the heel of my hand, I thump again.

Finally I hear Mrs Barrett's muffled voice calling out and stiff bolts being drawn back. She opens the door, and when she sees it's me, her annoyed expression dissolves.

'David! I was in the kitchen making tea, with the radio on. Why on earth didn't you just come around the back?'

'Can I come in?' I ask.

She stands aside and I step into the hallway.

'What is it?' She closes the door behind me. 'Are you upset?'

I press my finger to my lips, but I can't hear any voices from the garden. The back door must be closed.

Mrs Barrett puts her hand on my arm.

'David, are you feeling quite well? Have you taken your tablets today, or—'

'She's out there,' I hiss. 'Talking to *him*.'

'Talking to who, dear?' She shakes her head at me, frowning with concern. 'Come on now, you're not making much sense.'

'Mr Brown is with Holly in the garden. What are they talking about?'

'How should I know? I'm not the girl's keeper.'

'Yes, but—'

'Yes but *nothing*. You've got to get past this thing with Mr Brown, David, or it's going to ruin your life.'

'He already *has* ruined my life.' I spit out the words like bitter pips. 'I don't care what you, or Mother, or anyone else around here says… *it was all his fault*. He can deny it all he likes, but I know it.'

Mrs Barrett sighs and looks up at the ceiling as if she's searching for inspiration. Then she speaks slowly, precisely.

'David. We've talked about this before. You can't go around making these unfounded accusations, you just can't say—'

We both freeze as dishes clatter in the kitchen.

Mrs Barrett bustles down the hallway and stops at the kitchen door. Her voice is bright and thin.

'Holly, dear. Is everything all right?'

'Yes,' Holly replies. 'Are you OK? You look a bit… Oh, hello, David.'

'Hello,' I say, peering over Mrs Barrett's shoulder.

I hear the mower start up outside, and through the kitchen window I catch sight of Mr Brown at the bottom of the garden.

'Holly, were you talking to Mr Brown?' I ask.

Mrs Barrett throws me a warning look.

'Yes,' Holly says. 'He was just… he was telling me about the improvements he'll be making in the garden.'

She stares at me and presses her lips together.

I don't know why I call him Mr Brown. I ought to call him the Monster or the Liar. But somehow, referring to him as plain old *Mr Brown* helps me maintain a distance from him, helps me remove his threat and keep my mind calm.

'Right!' Mrs Barrett claps her hands. 'Holly, you go and get changed upstairs, and David, you can help me with tea if you're at a loose end.'

'I'm not at a loose end.' I clench my hands. 'I only came over to see… if everything was all right. With the water pressure.'

Mrs Barrett turns on both kitchen taps and the water gushes out at full pelt.

'There. Nothing at all wrong with it today.'

Before they can say anything else, I turn round and head back up the hallway to the door. I imagine their eyes burning into my back like laser beams.

They'll be talking about me when I leave, I just know it.

Mrs Barrett will explain to Holly that I have *a problem* with Mr Brown, and then Holly will ask why and the whole sorry state of affairs will be revealed.

I don't have Holly down as a gossip, but what if she is?

What if she blabs at work – maybe just by mistake, through simply not thinking – and Mr Kellington gets to hear about it and calls me into his office?

He might not believe my account of events. He might wonder if he's made a mistake in appointing me to such a responsible position in the company.

When I get back home, Mother is preparing a pasta sauce.

'Is everything all right, David?' The words sound muffled, as if she's saying them from behind a thick wall of glass.

I watch as she breaks up plum tomatoes with a fork, mashing and slicing the smooth elongated spheres of fibrous red flesh.

I often dream of doing the same thing to Mr Brown's face.

CHAPTER 28

Holly

Up in her bedroom, Holly stood back from the window and unbuttoned her blouse.

It had been an odd exchange downstairs. David had seemed very upset but she couldn't quite grasp why.

It felt like there were some pretty major things that were being left unsaid by the people around her.

She looked down towards the bottom of the garden.

Nick had ear defenders on and was pushing and pulling the mower from one side of the lawn to the other. As she watched, Cora appeared and walked down the garden. Nick shut off the mower and stood listening to her, his head bowed.

Cora's hands were animated, as if she wanted to add weight to whatever point she was making. After a minute or so, Nick nodded, and Cora walked back up toward the house, her lips pressed together in a grim line.

Holly took another step further back into the room, in case Cora looked up and caught her watching, although *she* certainly hadn't said or done anything wrong. She sat down on the edge of the bed and thought about Nick's words.

Watch him, he'd said. *That's all I'm saying. Watch him.*

Just a few words that had now planted a seed of doubt and discomfort in her mind. David did seem a bit weird in some respects, she'd already gathered that.

But he was harmless enough… wasn't he?

On the other side of the fence, she spotted Brian again. Smoking now, amongst the bushes and looking back up at the houses. She stepped back, keen to avoid drawing his eye.

She pulled on a pair of black leggings, the inner thigh seams rubbed and threadbare. As she slipped a long, baggy T-shirt over her head, she made yet another mental note about items to buy once she got paid. She was now beginning to regret throwing away some of her clothing when she'd first arrived.

As she hung up her clothes for the next day, she caught sight of the laptop. Cora had only just started to make tea, so she probably had another ten minutes or so before she was called down.

She sat on the edge of the bed and opened the computer, reaching under her pillow to pull out her small notebook and pencil.

She'd done so much work over the last eighteen months, trying to track down Geraldine and Evan in any way she could think of, but she had met an immovable brick wall in every direction.

It was the fault of what she called *the bad time*. That wasn't the official term; the doctors had termed it *repressed memory*, which sounded altogether more serious. She didn't feel like she was repressing anything; she just chose not to think about it.

Who'd want to keep revisiting those cruel, vile events? She had to think about herself, about preserving her sanity.

She'd told them this, but they'd said repressing memory was something that happened in the subconscious. She wouldn't have been aware that she was doing it.

The fact was, Holly had done too much over-thinking. She'd racked her brains about ways to trace the two of them and had simply lost track of everything.

So she had decided to start again. She would methodically and systematically work through each and every avenue or idea, no matter how trivial.

She'd started with the obvious biggies: social media and online clues.

She opened her fake Facebook account and inspected the list of names. She'd already crossed off ten possibles – she'd been focusing on Geraldine, trying different combinations of her middle name, maiden name, that sort of thing.

It wasn't an easy thing to do, to trace someone while trying to remain hidden yourself, but it wasn't impossible, and the private investigator she'd worked with briefly – until his ludicrous charges had eaten up her credit card limit in record time – had given her a few tips and tricks.

She added a few more names now, squinting at the thumbnail-sized photographs on the list of matching profiles, to no avail.

'Holly? Tea's ready, dear,' Cora called from downstairs.

She glanced at the clock display on the bottom right of her screen and was shocked to find that nearly twenty minutes had elapsed while she'd been absorbed in her thankless task.

'Coming!'

She crossed off the names she'd checked and set the laptop aside with a heavy heart.

Sometimes, like tonight, it really did feel like looking for the proverbial needle in a haystack. She closed the laptop and set it charging on the floor again.

Just before she went downstairs, she felt an irresistible pull to see Evan's face again. She rummaged in the drawer and gently peeled back the tissue paper, allowing herself to get lost in those beautiful eyes

Were they happy together, Evan and Geraldine? She was such a conniving, believable bitch, Holly couldn't blame him if he'd fallen for her lies. Hadn't she herself been sucked into her world, believing that Geraldine truly cared about her?

What a fool she'd been.

She knew deep down that Evan loved her just as much as she loved him. He was probably searching online himself, hoping to track her down. It was torture having to remain hidden when she knew the love of her life was desperately trying to find her too.

One day they'd be together again, she knew it.

She had to believe that, because the alternative meant life would no longer be worth living.

CHAPTER 29

Holly

She'd felt so full of dread, waking up after that first night in the Manchester drug den.

Despite her initial determination not to sleep, she'd ended up drifting off.

She'd snapped awake and found the room was now light, with Markus still sleeping soundly beside her. She had immediately looked around, heart pounding, but thankfully their luggage was still safe; in fact, Markus was using his holdall as a makeshift pillow.

The vile smell had seemed more pungent than ever upon waking, and she'd clamped the handkerchief to her face once more.

Her eyes had soon become accustomed to the daylight, and the urge to just run as far from the place as she could manage filled her again.

The darkness of the previous evening had been preferable, she'd realised. Then, she had seen only vague shapes. Now those shapes were revealed to be wretched, skeletal people surrounded by used syringes and bits of ash and foil.

She'd reached over and shaken Markus.

'Wake up!'

He'd stirred, still in the clutches of sleep, and she had pulled the holdall aside so that his head clonked to the floor.

'What the…? Ow…'

Reluctantly he'd sat up, squinting and rubbing his temple, his nose wrinkling as he registered the stench.

'It's six thirty,' Holly had whispered, still incredulous that she could have slept at all.

They'd both sat for a few seconds, looking around them in disbelief.

Holly had counted four other bodies in the room; she'd thought of them as that because, apart from the rise and fall of their chests, they looked exactly like identical corpses. People who were very overweight often shared the same bunched-up facial features, their eyes disappearing into dough-like cheeks like small currants. These souls had all resembled grey-skinned skeletons with sucked-in, angular cheeks and jutting bones.

A couple lay in the opposite corner, their emaciated limbs tangled together as if that was all that was tethering them to the physical world. Two young males lay separately, and comatose, alongside another wall.

'You're right,' Markus had said grimly. 'Let's split before the waking dead arise.'

His apt analogy had got Holly to her feet in no time, and she'd found to her horror on standing that she was desperate for the loo.

'I hope you are joking. I saw the state of the bathroom last night when we arrived,' Markus had told her grimly. 'Makes this room smell like a flower shop. If I were you, I would go in the garden. That's what I intend to do.'

Easy for blokes; they could pee anywhere, Holly had thought at the time. But mortified though she'd been, that was exactly what she'd done.

Markus had stood with his back to her to offer a little privacy at least, as she'd crouched in the long grass hoping the neighbours weren't watching.

Ironically, she'd thought, although she and Markus had just been classmates at school, never seeing each other outside of lessons, they were already getting to know each other very well indeed.

Ten minutes later, they were lugging their holdalls towards the busy main road.

Holly had never felt so glad to see the welcome sight of a dark-red-and-white Costa Coffee sign on the corner. She felt the prickle of tears of relief when she realised it was one of the early-opening branches.

Markus had bought her a croissant and a latte and sat her down in the corner of the nearly empty shop with their bags.

'I'll be back soon as I can,' he'd said, checking his phone. 'I need to make some calls and sort out where we're going from here. Will you be OK?'

'Fine.' She was still enjoying the wonderful sense of relief she'd experienced the second she'd escaped the house of horrors around the corner.

She'd whipped out her book and had sat quite happily in the corner. Nobody bothered her or asked why she didn't leave after she'd drunk her coffee. The staff didn't seem enamoured to be there and stared glumly out of the window, barely glancing her way at all.

As she'd expected, the café grew steadily busier as time ticked on, mostly with commuters grabbing their takeout coffees en route to work.

After about an hour, she'd been contemplating buying another coffee herself – a serious decision when she had so little cash and no job as yet on the horizon – when the door opened and Markus appeared again.

'We're being picked up outside in about thirty minutes,' he'd told her. 'We can stay and have another coffee here and then you shouldn't have to see this shitty part of Manchester again. How does that sound?'

'Perfect,' she'd replied, beaming at the thought of finally leaving the place.

He bought more coffees and sat back down.

'We could freshen up in the bathroom here,' he suggested, closing his eyes briefly as he savoured the creamy warmth of his drink. 'You go first. This guy who's picking us up, Brendan, he's my boss, so I'd like to look half decent, and you never know… there may be an opportunity for you too.'

Holly had used the disabled loo because there was more space. She locked the door behind her and peeled off her top, washing under her arms and applying deodorant at the small sink. She brushed her hair and slicked it back with water, pulling it into a short ponytail and securing any sticky-out bits with hair grips.

'That's better,' she told her reflection. Then, noticing the dark circles under her eyes and her slightly jaundiced complexion, she'd reached for her meagre make-up bag.

She'd applied a few dots of concealer to mask her lack of sleep, and then brushed on a little mascara and bronzer. A touch of dark pink lipstick and, she had to admit, she looked almost passable. Perhaps even like the kind of person Markus's boss would want to employ.

'Wow,' said Markus when she returned to the table. 'You look knockout.'

'That's a bit of an exaggeration.' She'd rolled her eyes but felt secretly pleased at his compliment. 'But at least I don't look like I just spent a sleepless night in a local drugs den.'

Markus had grinned. 'It will soon get better, I promise you.'

Again she wondered why he'd given her the impression before they left Nottingham that everything was organised and in hand. Again she quickly dismissed the thought, deciding not to challenge him now that things seemed to be improving at last.

Markus finished his coffee and paid a visit to the bathroom himself.

When he returned, she'd glanced at her watch.

'We still have ten minutes,' she'd ventured. 'What line of work is this guy Brendan in?'

'Hospitality, I suppose you'd call it,' Markus had said, surprising her with his willingness to talk at last. 'He owns several bars and restaurants dotted around Manchester and further afield. He needs people he can trust for all kinds of jobs. I've been helping him with his social media presence.'

Holly knew Markus was skilled-up when it came to IT. He'd been involved in all sorts of initiatives at school and had told her he didn't need a part-time job as he made lots of cash in hand from designing websites for people and organising online advertising and communications for small companies.

She'd felt a frisson of excitement. 'Sounds like there's a good chance he might have some waitressing or bar work I can do, at least to get me earning something.'

'Absolutely. In fact I've already mentioned this to him and he seemed quite keen.'

Her mood had instantly lifted. Suddenly a very bad start seemed to be turning into something altogether more positive.

Markus had been right after all, she reassured herself. It was all going to work out just fine.

Except, of course, it didn't.

CHAPTER 30

Holly

It was late on Thursday afternoon that, out of the corner of her eye, Holly saw a suited young couple approaching.

'Looks like we have some late customers.' She sidled over to Emily, hoping to ignite a little camaraderie for once. But Emily merely glanced at the couple and grimaced.

'Time-wasters,' she hissed, turning her back. 'This is the third time they've been in this week, supposedly looking for a suite. They're both on teachers' salaries, obviously well out of their league in here.'

'Hi,' the man said as he reached them. Holly smiled but Emily didn't look around. When he saw Emily's obvious lack of interest, the man's cheeks began to colour up, matching the pale red of his hair. 'We'd like to take another look at that corner suite in the window, if that's all right.'

'You mean the Brooklyn suite you looked at yesterday?' Emily replied frostily. 'The one that's priced at nearly eight and a half thousand pounds?'

'That's the one,' the young woman replied pleasantly. 'It's such a lot of money to spend in one go and we just need to be sure, you see.'

'You know, you'd probably find something quite similar for a third of the price at one of the chain furniture stores on the edge of town,' Emily offered bluntly. 'No doubt there'll be pieces there that are far better suited to your budget.'

Holly cringed inwardly as the young woman's face dropped.

'Excuse me,' Emily said brusquely, brushing past. 'I've just remembered an urgent call I need to make.'

Holly and the couple looked at each other awkwardly for a moment or two.

'Sorry about that,' Holly said, a little over-brightly, noting their disappointed faces. She held out her hand. 'I'm Holly. I'm new here but I happen to know all about the corner suite you've got your eye on. It's a beauty, isn't it?'

Josh had taken her around the showroom and given her a brief overview of everything currently for sale, but she had to admit she hadn't taken a great deal of notice, as there had been so much information to absorb.

The woman's smile returned. 'Thank you, Holly, we'd appreciate your help. I'm Alice and this is my husband, Luke.'

They shook hands, Holly smiling but silently praying she didn't mess up her first big sales opportunity.

'I've done nothing but think about this suite ever since we first set eyes on it.' Alice's pale, drawn face was suddenly glowing and animated. 'It would look *so* beautiful in our new apartment.'

'It really is very special,' Holly agreed. 'Let's take another look together.'

They walked over to the outsize three-piece silver-and-bronze suite that sat regally in the window. Holly checked the information sign in front of it.

'So, here we've got a crushed velvet grand corner sofa complete with eighteen cushions, a double snuggle chair and a large studded velvet footstool. And the total comes to...' she glanced at the price card at the side, 'eight thousand four hundred pounds.'

Her heart rate picked up as realisation dawned on her.

This morning, at the five-minute staff briefing Josh conducted before the start of business each day, they had discussed this very suite.

'Mr Kellington wants window space for another suite that's arrived unexpectedly early,' he had told them. 'I'll be reducing the Brooklyn to six and a half grand tomorrow. Just so you know, if you get anyone interested, you can go down to that price today if it swings a quick deal.'

'The suite has a solid beech frame, natural fibre seat cushions and is made locally by a very reputable manufacturer,' Holly continued, hoping she'd got the details right.

'We were concerned the colour is maybe just a tad too light,' Luke murmured. 'Could you order it in another colour if necessary?'

'Of course we can, if that's what you want,' Holly said, thumbing through the fabric swatch draped over the back of the sofa to hide her dread that they might do so. She looked furtively around the shop, remembering Emily's endlessly successful technique. 'Look, I shouldn't really be telling you this, but if you decided to take the showroom model, I could probably get you a very good deal on the price.'

'Really?' Alice's eyes widened. 'That would be brilliant, wouldn't it, Luke?'

'Hmm,' he mused, less convinced. His eyes roamed over the suite. 'I'd imagine customers have been sitting on this model, though; kids with sticky fingers perhaps. Whereas a brand-new one would be—'

'I can assure you very few people have sat on this particular suite.' Holly shook her head. 'It's been in the window for most of its short time here, and… well, as you can imagine, we don't get a lot of kids with sticky fingers running riot in the showroom. Have you sat on it yourselves yet?'

'Only very briefly,' Alice said. 'It's one of the reasons we came in again today.'

Holly smiled. 'Then let's put that right now.'

The next few minutes saw Alice and Luke cooing at the luxurious comfort of the sofa. Holly perched on the edge of the matching snuggle chair, watching as they muttered together in low voices.

'Another good thing about taking this showroom model is that it's also had a full stain-guard protection treatment that would usually cost three hundred pounds,' Holly added, standing up again. 'Tell you what, I'll give you a few minutes of privacy. If you decide to take it, I'll do my utmost to get you the best price and arrange for free delivery within five days. How's that sound?'

To her dismay, Luke stood up and helped his wife to her feet.

'Actually, Holly, I think we've seen everything we need to. We're going to sleep on it, and if we decide to take it, we'll be back first thing tomorrow morning. Hope that's OK?'

'Of course,' Holly said, trying desperately to keep the disappointment out of her voice. She handed Luke her business card. 'Take all the time you like, and if you think of anything else, don't hesitate to give me a call.'

She watched them leave, her heart a little heavier.

'Told you!' a triumphant voice announced behind her. 'Timewasters. I can spot them a mile away. You'll learn too, when you're not so wet behind the ears.'

Holly turned, and for a second was extremely tempted to slap Emily's smug, mocking face.

'I just think it's a big purchase for them,' she said lightly, hiding her irritation. 'It's understandable that they want to be absolutely sure before buying.'

'Ha! You're so naïve, Molly.' Emily tossed her glossy bob back from her face and laughed. 'If they were wealthy enough to buy that suite, they wouldn't think twice about it. They'd just—'

'It's Holly.'

'What?'

'My name is *Holly*, not Molly,' she repeated slowly, fully aware that Emily knew exactly what she'd called her. 'And actually, I find it *naïve* to dismiss the fact that there are lots of people out there who value their hard-earned money. They care enough to make an informed decision. Not everyone is as shallow as your air-kissing Fenwicks, you know.'

With that, she turned on her heel and walked away feeling quite triumphant.

When she was halfway upstairs to Josh's office, she looked down to see Emily still standing in the same spot with her mouth hanging open.

'She looks like she's catching flies.'

Holly turned back with a start to see David just above her, descending the stairwell.

'David.' She forced a weak smile. Nick Brown's comments and David turning up at the door like that last night had unnerved her a little.

David had seemed OK to her before, but now she felt a slight prickle of unease.

Whatever had happened two years ago sat between Holly and the rest of the street like the elephant in the room. Nobody seemed to want to talk about the mystery event, but it hovered in the air like a swarm of black flies. And it was high time she tackled it.

She looked up to find David still staring at her.

'Emily's not happy with me, I'm afraid.' She shrugged.

'Oh dear.' David tapped his fingertips on the stair rail as if he'd run out of words.

'You seemed a bit stressed out when you came round to the house last night,' Holly said lightly. 'If you fancy a quick chat one lunchtime, just let me know.'

He looked startled, like he'd been caught in a dazzling light.

'I don't have a lunchtime as such because I finish my shift at one,' he said quickly. 'I have to go straight for the bus.'

'I see,' Holly replied, feeling a poke of irritation at his description of yet another stringent routine. 'See you around then, Dave.'

'It's... David,' he said. 'I prefer to be called David... if that's OK.'

'Course.' Talk about uptight, she fumed inwardly. 'See you soon then, *David*.'

She carried on climbing up the steps, but he didn't move.

'What did... Mrs Barrett say last night when I'd gone back home?'

'Say?' Holly shook her head, a puzzled expression on her face. 'About what?'

'About *me*,' he said tersely.

'She didn't say anything about you.' Holly shrugged. 'David, are you sure you're feeling OK?'

Just watch him. Nick's voice echoed in her head.

'Yes,' he said, seeming to shake himself and focus on her face again. 'Yes, I'm fine.'

Before she could reply, he stepped aside and carried on downstairs without looking back.

CHAPTER 31

Holly

Holly's plan had been to carve out an ordered, calm life for herself. Not to become embroiled in a whole new set of dysfunctional people.

In her experience, everyone had a facade, and around here, she was still to some extent heavily reliant on people's opinions about each other.

It was difficult to sift through the information and decide who and what to believe.

Patience was the key, she felt. Fresh starts could take some time to come good. That had certainly been the case in Manchester.

That first morning after surviving the drugs den, she and Markus had stood outside the coffee shop with their bags stacked beside them and waited for his boss, Brendan, to pick them up.

Holly had turned at a screech of brakes and watched as a big black jeep pulled up at the kerb. It parked on double yellow lines, narrowing the lane and causing passing drivers to beep and curse.

'Wow, a G-Wagen. I love it.' Markus had given a low whistle.

A tall, broad-shouldered man who Holly guessed was probably in his late thirties had jumped out of the driver's side and given the middle finger to an openly cursing passing driver. He grinned and grasped Markus's hand warmly in both of his.

'Good to see you, man,' he'd beamed, and then turned to Holly. 'And this is your lovely friend you told me about, yeah?'

He'd said it without mockery and Holly felt full of confidence. She'd smiled shyly and shaken his hand.

His face had been deeply tanned in that way you couldn't get from just the odd week abroad. She'd thought he looked as though he probably went on holiday a lot and topped up his tan regularly. He had a wide smile and even white teeth. She'd felt a stir inside as she noticed his generous mouth... such soft, cushiony lips.

He'd been far too old for her, of course, but there was no harm in looking, was there? She'd felt so glad she'd taken Markus's advice and freshened up a bit in the café. At least she didn't look quite as rough any more.

'OK, so let's put your bags in the boot before I get into a fight out here.' Brendan had winked at her and grinned.

He'd opened the back door and she'd ducked under his arm and slipped inside the vehicle, inhaling the scent of the obviously new cream leather. She'd sighed in contentment, at last managing to push the hideous images of last night's accommodation out of her mind.

This was more like it, she'd thought to herself. *This* was what she'd come to Manchester for.

How she'd love to see the faces of all those bitchy girls at school right now, the ones who'd looked down on her and treated her like she was nothing, like she'd never achieve anything. What would they think seeing her sitting there in a vehicle that she suspected had probably cost more than a small house?

Markus and Brendan had still been in deep conversation outside. Every now and then, Markus would point to a feature on the car, and Brendan would nod and explain.

The beeps from other drivers hadn't stopped as traffic was forced to slow and squeeze around the big jeep. Brendan was so good-looking, and Holly had found she liked his arrogant attitude, forcing the traffic to wait until he was ready to go.

They'd eventually set off, and about twenty minutes later, the jeep had turned into a car park just off a busy road, crawling slowly towards an impressive steel-and-glass building. A black-and-gold sign had displayed the words *The Panther Bar* in fancy scripted letters.

Brendan had steered the jeep around the club and parked up at the rear.

'Is this your place?' Holly had asked, staring up at the impressive terrace dotted with lounge furniture and leafy potted palms. Underneath the decked area there appeared to be an entire wall of smoked glass.

'It certainly is.' Brendan had nodded, opening the boot and setting their bags on the gravel. 'One of them, anyhow. But I keep my office here.'

A heavy-set man dressed in a black suit had appeared and picked up their bags without speaking.

Inside, a petite middle-aged woman had greeted them and offered them drinks. 'A pot of coffee and some biscuits would be great, thanks, Myra,' Brendan had told her. 'Bring them through when you're ready.'

He'd opened a door on the left and they stepped into a large rectangular room featuring an entire glass wall overlooking the car park. Holly guessed this was the wall of smoked glass she'd spotted when they'd first arrived. It was crystal clear this side, whilst looking out, but a completely private screen for anyone trying to see in.

At one end of the room was a large round glass table with ten matching Perspex chairs; at the other end a smaller, individual glass desk and pedestal chair.

Holly was struck by the modern, minimalist look of the place, and it also occurred to her that the desk was probably the tidiest she'd ever seen, with barely a thing on it.

'This place is amazing,' Markus had said, slowly turning in a circle to take it all in.

'Thank you. I like it,' Brendan replied simply.

He'd pulled out one of the chairs at the conference table and lowered himself into it. 'Both of you, please, sit down.'

Myra had brought in a tray of coffee and biscuits and set it down before leaving the room again.

'So, Markus, we can talk about the IT stuff in detail a little later when my business partner gets here, but in the meantime,' he'd turned to Holly, 'Markus tells me you might be looking for a job yourself?'

'Oh, yes!' she'd managed, a little taken aback. 'I'll do anything. Bar work, waitressing… anything you've got, really.'

'That's what I like, a young person who's willing to graft.' Brendan had nodded appreciatively. 'Actually, I have got something in mind, but it's a bit different from what you're suggesting.'

She'd waited, all ears.

'My wife needs a bit of help in the house. Cleaning, ironing, but mostly companionship. She gets a little lonely at times, with me working so many hours.'

'That sounds really interesting,' Holly had said. She could clean and iron, so that was a start, she'd thought to herself.

'And… what are you like with kids?'

That had taken her aback. She didn't really know any kids; she was only just past being one herself.

'Fine,' she'd heard herself say. 'I love kids, get on really well with them.'

'That's good.' He'd nodded. 'Not for us – we haven't got kids – but some of the team bring them in here and it would help if you could keep them entertained for the odd hour or two, you know?'

'That sounds… perfect.' She'd made a great effort to keep her voice level because she'd actually felt like dancing around the office and punching the air. Could it really be this easy?

All the suspicion and dread she'd had about Manchester before that moment completely drained away in an instant.

CHAPTER 32

Holly

The next day at the briefing, Josh informed everyone that Emily would be in an hour later than usual as she'd had to make an emergency dental appointment after losing a filling the previous evening.

'As discussed, I'll be discounting the Brooklyn corner suite at some point this morning.' He hesitated. 'Bad luck, Holly. Emily told me you were certain you had that sale in the bag yesterday.'

The other sales staff pulled sympathetic faces at her.

Holly shrugged nonchalantly but the back of her neck bristled as she imagined Emily making fun of her to Josh.

'And don't forget, folks,' he added, 'we need to really push the Lalique vase, as Mr Kellington bought it not realising the new collection will be out in a couple of weeks' time. Several of our customers are avid collectors, and once they realise, we could get saddled with it and lose some serious money.'

Both Ben and Martyn, the other sales assistants, asked Holly how she was doing and told her to just ask if she needed help at any point.

'Thanks, guys,' she said, thinking how pleasant they were compared to Emily.

She didn't think it was her imagination that, thanks to Emily's absence, the atmosphere today was so much more relaxed and cordial between the staff.

Josh had barely finished unlocking the doors when the first customers of the day arrived. Holly immediately recognised them as Alice and Luke, the young couple interested in the corner suite.

'Hi, Holly!' Alice waved as they walked across the shop floor, and Martyn, who was nearby and already approaching them, nodded to Holly and fell back.

'Hello again.' Holly beamed when Alice gripped the top of her arm in excitement.

'Holly, if you can get us some money off, we're going to buy it!' Alice spluttered, unable to hold in her glee. 'Right, Luke?'

'Right.' He smiled at his wife. 'Thanks for being so patient and giving us a bit of space, Holly. We just needed to be absolutely sure.'

'Really?' Holly's eyes widened but she tried to look as if she pulled off this kind of sale every day. 'That's fantastic! And I totally understand you needed to be sure; it's a lot of money to invest in your home.'

'My aunt died recently and left us a bequest, you see,' Alice explained. 'We'd never ordinarily be able to shop at Kellington's, but her gift has enabled us to put a big deposit down on a spacious new apartment and treat ourselves to something really special here.'

So Emily had been right after all. Alice and Luke weren't the typically wealthy Kellington's type of customer, but that didn't matter. They still had ready cash to spend, and that money was as good as anyone else's.

Emily obviously hadn't factored *that* little consideration into her snobbish assumptions.

'I'm so sorry to hear about your aunt,' Holly said kindly. 'But it's wonderful that you're going to use her gift for something that will give you so much pleasure and comfort.'

'Thank you, Holly. It will.' Alice gave a small regretful smile.

'Give me a sec then and I'll see what I can do about the price,' Holly said.

She disappeared into the back office and was relieved to find it empty. She timed exactly one minute on her watch before walking back out.

'I've just spoken to Mr Kellington and I'm pleased to say he's given me special clearance to discount the suite for you today.'

Alice bobbed up and down on the balls of her feet, completely unable to keep her face from splitting into a wide smile.

'I can make it a nice round eight thousand; that's nearly a full five per cent off.'

Holly watched as both their faces dimmed.

Alice bit her lip and looked at Luke.

'I was hoping for perhaps ten per cent off,' he said. His feet shifted, showing that he was clearly uncomfortable in a negotiating situation.

Holly glanced around her, scanning the shop floor, as she'd witnessed Emily doing countless times.

'Look.' She spoke quietly. 'I'll probably get into trouble for doing this, but I'll go down to seven thousand eight hundred. That's nearly seven and a half per cent off… you'll save six hundred pounds.'

'*Six hundred pounds!* It's a lot of money, Luke.' Alice nudged him, her expression hopeful. 'That would cover the new bedding and curtains we liked.'

Luke held Holly's gaze for a moment, and then he grinned, blowing air out of his mouth.

'Deal!' he announced, laughing as Alice launched herself into his arms.

'Amazing!' Holly exclaimed before remembering to stay professionally calm. 'I'm so pleased for you both. What a stunning piece you've purchased for your new lounge – congratulations.'

After agreeing a delivery date for the beginning of the following week, Holly escorted the couple over to the payment station, where Josh and Mr Kellington now stood, discussing the layout of the displays.

'Luke and Alice have just bought the Brooklyn suite at a special price,' Holly told Sue, the cashier, in a loud voice. 'Seven thousand eight hundred pounds all in. Delivery slot for Monday, please, Sue.'

She glanced at Josh, who briefly raised an eyebrow and winked at her.

Mr Kellington introduced himself, shook Alice and Luke's hands and generally made a fuss, congratulating them.

'Thanks so much, Mr Kellington,' Alice gushed. 'For agreeing to the discount, I mean.'

Holly's heartbeat seemed suddenly to relocate to her head as her fib was revealed, but she needn't have worried.

'You're most welcome, my dear,' he replied graciously and without hesitation. 'I'm pleased Holly has been able to assist you in finding something you love.'

'She's been brilliant.' Luke nodded. 'To be honest, we were on the brink of walking out of the store yesterday after that other snooty saleswoman told us to go and look elsewhere, but Holly looked after us and answered all our questions. She gave us the time and space to make our minds up.'

Holly's cheeks nearly burst with gratitude. She looked modestly at her hands.

Mr Kellington continued to nod and smile at the customers, but Holly hadn't missed the shadow that passed over his face the instant Luke made reference to Emily's snub.

That would teach Miss Emily Beech to gossip about Holly's supposed failed sales with Josh, and it would keep that smug look off her face, at least for a while.

Holly couldn't stop smiling to herself, even when her customers had left the building.

The old cliché was true. Revenge tasted very sweet, like nectar.

CHAPTER 33

Holly

'You've done incredibly well, Holly,' Mr Kellington said when she returned to her desk. 'A very clever little ruse you used there, too, telling them I'd authorised a discount.'

Holly felt a flare of heat beginning to climb up her neck. She wasn't sure Mr Kellington would approve of her lying to customers.

'I'd already told them I was new, you see,' she said quickly. 'I had to, because when Emily walked away… well, I wanted to be honest with them about just having started here… in case I couldn't answer all their questions. And they were so overjoyed at buying such a beautiful suite from Kellington's, I decided to make it extra special by saying you had personally authorised their discount.'

Mr Kellington beamed at her. 'Very astute, and just the kind of added value we like to give our customers, Holly. But from what I understand, their experience was almost ruined.' His unkempt brows met in the middle.

Holly looked down. 'Yes, well… I know Emily is very experienced, but it turns out she was wrong in her assumption. They weren't time-wasters after all.'

'So that's her game, is it?' he blustered. 'Categorising people on sight, at their point of entry to the store?'

'I… I'm sorry,' Holly stammered. 'I didn't mean to speak out of turn, I…'

'You have nothing to apologise for, my dear. I can see the spirit of Kellington's in you where it may be missing in certain other members of staff.'

Holly excused herself and disappeared upstairs to the staff bathroom. Once inside, with the door locked, she did a little jig.

Mostly because of the juicy slice of commission that would be coming her way at the end of the month. But, she had to admit, also to celebrate dropping Emily in it.

She had tried her very best to like and get to know her colleague, but she had been snubbed at every turn. And it had hurt.

To her delight, when she got downstairs, Josh brought a cup of coffee and a vanilla slice over to her sales desk. 'It's a bit of a Kellington's tradition we like to uphold when someone gets a big deal,' he grinned.

Ben and Martyn came over to offer their congratulations, followed by Mr Kellington himself.

Holly sipped her coffee and allowed herself to bathe in the glory of their compliments.

'Let us into your secret, then,' Ben urged. 'I've been here three years and the biggest single purchase I've managed is five grand.'

'Yeah, you've been here literally five minutes and you're already in front of the entire sales team,' Martyn added good-humouredly.

Holly could tell they were both genuinely chuffed for her, although she felt sure it would be a different story altogether when Emily heard the news.

Speak of the devil and she shall appear was the phrase that popped into Holly's mind when Emily suddenly entered the shop floor via the back door.

She looked her usual striking self in a black pencil skirt and purple fitted jacket. Her long, slender legs were sheathed in sheer black stockings and her customary black patent heels, and she wore her hair pinned up in a neat French roll.

Holly watched as she strode across the shop, tall and authoritative, clutching her expensive-looking oversized handbag. She acted as if she owned the place.

'Send Miss Beech up to my office right away, please, Josh,' Mr Kellington said curtly, heading back across the showroom without waiting for Emily's approach.

'Uh oh,' Holly murmured.

'There's nothing for you to worry about,' Josh reassured her. 'You've done nothing wrong at all.'

'Somehow I don't think Emily will see it that way,' Holly grimaced. 'She'll probably think I told Mr Kellington she called the customers time-wasters on purpose, but it just slipped out.'

'Emily has got no one to blame but herself.' Josh shrugged. 'She's worked here long enough to know how strongly the boss feels about providing a good customer experience.'

'Someone needs to tell that brainless jobsworth in the car park that there's a hierarchy around here and *he's* at the bottom of the pile,' Emily was complaining loudly as she approached. 'I should be able to park where the hell I like, not get shoehorned into some corner because there happens to be a vacant square on David's bloody clipboard.'

Everyone found somewhere else to look.

Emily sniffed scornfully as she reached the sales desk. 'What's this… the mice having fun while the cat's away?' Holly saw her swiftly take in the significance of the cream cake and the beaming faces of the other staff. 'Ah, I see. Who's bagged a good one, then?'

Nobody spoke.

'I… I have,' Holly said after a moment. 'I still can't believe it.'

'Go on – how much?' Emily sneered. 'Bet it's nowhere near *my* best one.'

'It's better, actually,' Josh said before Holly could reply. 'Nearly eight grand's worth in a single transaction.'

'I don't believe it.' Emily took a step back as if Holly had physically pushed her. 'How on earth did *you* manage… Hang on, it wasn't the Brooklyn corner suite, was it?'

Holly gave a little smile.

'*I* was first point of contact for that couple,' Emily raged, slamming her palm onto the desk. 'I spent at least half an hour with them in total over their two visits to the shop.' She rounded on Josh. 'You know full well the rule is that the first—'

'That rule is superseded if the sales person tells the customers they're time-wasters.' Josh cut across her coldly.

'I didn't tell them that!' she fumed. 'I only said that to… You little snake in the grass!'

Holly shrank back as Emily turned to her, pressing her bright red lips together until they resembled a knife slash across her immaculate face. She felt relieved when Josh stepped manfully between them, holding his palms up in the air.

'Some might say the rule is also superseded if the sales person suggests the customer goes elsewhere for their furniture. And the customer told Mr Kellington *that* himself.'

Emily sucked in air. 'I didn't mean it like that, Josh. I was just—'

'Save it. Mr Kellington wants to see you right away.' Josh dismissed her.

'I… I'll need to lock my bag in the staff room.'

Was it Holly's imagination, or was there a tremor to Emily's voice?

Josh shook his head. 'Go straight up there now, please, Emily. You can leave your bag down here.'

Emily dumped her bag by the desk without replying, then turned on her heel and stormed off towards the stairs.

'Look, I need to go up there too, but don't go blaming yourself, Holly,' Josh told her. 'Enjoy your moment. Mr Kellington thinks you're amazing.'

Ben and Martyn both went back to their end of the showroom and Holly found herself alone again. Unusually, the shop floor was completely devoid of customers, save for an elderly lady at the far end whom Ben was now assisting.

She took a few breaths and relaxed her shoulders.

Despite Emily's outburst, she had the distinct feeling that this was going to turn out to be a very good day.

CHAPTER 34

Holly

When Holly arrived home, Cora was upstairs. She stood outside the older woman's bedroom door and listened to the thump and slide of moving furniture, the laboured breathing.

Who'd have thought an ordinary mature lady like Cora would be keeping such an enormous secret to herself? One thing Holly had learned over the years was that people never failed to surprise you. And not always in a good way.

It would be nice if Cora voluntarily confided in her soon, but Holly didn't think that would happen. No. She'd be more likely to ask David or his mum, Pat, for advice... or perhaps even her gardener, Nick Brown.

She didn't think Cora would want that unpleasant man Brian to know. There was something about him Holly mistrusted.

She'd seen Brian smoking at all hours down at the bottom of their garden. Although he'd been over the other side of the fence at the time, his eyes had always seemed to be trained up at her window.

Some people would no doubt say she suffered from an overactive imagination, but Holly had previous experience when it came to this sort of thing. She knew how ordinary and innocuous a pervert could look, thanks to living with Uncle Keith.

She didn't disturb Cora. Instead she went into her own bedroom and lay on the bed to come down a bit from the excitement of the day.

She'd have to just put up and shut up for a bit longer in the interests of the idea that was forming slowly in her mind. Some things couldn't be rushed.

Sometimes it felt like her whole life had involved covering up the truth, staying quiet when she really wanted to speak out, or painting a picture of herself that didn't reflect the reality of who she actually was.

When Brendan had put her through her paces in a mini interview of sorts in his Manchester office, Holly had been forced to tell him what she thought he wanted to hear, rather than the unpalatable truth.

'Markus tells me you were traumatised by that hellhole you were staying in last night,' Brendan had said, surprising her with his bluntness.

'Well, it… it wasn't the best place,' she'd replied, glaring at Markus and wondering if Brendan had been the one who'd arranged for them to stay there and was offended in some way.

'I apologise,' he'd said, flashing her that irresistible grin again. 'I confess it's a little test I like to give any prospective employees of mine.'

'Test?'

She'd looked at Markus and he had shrugged apologetically.

'It tests mettle, you see,' Brendan had explained cheerfully. 'Anyone who can get through a whole evening in a place like that is the sort of person I can work with. Beats a load of pointless interview questions every time.'

For a moment Holly was speechless.

Markus coughed.

'It was an awful place,' she whispered. 'Those people...'

'They won't be helped, unfortunately,' Brendan said without emotion. 'It's a lifestyle choice that soon proves very difficult to escape from, once you've made the fateful decision to turn to drugs.'

'It's very sad nonetheless,' she said quietly.

Brendan had seemed so reasonable and nice, but given this new, cold attitude, she wasn't sure what to think.

She'd glanced at Markus, suddenly unsure of him too.

'I take it you knew that last night was a test?' She'd struggled to keep her voice level.

'I... I kept telling you things would turn out fine,' he'd said.

Holly had felt like punching him. During the coach journey from Nottingham, she had repeatedly asked him what the arrangements would be once they arrived, but he'd played dumb. Now it was evident he'd been fully aware how terrified she was last night and had still chosen to say nothing.

Brendan had clapped his hands and smiled.

'Forget about it. You'll be relieved to hear I've got a decent place for you both to stay, so I'll take you there later. If things work out, could you start work tomorrow, Holly? Does that suit?'

'Oh! Absolutely,' she'd beamed, pushing the previous night's ordeal to the back of her mind. It sounded a bit of a strange job that he'd outlined, but who cared? 'I can't wait. Thanks so much, Brendan.'

'No. Thank *you*,' he'd said, and reached over to pat her knee before turning to Markus again. 'Just a thought, mate, can you pop out to Myra and get Holly an application form? Ask her if there's anything else she needs.'

'Sure.' Markus had stood up right away, seemingly pleased to avoid Holly's dagger-like stare. 'I can do that now.'

Holly had felt a stab of self-consciousness, wondering how long Markus would be gone and what she'd talk to Brendan about in the meantime, but she needn't have worried.

'So.' He'd turned to look at her again. 'While we have a spare five minutes, why don't you tell me a little bit about yourself?'

CHAPTER 35

Holly

Holly had nodded and taken a deep breath. Her account would need to illustrate that she'd be an ideal employee. She didn't want to inadvertently mention something that might overshadow her qualities.

'Start right at the beginning,' Brendan had said. 'First of all, tell me about your parents.'

Holly had been a little taken aback. She'd not expected this kind of questioning at all. It was time to think on her feet.

Making sure to keep any traces of concern off her face, she'd begun to tell him about her parents. Only she'd described them as she'd have liked them to be, rather than the disaster that had been the real thing.

'Dad was born down south, in Devon, and Mum was from Nottingham. They both loved the Midlands, I don't think they would have ever moved if they'd still been here. When Dad came to work in the Midlands, he—'

'Hang on. You said *if they were still here*; are they…'

She'd nodded. 'They're both dead now.'

It was only after she'd uttered the words and Brendan had raised an eyebrow that she realised it had sounded perhaps a little too blunt. Callous even. She'd known instantly she'd need to remedy it right away.

'I'm sorry to just come out and say it like that,' she'd said, looking at her hands. 'I suppose it's a defence mechanism I've developed over the years. Growing up, it was always the thing I dreaded. *Where is your dad?* I was young and it was just much easier to tell people straight, to take the emotion out of it.'

'I understand completely,' Brendan had said, nodding. 'It must've been really hard for you.'

'It was.' She'd given him a weak smile. 'But I'm fine talking about it now.'

'And how – if you don't mind me asking – did it happen that *both* your parents passed away, so untimely?'

She remembered it had crossed her mind at that point that this was a pretty deep conversation to be having with a guy she'd only just met, even if he *was* to be her new employer.

Certainly this kind of in-depth questioning – it felt like a sort of interview – wouldn't happen in a regular job. There again, to be offered a position within a short time of meeting someone wasn't that standard either. She guessed it worked both ways.

'My dad was knocked down and killed as he crossed the road when I was only five years old, and my mum... well, she was a keen climber. She went out in adverse weather conditions in Derbyshire and slipped, falling to her death. That happened three years ago.'

'My God, you poor thing,' he'd murmured. 'So, what happened to you when your mum passed away? Where did you go?'

'My aunt and uncle took me in. I don't know what I'd have done without them.' She swiftly pushed aside thoughts of how she'd given the two of them a piece of her mind when she left the house.

Holly had paused at that moment, had wondered where the lies had come from. Her dad *had* been knocked over crossing the road, but she'd failed to add that he had been a certified schizophrenic who hadn't taken his medication for over a week.

Coming up with a cause of death for her mother had been easy too. Holly had mentally rewound to the days when her mum had loved walking in Derbyshire. She'd often go alone, saying it cleared her head and helped her to feel better. That had been years ago, in the days before her drinking began.

As a child, Holly would sometimes worry if it started to rain or the wind whipped up while her mum was out walking. She used to fear she might be blown off the side of Mam Tor or something similar.

Put on the spot by Brendan, she had managed to concoct a touching story. Far better than admitting her father had been mentally ill and her mother a hopeless alcoholic. That wouldn't have reflected very well at all on her own character, even though nobody had the luxury of choosing their parents.

They'd talked for a while longer, Holly managing to come up with some interesting filler about being taught to value education and feeling secure and loved at home with her aunt and uncle.

She managed to avoid telling Brendan how she'd twice been excluded from her old school for non-attendance. She could hardly say she'd been too tired to go to lessons after looking after her alcoholic mother, who'd been vomiting all night long.

She felt inordinately pleased with herself that she'd managed to create such a passable upbringing. If only it had been true, her life mightn't have been in such a mess.

Markus returned to the room and Holly realised that she and Brendan had been chatting for about half an hour and it had all been about her childhood.

'Well, you sound absolutely perfect for the role I have in mind, Holly.' Brendan had smiled. 'I'll set up a meeting with my wife tomorrow, how's that sound?

'That sounds wonderful,' she'd said, and for the first time in a while, she had spoken the truth.

*

The feeling of things going to plan felt incongruous now to Holly.

There had been so much disappointment, sadness and tragedy already in her life, she'd almost accepted it would always be her cross to bear.

But she hadn't anticipated the job at Kellington's going so well. Suddenly work felt like a massive priority to her. She thought of it as far more than a wage each month.

It was the key that would open so many doors.

If she continued with her successful sales record, she would soon have the money she desperately needed to enable her to change so much about herself and, more importantly, to fund whatever action was required to find Evan again.

It was the most effective tool in changing her world as quickly as possible.

She reached down for her laptop and opened it up on her knees, scowling at the bright screen.

The browsing history window was open on the desktop. She had a habit of closing all windows at the end of each session. Besides, she couldn't even remember looking at the browsing history.

Still, she had to smile when she saw the list of entries.

Searching for *missing persons*, *identity documentation* and *tracing information online*... it made her sound like some kind of secret agent or master criminal. If only her life were that exciting.

She entered a few names into the Google search bar.

David Lewis.

Nick Brown.

Cora Barrett.

Baker Crescent.

Nothing of any significance came up. She closed the laptop again in annoyance. Why couldn't she just get a break for once?

The people around her were keeping quiet about something that had happened to David. Nick Brown might have been involved too. And it seemed Cora knew all about it.

Holly hadn't been living here very long, but Cora trusted her enough to invite her to move into her home and give her her own set of keys… so why didn't she qualify to be told the big secret about David's traumatic past?

It only served to make Holly more curious.

CHAPTER 36

Holly

The following morning, Holly boarded the bus for work with a spring in her step.

After paying one of the now-familiar drivers and exchanging pleasantries, she took a seat in the middle of the half-empty vehicle.

The bus set off, lumbering past the park and the big houses that gradually got smaller and smaller towards the outskirts of the city. There, the terraces and converted Victorian villas began to morph into raw, Brutalist-style apartment blocks set on disproportionately small squares of scuffed grass edged with vandalised wooden benches that nobody ever seemed to sit on.

She felt lucky to be living with Cora in a nice spacious house in a leafy street in a good area. Not that things couldn't change.

She'd thought herself lucky to be living in a nice place all those years ago too.

When Brendan had first opened the door to the apartment in the Salford area of Manchester, he'd stood back and allowed Holly and Markus to enter first.

'Wow!' she'd breathed, hardly able to believe her eyes.

They'd stepped straight into a large open-plan lounge overlooking the water. A glossy white kitchen fitted neatly into one end and a sleek beech laminate floor led to double French doors with a Juliet balcony.

The room had been fully furnished, with petrol-blue couches, a compact dining table with four chairs, a fluffy rug, a coffee table and an impressive flat-screen television fixed to the wall.

'There are two bedrooms and a bathroom through there.' Brendan had pointed to another door, but Holly had her face pressed up against the window, taking in the view. 'That's the River Irwell you can see out there. I know this place is small, but it's just for the next couple of nights, until we get you sorted out properly.'

'A couple of nights?' Holly had stared at him. 'I could seriously live here for the rest of my life.'

Brendan had laughed.

'The business owns a few properties and we use this apartment for visiting delegates, that sort of thing. Trust me, it's quite basic.'

'It's brilliant.' Markus had nodded. 'Thank you.'

When Brendan had left, Holly turned and looked at Markus.

'Why did you lie to me?' she said accusingly. 'Why didn't you tell me that Brendan had arranged last night as some kind of twisted test?'

'I'm sorry,' he sighed. 'I didn't know where we were stopping for sure. I thought it best to keep it to myself so you didn't worry on the journey over.'

'How considerate of you, and I thought we were friends.'

'We are friends. I have myself to think of, too,' he tried to reason. 'I need to prove to Brendan that he can trust me to carry out his instructions. He told me you would be safe; that was the main thing.'

'But it didn't feel safe.' Holly scowled. 'You were scared too.'

'I'm sorry,' Markus said again. 'Still friends?'

'Suppose so.' She'd looked around the apartment then, and despite her best efforts to stay annoyed with him, her smile had returned.

She'd slipped off her shoes and danced around the room.

'Manchester is *simply the best!*' she'd sung to the Tina Turner tune. 'I never in a million years thought I'd live somewhere like this.'

'Well, like he said, it's just for a couple of nights,' Markus had said.

'Don't spoil it!' She'd sighed and sat down on one of the comfy sofas. 'I'm going to imagine this is home now. I'm not worrying about what happens in a couple of days' time. Let's enjoy it!'

'I'm just saying… let's not get our hopes up too much that this is how it'll continue.'

Holly had wafted her hand dismissively at his boring caution. More than anything, she wanted to immerse herself in this dream start to their new life in a big city.

She'd sprung up again and darted into the kitchenette.

'Small but perfect,' she'd announced. 'Just like the rest of it.'

She'd gasped in amazement when she opened the outsize refrigerator and found it was stocked with provisions.

A bottle of white wine, beer and orange juice sat alongside eggs, butter, yoghurts and milk. Likewise, the cupboards held pasta, bread and tinned produce, while further inspection revealed every piece of crockery or kitchen tool you could wish for, squirrelled away behind the immaculate glossy doors and drawer fronts.

Markus had headed across the room, and together they stepped into a narrow hallway with four doors leading off. There were two reasonably sized bedrooms, one with a river view, and a sparkling white fully tiled bathroom with a big glass shower, while the fourth door revealed a storage cupboard containing an ironing board, hoover and other cleaning tools.

'Neat.' Markus had grinned, finally seeming to relax a little. 'I suppose we might keep it, yes? Better than going back to last night's accommodation, I think.'

Holly had laughed without humour. 'I'd rather sleep on the street than go back there.'

'You can have the room with the view,' Markus had told her.

'Really? I would *love* to sleep in there. We can swap after tonight if you like.'

'It's fine,' he'd said. 'Knock yourself out, Holls.'

Holly had sensed he seemed a little withdrawn.

'Are you feeling OK? You're… I don't know… a little bit quieter than usual.'

'I'm fine.' He'd yawned widely. 'Sorry, I'm just so tired. In fact, I think I'm gonna crash right now and sleep through until morning.'

Holly had stared at him in horror. 'It's only six o'clock! I was going to cook us something. I—'

'I'm really sorry.' He'd shrugged, suddenly looking exhausted. 'I just need to sleep.'

When Markus had gone to bed, Holly sat alone in the living room. Even though it was cool outside, she cracked open the French doors slightly and stared mesmerised at the view.

The silence and thinking time allowed her to analyse the unfamiliar feeling in the middle of her chest. She'd had it for the last couple of hours: a sort of lightness, a feeling that everything was going to be fine. It made a change from the usual way she felt: that there was something in the air to fear or dread.

CHAPTER 37

Holly

The bus journey to work had gone quickly. Holly looked up as the bus pulled into the Victoria Centre bus station.

Sucking in a deep breath, she cleared her mind of swarming thoughts from the past and crossed the busy main road to walk down Huntingdon Street to Kellington's.

Feeling better for the fresh air, she quickened her step and focused her mind on the day ahead.

She couldn't stop old memories from surfacing, but neither could she afford to dwell on them all day. Although she couldn't completely ignore what had happened, the past was the past and she needed to focus all her energy on a better future.

So long as she kept reminding herself of that, she remained confident that she'd move forward in her life.

She turned up the narrow side street that led to the back entrance and the store's car park. For the first time since she'd worked there, she walked closer to the building and, as she passed, peered directly into the glass kiosk that presided over the car park.

David sat in there chewing the end of a ballpoint pen. His head bowed, he seemed thoroughly absorbed in studying the handwritten list on a clipboard in front of him. On his desk was a very neat row of coloured pens, a stapler and a telephone. Apart from the clipboard and a book, that was all.

She tapped on the glass and called out brightly, 'Morning, David.'

He jumped up, almost falling over his chair in the process.

Holly entered the building, managing to straighten her face as she stepped into the foyer.

David slid open the internal glass hatch, through which he usually handed customers their parking authorisation tickets.

'Morning, Holly,' he said, his glowing cheeks belying his casual tone. 'How are you? How is Mrs Barrett? How are you settling in here?'

She pressed an index finger to her pursed lips and assumed a puzzled look.

'Which question should I answer first?'

'I'm sorry. I didn't mean…' He took a breath. 'How are you?'

'I'm fine, thanks.' She smiled and reached for the door handle to enter the store, but then let her hand drop again. It wouldn't hurt to pass the time of day with him. Instead of thinking of cunning ways to get to the bottom of what had happened to affect David so badly, maybe she ought to wait for the right moment and then just ask him herself.

She turned towards him. 'I've had a really good first couple of weeks here, thanks, and I'm feeling quite at home at Cora's. How are *you*, David?'

'OK, I suppose. At least I was…' A muscle flexed in his jaw as if he was trying to fight saying something. 'It's just that… well, Brian has moved in with us now.'

'Brian is your…'

'He's Mother's friend,' he said morosely.

'I see.' She recalled the ruddy-faced bald man she'd seen in the garden.

She glanced at David's mouth, which was set in a grim line. 'Aren't you very happy about it then, Brian moving in?'

'He can be quite a difficult man,' David said slowly, tapping his pen on the counter. 'You know the sort.'

'Oh yes,' Holly said meaningfully as she spotted Emily's black Z4 enter the car park. 'I know *exactly* the sort of person you mean.'

David followed her eyes and nodded.

Something caught Holly's eye on the desk.

'Oh, you're reading *Rear Window*. That's one of my favourite films.' She beamed.

When she'd first arrived at Geraldine's, she'd loved nothing more than running a nice, relaxing bubble bath in her private en suite bathroom and taking an hour for herself with a good book. She'd loved the film and this was one of the titles she'd read.

'Yes, they made the film in 1954, you know. It's on at the Broadway cinema the week after next; they show a classic film matinee now every weekend,' David said matter-of-factly, breaking into her reverie.

'Is it? Nice. Are you going to see it?'

'No, no.' He began to tidy his already pristine desk. 'I don't generally go out at the weekends.'

'Is that because of… something that happened to you?'

He looked at her, frowning, and she felt her face heat up.

'Something that happened?' he repeated sharply.

'It was just something Cora said, when she first told me you lived next door… just that…' She was babbling. Why on earth had she chosen to tackle the subject now? 'Sorry. Forget I said anything.'

'I don't go out a lot because I have other work to do,' David said frostily. 'When I'm not here, that is.'

In a moment of placatory madness, Holly said, 'Well that's a shame, because I'd love to see the film again but I've nobody to go with.'

David stared at her, his face blank.

The outer door flew open and Emily stomped into the small foyer. David glanced out of his window at the car park and coughed.

'Miss Beech…'

'Don't start this morning, David,' Emily snapped, glaring first at Holly and then back at him. 'The car park is practically empty at this time, so save your whining for somebody else.'

'But you see, Mr Kellington likes designated spots for staff and customers, and you've just parked in a customer space.'

'I simply parked where there was an empty space. There's no sign telling me I can't park there, so you needn't bother complaining to Mr Kellington again.' She stormed past Holly and pulled open the door into the store before glaring back at her pointedly. 'Frankly, that's all I need, another jobsworth grassing me up.'

'Oh dear,' David said once she'd gone. 'Miss Beech seemed rather upset.'

'I wouldn't worry, David, she's prickly at the best of times.' Holly reached for the door handle herself. 'Right, I'd best be off. Have a nice day.'

'You too,' he called after her. 'See you soon, Holly… I hope.'

Holly walked straight upstairs into the staff office to lock her handbag away. Some of the other staff were already in there and murmured their good mornings. Martyn pulled the corners of his mouth down behind Emily's back to indicate to Holly that their colleague was in a bad mood.

It wouldn't have taken much to guess, even if Holly had not already witnessed it in the foyer. Emily tossed her flat driving shoes into her locker and then pushed her stockinged feet aggressively into a pair of heels that she plucked forcibly from its depths.

Holly watched her surreptitiously from behind.

Today Emily had styled her hair into a sleek swept-back style, held firmly in place with a dramatic gold clasp. She wore wide black culottes and a fitted black jacket with shiny brass buttons over a neat white blouse. She always seemed to be able to make sartorial elegance look effortless.

Holly brushed the slight creases out of her own cheap navy skirt and glanced into the small mirror on the wall while she straightened the collar on her tired cream-coloured blouse.

She'd made a bit of an effort with her own hair and make-up before leaving the house this morning.

Her hair was desperate for a cut, so she'd tucked it back behind her ear on one side and fastened it there with a pretty diamanté hairgrip. Her roots were starting to show through from her last cheap and cheerful home colour session, but a professional retouch was going to have to wait until her first payday.

She barely owned any make-up but had dusted on a little of Cora's blusher, which she'd found in the bathroom cupboard, and some old mascara that frankly had smelled a bit off but still managed to accentuate her dark eyes. Unfortunately she'd no concealer to help with the shadows under her eyes.

Finally she'd applied a lick of her own raspberry-coloured lip gloss, though amateur that she was, she realised she'd forgotten to bring it with her for a reapplication at lunchtime.

Sadly, next to Emily's skilfully made-up face, Holly looked like she'd just fallen out of bed without making any effort. She might as well not have bothered in the first place.

Behind her, Emily cleared her throat.

'Sorry!' Holly stepped aside. 'I didn't realise you were waiting for the mirror.'

'No. Seems you don't realise a lot of things, doesn't it, Holly? Like *not realising* you'd dropped me in it with Mr Kellington.'

Holly opened her mouth and closed it again. Martyn raised an eyebrow as he and the other staff filed silently out of the office, leaving the two women alone.

'Look, Emily, I'm sorry if—'

'Save it, why don't you?' Emily smoothed the sides of her already immaculate hair with flat palms and turned around to face her. 'You *knew* I'd dealt with those customers first. You knew the sale belonged to me.'

'But you weren't interested in them,' Holly protested. 'You tried to send them to another shop!'

Emily took a step towards her and glared down from her towering heels. She jutted her chin out, pressing her face closer to Holly's to complete the intimidation.

'If I hear you say that once more, I swear I'll rip your tongue out.'

Holly gasped, recoiling from her colleague's vitriolic words and the unpleasant strong smell of coffee on Emily's breath.

'You can't threaten me like that.'

'I can say exactly what I like, because this time, you have no witnesses.' Emily smiled sweetly. 'I got rid of the last silly cow who came here thinking she could snap at my heels, and I'll have no problem getting rid of you too. Just give me time.'

CHAPTER 38

David

Holly seems so different to anyone else I know… perhaps have *ever* known.

She is bright, articulate and friendly but not at all overbearing.

Best of all, she speaks to me as if I'm her equal. She's patient when I'm trying to make myself understood.

I've finally realised this is what it must feel like to be a regular person who fits in with the people around you without any effort or awkwardness.

I pack my empty snack box into my rucksack. Sometimes I wish I could stay here all day, particularly as I might have a chance of seeing Holly on the bus after the store closes.

I don't want to go home any more, especially now *he's* living with us.

'Everything OK, Dave?' Paul sticks his head in through the office door. With the swivel chair taking up most of the floor space, there isn't room for two of us in here.

'Yes. Everything's fine, Paul,' I say. 'And I'd prefer it if you could call me *David*. Remember?'

'Sorry, David. I forgot.'

Paul's smile wobbles a bit, and then, of course, I feel bad. I've been correcting him about my name most days for the past ten months. But things don't stick in Paul's head the way they do with others.

'I've left you a list of registration numbers and vehicle makes and models. If you could copy all those out neatly, that would be great,' I say slowly so I know my words are registering.

Paul nods at me like a puppy, eager to please.

'And I want you to keep a special lookout for that silver BMW. He's a cheeky so-and-so and managed to get back to his car just as Bob from Clamp 'Em arrived the other day. Foiled our attempts again.'

I still feel irked when I think about the arrogance of that Beamer driver. The cocky swine actually gave us a thumbs-up and shouted gleefully, 'Good morning, gentlemen!' when he returned to his vehicle. He had a hint of a foreign accent, which of course set Bob off on one of his pro-Brexit rants.

Sadly, the driver jumped back into his car before Bob could slide from his cab.

In line with Mr Kellington's expectations, I always think of jobs to keep Paul busy during the afternoon, even though nine times out of ten they are completely unnecessary.

'I'll ring Bob right away if that BMW asshole driver comes again.' Paul scowls.

'Good man.' I pat him on the shoulder and leave the office.

He's all right, is Paul. I should make an effort not to get so ratty with him. He's Mr Kellington's nephew and he works the afternoons to my mornings.

'I'd like you to act as a bit of a mentor to young Paul, if you would, David,' Mr Kellington explained on my first morning. 'He's a hard-working, very loyal lad but nobody will give him a chance in the world of work because he went to Aspley Brook.'

I know Aspley Brook well. It's a special school, located on the outskirts of Nottingham.

Mr Kellington replaced the retiring full-time parking officer with myself and Paul, so I couldn't go full-time now even if I wanted to. I can't imagine Paul will ever leave.

Still, I feel honoured that Mr Kellington trusts me to keep an eye on his nephew. I take it very seriously, and anyway, I have my other role to fulfil at home during the afternoon. It might be an unpaid position, but that doesn't make it any less important. Someone has to keep an eye on Mr Brown.

As I walk up to the bus station, the thoughts about Holly start to whirr around my mind again. I don't know if I've got confused with the thing she said about the film.

Part of me thinks I must have the wrong end of the stick, but another bit of me says I'm not imagining it, that she as good as invited me to the cinema.

I know she didn't mean it like a *date*. It was said in the spirit of friendship, a *no big deal* thing that a friend might suggest.

Friend might be a strong word. I check myself. Acquaintance, then. Colleague, even.

Yet friendship can lead to other things. I'm not saying it would. I'd never go down that road again unless I was absolutely certain I wasn't imagining things.

That was the trouble last time. I thought I knew what she was getting at and it turned out she meant something else altogether. Like Mother said at the time, some people are very good at sending out mixed messages.

I've seen quite a bit of Holly this week. I'm quite clever about picking my moment.

For example, on Tuesday I spotted Mr Kellington popping out to the little tobacco shop down the road. He never tells anyone he's going, but of course he has to come past my office. Once he'd left the premises, I went into the store.

And yesterday, when I knew he planned to spend the morning in the warehouse, talking to the staff there, I went upstairs pretending to look for him.

Nobody ever gives me a second glance in the store unless I bump into them or suchlike. It feels as I'm wearing an invisibility cloak at times.

The upside of being ignored is that it's perfectly easy to linger on the floor above, looking down onto the showroom, and watch her for a short time.

And that's what I did, both times.

She goes quietly about her business. She's not in the least bit pushy with the customers. And when she stopped to say hello at my office this morning first thing, she was so respectful and unassuming. Completely unaware of her own loveliness.

She doesn't need lashings of make-up on her smooth olive complexion, and those kind dark eyes shine all on their own without needing to be lathered in garish eyeshadow.

A natural beauty, that's what she is.

Apart from Mr Kellington and occasionally Josh – usually when he wants his car washing – nobody here ever thinks to pass the time of day with me. Especially that attention-seeking tart that Holly works with, who gives me nothing but trouble.

Emily Beech goads me by purposely parking badly and then speaks to me like I'm nothing, just something nasty on the bottom of her shoe. It's obvious she thinks herself above me. She's what Mother might describe as being *full to the brim* of herself.

After all, I'm merely the parking officer, while she's the hotshot top sales person. If you ask me, she's well overdue for someone to take her down a peg or two.

There have been times I've sat in my office imagining just how I'd do it if I got the chance, but I can't afford to dwell on that stuff for very long, I know that.

Still, I often feel like giving her a few home truths.

Where would she be if her well-heeled customers couldn't park up in their gleaming Jaguars, Mercedes and BMWs? They'd go elsewhere for their fancy furniture.

Nobody here seems to realise it, but without me policing the outdoor facilities in all weathers, they wouldn't even *have* a business.

CHAPTER 39

David

I turn the corner into the crescent and spot Brian's battered old van outside the house.

A fog gathers around my head.

I've tried to get his routine mapped out, but it soon became apparent that he doesn't really have one. He's out at the pub an awful lot, but only when the mood takes him; he doesn't go on certain days or anything like that.

I walk into the kitchen, where Mother is busy making sandwiches.

'Hello, love.' She smiles without looking at me. 'Lunch will be ready in ten minutes. Had a good morning at work?'

'Yes thanks.' I carry on walking and head upstairs.

The living room door is closed, but I can hear the television is on in there. Football, yet again.

Before Brian moved in, Mother and I would often sit and have a cup of tea and a biscuit together while we watched the headlines on Sky news.

I'd tell her about anything eventful that had happened at work during the morning. She always seemed very interested.

She often asked questions about the processes I'd implemented at Kellington's, which I enjoyed explaining fully to her, even impressing myself on occasion with my extensive knowledge of parking regulations.

Then she liked to take her afternoon rest while I caught up with my paperwork for a couple of hours upstairs.

Late afternoon we'd watch *Homes Under the Hammer* together. Then, as it got to the time when the residents of Baker Crescent began to arrive home from work, I'd go back upstairs to begin my evening monitoring session.

At one time, Mother would have known all about the BMW driver who nearly got clamped yesterday. I don't bother telling her all that sort of stuff now, because Brian can always be relied upon to appear in the kitchen, spouting his unwanted opinions at us.

'Parking violation?' he spluttered last week when I was in the middle of telling Mother about a devious customer who'd parked up, looked around the store and then nipped out of the front entrance and across the road.

The woman had enjoyed the next two and a half hours perusing the Victoria Centre shopping mall, courtesy of Kellington's free parking. Later, she had blatantly admitted, when standing in front of her clamped car close to tears, that she'd thought – to quote – *you wouldn't notice.*

'Incredible!' Mother exclaimed.

'You can't blame folks for using their head and maximising the local facilities,' Brian offered, even though it had precisely nothing to do with him. 'It does no harm. She'd been in the shop, hadn't she?'

'Yes, she had, but it states clearly on the authorisation ticket I issue that customers can only park there for an hour, maximum. Buying furniture never takes longer than that.'

'Says who? You've never bought a piece of furniture in your life, Dave. Everything's always been provided for you, hasn't it?'

As usual when Brian embarks on one of his rants, Mother found something pressing that needed doing in the other room.

'They are the rules,' I said calmly, staring blindly at the muted television. 'And rules are there to be adhered to.'

Brian let out a hacking laugh.

'Ha! You're a fine one to talk. What about the rule that says fully grown men are supposed to move out of their mother's house and stand on their own two feet well before they turn forty years of age? How do you justify flouting *that* rule?'

'It's not the same thing at all,' I said tightly, trying to focus on keeping my breathing regular.

'No, I didn't think it would be.' Brian jutted his chin forward aggressively. 'Here, I've got another useful rule for you… Don't mooch around in your bedroom half your life and sponge off your mother. Is that a rule worth observing?'

I've always known there's absolutely no reasoning to be had with Brian. Since he's officially moved in here, he seems to have become even more belligerent in making his bigoted opinions known.

'Excuse me.' I threw my shoulders back and walked past him to the hallway. 'I've got things to do.'

'Like what?' His mocking tone followed me upstairs like a lingering bad odour. 'Spying on people from your bedroom window, you mean? Lusting after that new girl next door while she gets undressed at her bedroom window?'

It's precisely that kind of unpleasant altercation that has made me decide to change my routine and head directly up to my room when I get home from work each day.

Mother hasn't commented on this new behaviour, but she now calls me when lunch is ready and I go down and bring the food back up to my room.

I haven't got a television up here, have never needed one, but it doesn't matter. I can watch most things online anyway. It's far preferable to having to put up with Brian's company.

I unclench my fists and see that my fingernails have left livid half-moons all over the fleshy mound of my palm.

People have always tended to underestimate me. They think I'm meek and harmless because I don't make much noise, because I walk away rather than challenge.

But there's a part of me they don't know.

Sometimes, like now, I have a sense of a powerful uncurling sensation inside. Like a hungry snake awaking from a long slumber.

I open my laptop and check the CCTV camera footage. Part of my morning routine before leaving for work is to set both window cameras up at my bedroom window.

Providing I angle them correctly, they cover a satisfyingly large span of the rear gardens of this house and the surrounding properties.

One faces the left of the crescent, one the right. They're motion-activated so it doesn't take me too long to whip through the footage. I generally like to make it my first job of the afternoon.

There are three scenes lasting longer than the usual two-second blips of a bird or a cat that activate the cameras regularly.

At 11.51, Mrs Barrett took the rubbish out to her bins. At 12.11, Mother put some crumbs out on the bird table.

I press play on the final clip and watch as Brian walks down to the bottom of the garden. He peers into the thick tangle of bushes there and then turns around, staring back up at the house. He lights a cigarette and stays there for a few minutes before walking back up the garden until he is out of sight of the camera lens.

There is nothing there that needs further investigation, so I select all the footage and click delete, resetting the cameras for the next stint.

Using this method, and in conjunction with the hours I'm here at the window in person, I can ensure that our house and the surrounding properties are monitored constantly.

The people living in the vicinity don't realise it, but they have their very own guardian angel watching over them every hour of every single day.

CHAPTER 40

Holly

All four of the showroom staff had enjoyed a steady stream of customers throughout the morning. Holly herself had made two reasonable sales of a stylish floor lamp and a set of cut-glass tea-light holders.

Her commission today had only amounted to fifteen pounds, but who cared? Thanks to the big sale she'd pulled off yesterday, she was set for the month now, even if she didn't earn another penny of bonus leading up to payday.

She'd enjoyed being busy. The time had gone quickly, but despite the distractions, Emily's words still kept drifting back to her:

You knew *I'd dealt with those customers first. You knew the sale belonged to me.*

Holly sighed. What use did it serve to keep replaying it over in her mind?

It was obvious to everyone here that Emily had been deluded about this particular transaction. She was clearly just sour because she'd got it wrong. She had underestimated the customers and lost out on a sale. It was as simple as that.

But there was something else she had said that kept repeating on a loop in Holly's head:

I got rid of the last silly cow who came here thinking she could snap at my heels, and I'll have no problem getting rid of you too.

She had all but admitted that she'd ousted the last sales assistant who'd tried to make a go of it. Holly didn't like Emily one bit, but she knew she'd be a fool to underestimate her.

Although she was doing well here, she was under no illusion that it was early days. She was still the new kid on the block, while Emily had the benefit of more experience, and Mr Kellington and Josh knew just how consistently successful she was.

She'd really need to keep her wits about her from now on, because Emily could strike at any given time. She decided it was best all round if she just stayed as far away as possible from Miss Emily Beech and her spiteful intentions from here on in. That woman was trouble she didn't need.

As Holly rearranged a little cluster of silverware on one of the occasional tables in the middle of the shop, she thought how that day she'd left for Manchester had been one of the few times she'd had the sense that her life was taking a turn for the better.

She had the same sensation right now, despite her concerns about Emily.

She enjoyed working here at Kellington's, and although Cora sometimes acted a little oddly, she liked living in her comfortable home.

Perhaps, she pondered, a quiet word with Josh about Emily's threat this morning might not go amiss. Speaking to Mr Kellington himself was a frightening prospect, but if she had to do it, she would.

She already knew that he thought well of her, and after the events of yesterday, maybe he had begun to get the measure of Emily.

She continued to tinker with the accessories, and before she knew it, her mind had drifted away from the task in hand.

*

She'd slept well that second night in Manchester. There had been no disturbances from Uncle Keith's hacking cough in the next room, and no worrying for her life or about the half-dead drug addicts she had to share a space with, as had been the case the night before.

She'd fallen asleep with the curtains open. Although it had been too dark to enjoy the view, she'd taken great pleasure knowing it was there, and in the morning, she'd opened her eyes with that childlike, delicious sense of not quite knowing where she was and yet also sensing it was somewhere nice, and then seen the river thrashing around outside the apartment window.

She'd found it impossible to simply lie there staring at the ceiling. Instead she went out to the kitchenette, made a cup of tea and pulled a dining chair across to drink it in front of the French doors.

Despite the fact it was not yet eight o'clock, dog walkers meandered along across the bank, enjoying the early sunshine. She'd spotted a cyclist and two joggers and, to her delight, a fleet of racing rowers had skimmed past on the water.

She had sighed with a contentment she'd barely felt so far in her life. She wondered, could it actually be possible to live in a place like this, if her new start was successful?

She'd jumped slightly at a noise behind her as a sleep-addled Markus appeared in the hall doorway.

'Morning,' he'd said, his voice gravelly. 'You're addicted to that view.'

'Morning.' She'd grinned. 'You're right, I am. I could sit here all day.'

'No chance of that, I'm afraid,' he told her. 'Brendan just texted to say he'll be here at nine to take you to meet his wife.'

'What?' She'd jumped up then, spilling a few drops of tea onto the laminate floor. 'I'd better get ready.'

She'd bent down and wiped up the drops with a tissue, a feeling of sick panic rising in her throat. It was both exciting and terrifying that she'd be meeting Brendan's wife... Geraldine, he'd said her name was.

She'd been painfully aware that her future lay in Geraldine's hands. What if she decided she didn't like Holly? The job opportunity could dry up in a matter of minutes, and then where would she be?

'You look like you're about to burst into tears,' Markus had said drily, rubbing his eyes. 'I'm making some toast. Want some?'

'No thanks.' She felt certain she'd choke if she ate anything on top of the nerves. 'I just... I'm nervous about meeting his wife. I want her to like me.'

'Chill, doll. Don't you know you're adorable?'

She'd grinned at his silly fake American accent and headed for the bathroom.

The shower had been good. She'd stood under the scalding needles of water, her face turned upwards with her eyes squeezed shut. The stinging pain had felt invigorating, as if she were purging herself of the doubt and dithering.

She'd wrapped a fluffy towel around herself and returned to the bedroom, cursing the meagre choice of outfits she had to choose from. Everything looked old and worn. There was nothing smart that would remotely impress anyone of Geraldine's calibre.

She'd dried her hair – someone had thoughtfully placed a hair dryer on the dressing table – and pinned it back from her face. Then she applied a bit of make-up and felt gratified that she looked passable – mostly thanks to the glow the shower had afforded her.

She'd dressed in her less frayed pair of black jeans, paired with a neat blue wool sweater.

By 8.55 she was sitting waiting for Brendan's arrival. Markus had seemed a little distant and had already gone back to bed with his tea and toast.

CHAPTER 41

Holly

Brendan had led her out of the apartment block to a glittering black sports car that looked like it belonged in a Batman movie.

'Wow, what make is this?' she'd said, immediately regretting her naïvety.

'It's a Ferrari,' he'd laughed, opening the passenger door. 'Jump in.'

The car had growled like a disgruntled beast as it shot away from the kerb.

'It's about a twenty-minute drive to my place,' Brendan had told her. 'Relax and enjoy the ride.'

Holly had taken a deep breath and allowed herself to sink back into the plush cream leather seat. Watching as the streets of Salford passed her window in a blur, she'd felt like pinching herself more than once.

Brendan's aftershave had smelled lovely: a mix of nutmeg and spice but not overpowering. He wore well-cut jeans and a plain black Hugo Boss T-shirt that tantalisingly hugged his firm, athletic physique.

She'd forced herself to focus on what was outside the car rather than in it, cringing when she realised that theoretically, Brendan was old enough to be her *dad*.

Easy conversation had punctuated periods of not talking. Chill-out tunes had played faintly in the background, and just when she'd thought she could no longer fight the urge to close her eyes, the car had slowed and taken a sharp turn to the right.

Brendan had held up some kind of remote in front of him, and the next minute, eight-foot-high fancy wrought-iron gates had swung open in front of the car.

Holly had bitten back a gasp. Brendan must already think her a hillbilly from the sticks, she was so embarrassingly over-impressed with everything.

The car had crawled through the gates and up a long gravelled driveway. Brendan drove around a fountain that formed a kind of roundabout at the top where the driveway widened out and parked outside the front door of the palatial white-pillared mansion.

The double-width front door had opened right away and a petite woman with wavy shoulder-length dark hair appeared. Brendan had jumped out of the car and opened the passenger door for Holly.

'Welcome to our home,' he'd said.

'Hi, I'm Geraldine, Brendan's wife.' The woman stepped forward and held out her hand. 'Welcome to Medlock Hall. I've been dying to meet you.' She was dressed in jeans and a plain white blouse. Fluffy pink slippers completed her casual outfit.

'Pleased to meet you. I'm Holly.'

Holly realised she'd made the assumption that Brendan's wife would be some impossibly glamorous model-like creature who was probably dripping in jewels and wearing inch-thick make-up.

She was certainly attractive, but seemed ordinary and not full of herself at all.

They'd waved Brendan off – apparently he had to get straight back to the office for an important meeting – and seconds later, the growling Ferrari was rumbling back down the driveway.

'Come on.' Geraldine had guided Holly through a spacious hallway framed by a sweeping glass staircase at either side. When

Holly looked up, she saw an open landing, studded with closed doors leading, she assumed, to bedrooms. 'Let's have a drink and a chat.'

They'd walked across a striking parquet flooring, through double doors and into a stunning room that literally took Holly's breath away.

Geraldine heard her tiny, inadvertent gasp and smiled, seeming pleased with her reaction.

The vast space was carpeted in a cream wool Berber rug. Two enormous black leather corner suites faced a wall of bi-folding glass doors that looked out onto an enormous decked area peppered with lavishly cushioned outdoor furniture, with what looked to be around an acre of landscaped gardens beyond.

'Please sit down, Holly,' Geraldine had said without looking once at the commanding view. 'I'll get us some coffee.'

Instead of heading off to the kitchen, she'd rung a small silver bell on a side table.

A plump Filipino lady had appeared as if by magic carrying a tray laden with coffee and biscuits. She'd offered Holly a reserved smile.

'Thank you, Patricia,' Geraldine had said briskly. 'You can pop the tray just there, on the table.'

'Anything else, madam?' Patricia had said whilst staring at Holly.

'That's it, you may go. Thank you.' Geraldine turned back to her. 'Now, Holly, tell me all about yourself and why you decided to come to Manchester.'

Holly had reiterated a lot of what she'd already told Brendan. Dithering, pessimistic Holly, who fretted constantly about whether her new start would materialise, had been suddenly replaced in her account of the last year or so by a confident, ambitious young woman who was determined to do well.

'I don't know how much Brendan has told you about exactly what we're looking for,' Geraldine had said. 'It's an unconventional appointment in a way, and therefore essential that we get the right person. It's not a position we can fill with just anyone.'

Holly's mood had instantly dipped. She'd lived her young life so far as the girl who nobody chose as a best friend, who nobody wanted on their netball team and who had gone unnoticed by all the boys at school, and at college too.

There had been no reason to believe Geraldine would see anything different in her.

'I can promise you I'll work really hard to do a good job,' she'd heard herself say, before biting down on her tongue before she could embarrass herself further.

Geraldine had smiled.

'That's good to hear.' She'd nodded. 'Because I'm looking for a very special kind of person indeed.'

CHAPTER 42

Holly

The showroom hit a quiet patch, so Holly took the opportunity to sit at her desk and begin to tidy up her mounting paperwork.

Out of the corner of her eye she watched as Emily put her current victims through their paces. She could almost lip-read the stages of Emily's patter, and it was obvious that she was currently at the 'Look, I might get into trouble but…' stage, no doubt poised to fleece the unsuspecting buyers of an extra few hundred pounds on the back-room sales price.

Incredibly, this time the customers didn't fall for it. The man held up his hands, then they thanked Emily profusely and left the shop empty-handed.

Emily stood motionless for a few moments, staring out of the window. There was something just a little off kilter about her today, Holly observed. It was difficult to pin down why the thought occurred to her, but for one thing, Emily had seemed a little *too* pushy with the customers, a little bit manic even.

Josh sauntered over and spoke to Emily in a low murmur that Holly couldn't quite catch. Emily nodded and shrugged.

Holly thought he'd probably offered her sympathy. She could imagine him saying, 'You win some, you lose some.' That seemed to be one of his favourite phrases.

They walked back to Emily's desk together, and as they passed her, Holly called out to Josh.

'I might have a buyer for the Lalique vase later today. A customer is calling back to view it again.'

'Brilliant, Holly… fingers crossed!' He winked at her but continued walking. 'Mr Kellington will be delighted if you close that deal.'

She saw Emily's face tighten and enjoyed the frisson of pleasure that resulted from it. Emily was quite obviously grossly irritated by the thought of Holly pulling off another high-profile sale.

When Josh left the shop floor, Emily turned her back and picked up the telephone, speaking in a low enough voice that Holly was unable to hear the detail. When she'd finished the call, she replaced the handset and turned towards Holly, flashing her a self-satisfied grin.

Holly felt like asking what the smug attitude was in aid of, but she bit back the retort and continued to record her sales chits on the database that Josh would authorise before sending it through to the wages department at the end of the month.

Emily walked over to the large expanse of window that over-looked the busy main road. Holly noticed that her demeanour had changed yet again. She now seemed to hold less tension in her body and, in the short time since her customers had abruptly left, her face had softened a little. She appeared… mildly excited, almost as if she were looking forward to something.

Holly was helping Ben to rearrange the accessories in one of the room mock-ups at his end of the showroom when the doors opened. She looked up and smiled a welcome as the Fenwicks swept into the store.

'Mr and Mrs Fenwick,' she beamed, walking over to them. 'I wanted to formally introduce myself. I'm Holly, the new sales assistant here.'

'How nice,' Mrs Fenwick simpered, taking her hand. 'And how lovely that you already know our names!'

'I'm not surprised, the amount of time and money we spend in here,' Mr Fenwick muttered drily as he grasped Holly's hand.

Holly mischievously thought that if she could grab them quick and make a sale under Emily's nose today, it might just be enough to finish her off. She fought a grin as she imagined the pristine Emily crumbling in a puff of smoke with nothing left but a pile of clothes, just like the Wicked Witch of the West. But before she could progress her amusing idea, Emily appeared at her side out of nowhere, as if by magic.

'Mr and Mrs Fenwick!' Her face lit up like a lantern. 'Thanks *so* much for calling in on your way home. Did you have a super lunch?'

'We did, darling. It was marvellous. And Holly here has just introduced herself, which we thought was *so* lovely of her.'

'Oh that *is* nice of you, Holly.' Emily turned to her with a dazzling, stretched smile and the manic glint still in her eye. 'But don't worry, Mr and Mrs Fenwick are quite safe in my hands now. In fact, I think Josh was just looking for you.'

Holly smiled at her prompt dismissal. Fair dues, she'd been rumbled. It was fun while it lasted.

'Now.' Emily clapped her hands and turned back to her clients. 'Let me show you that wonderful Lalique vase I called you about. I think it would be the perfect piece for your stylish lounge.'

So *that* was her game.

Holly realised that when she'd mentioned to Josh earlier about the possibility of one of her customers returning to view the vase again, Emily had instantly determined to try and flog the item before she had a chance to add to her already impressive commission total.

Holly could read her like a book.

She watched as the three of them moved slowly across the shop, chattering on about the *sublime* fine dining menu at the *astounding* restaurant in Castlegate the Fenwicks had just tipped out of.

Some of these people were just a mine of superlatives with little substance behind them.

When Emily presented the vase, Mrs Fenwick threw her hands in the air and audibly gasped at its beauty.

No doubt the next few minutes would be spent with the two women shoehorning Mr Fenwick between a rock and a hard place in a bid to convince him to produce his battered credit card yet again.

Holly waited.

The first sign that something was wrong was when Emily took a big step back, her hands flying to her mouth. She spun around, her eyes wide and searching the store.

'Bloody hell, what's up with Em?' Ben whispered, sidling up to Holly. 'Have the Fenwicks finally refused to pay over the odds?'

Holly couldn't help smiling at his comment, but when Emily dropped her hands, she saw that her face had totally drained of colour. Two bright spots of blusher and her vivid pink lips stood out incongruously against her pallor.

The obviously shocked Fenwicks backed away from the display pedestal a little, as if suddenly the vase had grown sharp teeth.

Holly walked slowly towards them. They had the look of wild deer that might scatter at any moment. A few other customers browsing nearby began to watch proceedings with interest.

'Emily… is everything all right?' she called as she neared the small group.

Emily shook her head, and then, noticing that people were watching, pushed her shoulders back, standing up a little straighter.

'You'd better get Josh down here right away, Ben,' she said coolly.

Ben dashed towards the stairs without a word.

'Emily…' Mr Fenwick glanced at his wife, who gave a small shrug of agreement. 'To tell you the truth, we're rather pushed for time today. We'll get off now and you can give us a ring when there's something else to see. I do hope everything gets sorted out.'

Emily gave him a vague nod, for once seeming quite distracted.

Martyn, the other salesman, walked over and ushered away the spectators. Emily's eyes were fixed on Holly.

'What?' Holly asked. 'Why are you looking at me like that?'

'You'll find out soon enough,' Emily said, in such an unexpectedly pleasant tone that goose bumps popped up on both Holly's forearms.

CHAPTER 43

Holly

'What is it?' Josh rushed over to Emily, a little breathless. 'Mr Kellington's on his way down. What's the crisis?'

'It appears that someone has vandalised the Lalique vase,' Emily said with a pained look.

Josh walked over to the pedestal and bent closer to it, narrowing his eyes.

'Bloody hell, the flowers have been damaged. How has this happened?'

'Exactly the question I've just been asking myself,' Emily said, the tip of her pink tongue shooting out and licking her lips. 'The Fenwicks came in to view it and I'm afraid *this* is what they were confronted with.' Her nostrils flared. 'Needless to say, they couldn't get out of the shop quickly enough.'

'This vase is now unsaleable,' Josh announced, his face grim. 'It's unlikely that a customer has damaged it walking past, because it's behind the security rope and...' he inspected the base of the marble pillar, 'there are no pieces scattered on the floor as you'd expect with accidental breakage.'

'What's happening here?'

Everyone jumped a little at the sound of Mr Kellington's voice booming from behind them.

'I'm afraid the Lalique vase has been badly damaged,' Josh said gravely. 'Some of the flowers have been clean chipped off. It's unsaleable and unreturnable.'

'Was it a customer accident?'

'I don't think so.' Josh shrugged. 'It might've been done a while ago, because the broken bits are nowhere to be seen.'

Holly watched in trepidation as Mr Kellington's usually pleasant expression grew thunderous. 'What? And it's only just been noticed? How can this have happened?'

Everyone shuffled, speechless, until Emily's clear voice broke the silence.

'I hate to say it,' she sniffed, looking nervously at her hands as if it were torturous for her to issue a slight. 'But as far as I'm aware, the only person who has touched the vase is Holly.'

All eyes turned immediately to Holly, and she felt her face ignite with a blaze of colour.

'It was intact when I unpacked and dusted it two days ago,' she said steadily. But the more she tried to focus on keeping calm and rational, the more she felt concerned it might look as if she was trying to cover something up.

Was it more natural to get annoyed? she wondered, and then berated herself. Such thoughts were ridiculous.

'And when you unpacked it, you noticed nothing wrong at all... all the floral decoration on there appeared to be intact?' Emily demanded, as if *she* were the showroom manager.

'Of course I didn't notice anything amiss. Don't you think I might have mentioned it?' Holly allowed a little more outrage to creep into her voice. Emily was a first-rate actress and she didn't stand a chance unless she matched her skills.

'You mightn't have mentioned it if you were the one who knocked the flowers off it,' Emily muttered, turning away.

'Now, now, let's just calm down a little,' Mr Kellington urged. 'There's no joy to be had in pointing the finger and directing blame. It is, however, important that we at least *try* and establish how the damage occurred so we can avoid a similar situation in the future.'

'It's never happened before,' Emily huffed, the implication being before Holly joined the company.

'Perhaps we should have a search around and try to find the flowers,' Holly suggested. 'That might give us a clue as to what happened.'

'I've already looked and there's nothing on the floor or surrounding area at all,' Emily said dismissively.

'The cleaner has been in twice since the vase went on display,' Josh pointed out. 'It's possible they've already been vacuumed up.'

'I'll have my secretary call her and ask if she found anything during her clean,' Mr Kellington muttered, scratching his head.

'I... I just wondered... what if it happened this morning?' Holly ventured. 'I mean... surely one of us would've noticed before now if it had been damaged for some time.'

'It seemed to me the vase had been turned to purposely conceal the damage.' Emily narrowed her eyes. 'The chipped flowers were at the back where it wouldn't seem so obvious.'

Holly said nothing and let her colleague's peevish comments hang in the air. It would be clear to everyone, as it was to her, that Emily was persisting in her ploy to point the finger very firmly in Holly's direction, despite having zero evidence.

'Very well, let's leave it there,' Mr Kellington intervened. 'We're getting nowhere fast, and frankly, it's rather unpleasant and not at all conducive to a happy workplace.'

The afternoon dragged on, as if something unspoken hung in the air. Holly even caught a subdued Ben and Martyn glancing at her a couple of times, as though they were trying to weigh up whether she was guilty of the damage or not.

Emily was the only one who seemed to get a second wind. She laughed more loudly with her customers, swept past Holly without acknowledging her in an overbearing cloud of Gucci Rush and stalked around the shop floor even more aggressively than usual.

Josh smiled at Holly when he passed, but he didn't say anything, didn't tell her not to worry, or reassure her that everything would be OK.

After yesterday's high of being the sales golden girl, she felt quite the outcast.

CHAPTER 44

Holly

The first time Holly met Brendan's wife, she'd got the distinct impression that Geraldine was looking for more than an employee; that she wanted a best friend.

Of course, she knew that couldn't be the case; being someone's friend was hardly a paid position.

'Although we haven't got kids yet, I hope we will have one day.' A shadow had passed over Geraldine's face but she'd quickly recovered. 'Brendan works really hard and we have an amazing life, but it gets lonely and…' She'd hesitated. 'I'm not a friends sort of person, I suppose. I have difficulty trusting people.'

Holly had nodded, but she was far from being sure of exactly what Geraldine was trying to say.

'As you can see, we have Patricia to do the housekeeping, so there wouldn't be that much to do around the house. You'd be mainly hanging out with me and accompanying me to various places… Is that something that might interest you, Holly?'

Was she joking? Holly had thought. It had sounded like a dream… one she intended snapping up.

'It sounds perfect. I'd love to work for you, Geraldine.'

'Excellent! Well then, consider yourself hired. Myra at the office can sort out all the boring paperwork.' Her eyes had flickered over

Holly's outfit. 'We'll go out shopping right now and get you some
new clothes and anything else you need.'

Neither Brendan nor Geraldine had mentioned salary or
working hours yet, but Holly felt a bit awkward bringing it up.
She'd hopefully get a chance to broach the subject later.

'I have some clothes back at the apartment,' she had volun-
teered. 'I can go and get changed if you'd prefer me to.'

'Oh no, you don't need to go back there. Come on, I'll show
you to your bedroom.'

Holly had found herself ushered back out into the hallway and
up one of the flights of stairs. She felt a little twinge of sadness
when she thought about the neat little flat with the river view.
She felt sure she could have been happy there.

This was an amazing house for sure, but it occurred to her
that living full-time with her boss might prove a little stifling on
occasion.

Her mind had been swiftly wiped clean of any doubts whatsoever when Geraldine opened a door and they stepped inside a
bedroom so beautiful it literally took her breath away.

There was a large double bed centre stage with a diamanté-
studded cream headboard, champagne-coloured bedding and a
matching sparkly throw. Fitted mirrored wardrobes entirely lined
one long wall.

Geraldine had walked over to a door, opening it so that Holly
could see the stylish black and white en suite bathroom beyond.

'It's so beautiful,' Holly had exclaimed.

She'd stood by the large picture window that overlooked the
front of the house and spotted the fountain Brendan had driven
around earlier. From this vantage point she'd been able to see that
the gravelled driveway was flanked with mature bushes and trees,
with just a glimpse of the imposing metal gates beyond.

Suddenly Geraldine had been beside her, encasing Holly's hand
in her own warm, dry fingers.

Holly had managed, somehow, to keep the startled look from her face.

'Do you think you could be happy here, Holly?'

'I do.' She'd placed her other hand on Geraldine's arm, overcome by a rush of gratitude. 'I really do think I could.'

The next twenty-four hours had been a whirlwind.

Geraldine wouldn't hear of Holly going back to the apartment for her belongings.

'Brendan will arrange for someone to pick up your things. Probably best to throw most of it away anyway,' she'd said dismissively. 'You've probably noticed we prefer clean and new here at Medlock Hall. No bad memories, no insecurities that old stuff keeps hold of, you know?'

Holly had nodded in agreement. She'd known exactly what Geraldine meant.

All the clothes she'd brought with her to Manchester had memories attached. Of feeling less-than while wearing them. Labelled an ugly duckling and never quite matching up to the other girls at school. She wouldn't be shedding any tears by letting them go.

'I'll give you a tour of the house later. We have a gym and pool in the basement that you can use. It'll take no time at all to get rid of that puppy fat.'

Holly had swallowed down the lump in her throat. The girls at school had called her *lard ass* every day during her last year. *Puppy fat* was a kinder term, but everyone knew it meant the same thing.

Just before lunchtime, Brendan had swept back into the house.

'She's going to stay!' Geraldine had clapped her hands childishly as he embraced her.

'Brilliant news,' he'd beamed, opening his briefcase. 'I got Myra to draw up a contract on the off chance. Nothing to worry about, just covers us and protects you, you know the kind of thing.' He'd waved a silver pen at Holly. 'Have a read-through, make sure you're happy with everything and sign at the bottom.'

Holly had accepted the proffered pen and started to read through the contract, although it had been difficult to focus on it because Brendan had continued talking to her.

He'd told her briefly that Markus had begun his new job as assistant manager at one of his nightclubs.

'One of my guys will bring your stuff over from the apartment later,' he'd said. 'Markus has already left for Newcastle.'

'*Newcastle?*' She'd stopped reading and looked up at him in surprise.

'That's where the club is.' He'd shrugged. 'Got to follow the work, right?'

What he'd said was true, of course. Markus had to pursue his own new start, but she'd felt unexpectedly vulnerable at the news that he'd already left. There was nobody here she knew well any more. She was alone in a strange city.

'Hey, don't look so put out.' Brendan had smiled kindly. 'We'll look after you.'

She'd smiled back gratefully. She had no right to feel sorry for herself, living the dream like this.

'Holly… come and see!' Geraldine had called brightly from the hallway.

She'd pushed the contract aside and stood up.

'Can you just sign that before Geraldine commandeers you? Myra will chew my ear off if I go back without it, and I have another bloody meeting in an hour.' Brendan had held out his hand for the paperwork.

Holly had hesitated. She'd hardly read any of the contract yet, and there were four double-sided stapled pages filled top to bottom with official-looking typed clauses.

'I'll bring a copy back with me later so you can read through it at your leisure,' Brendan had added. 'Is that OK with you?'

She'd smiled and nodded, signing and dating the document on each page, as indicated.

Why give it a second thought? She'd got to stop acting like everyone was just waiting to do her down. She reminded herself that she'd left that all behind now. She was among professional people who were going to help her make a better life.

'We'd usually want references, but I think we're pretty good judges of character, and we know Markus,' Brendan had said. 'You seem like a good sort to me.'

She'd blushed. Then Geraldine had called her name again.

'Thanks, Brendan,' Holly had said before leaving the room. 'I really do appreciate what you're doing for me.'

CHAPTER 45

David

Two years and three months ago, I found out that Mr Brown, who lives two doors down, was having an extramarital affair.

I'd realised over time. Although I've always kept an eye on proceedings from my bedroom for Neighbourhood Watch purposes, I had a full-time job at the printing firm at the time, and in those days I enjoyed visiting the local library's reading room so I didn't sit at home in my room as much.

Mr Brown had lost his job and been out of work for a few weeks, and Mother had told me that Mrs Brown, who sometimes took tea with Mrs Barrett of an afternoon at the local café, had been forced to increase her hours at the local dental surgery when their income dropped.

The surgery opened at eight a.m. prompt, and Mrs Brown, who struck me as an organised, efficient individual, would leave the house at seven fifteen in the morning, five days a week.

It just so happened that at that precise time, I'd already taken my shower and would be getting ready in the bathroom for work myself.

I'd always have the side-opening window ajar to help disperse the trapped steam, and as I stood in front of the mirror combing my hair one particular morning, I noticed that, fifteen minutes after Mrs Brown had left, a black cab pulled up.

A woman – who, it had to be said, looked quite a bit younger than the lady of the house – got out and was met at the door by none other than Mr Brown himself.

Truthfully, I didn't think much of it at the time, but when it happened twice more that week, my interest was most definitely piqued.

The third time the taxi dropped the young lady off, I gave in to an impulsive whim. I called work and informed the office that due to a minor medical matter, I'd be a little late in.

I left the house and waited at the end of the crescent, where I had a good view of all the houses. Within the hour, Mr Brown's front door opened and he kissed the young lady goodbye in full view of anyone who cared to watch. There was no cab to collect her, and she walked down to the main road, towards me.

When she passed me, I looked at my watch as if I was waiting for someone. She was young and pretty and smelled faintly of talcum powder.

That was the first time I'd been close to Miss Della Carter, and as soon as she'd disappeared around the corner, I had a very strong urge to get close to her again.

CHAPTER 46

Holly

At the end of the day, the staff gathered their belongings. Martyn was first out, calling goodbye to the others.

'Damn it!' Holly and Ben both turned at Emily's loud cursing as she came downstairs in her flat driving shoes, rifling in her handbag. She stomped over to her desk and dumped the bag on there.

'What's up?' Ben asked.

'I can't find my car keys,' she muttered. 'But they've got to be in here somewhere.'

Josh passed on his way out of the shop and stopped to watch, mildly curious.

'On overtime, Em? You're usually first out the door,' he teased.

'Yeah, well, that was before my car keys decided to do a bloody disappearing act,' she growled, both hands immersed in her vast cavern of a bag. 'Sod this, I've got a nail appointment in fifteen minutes. Drastic measures are called for.'

She upended the bag onto her desk, and Holly watched as Ben and Josh both peered down at the mountainous heap of items that emerged.

'Blimey!' Josh said. 'It's true what they say, Ben. Everything in there but the kitchen sink.'

The two men sniggered, and then Josh's face grew more serious. He scowled and peered closer at the tangle of tissues and mints and make-up.

'Isn't that...' He cocked his head to one side and squinted, as if trying to make sense of something.

'What is it?' Emily snapped. 'It's keys I'm looking for.'

Her jaw dropped as she followed Josh's pointing finger and looked down at her belongings.

'Isn't that one of the glass flowers from the broken vase?' Ben said, incredulously. 'Look, there's another...' Only then did he seem to realise the implication of his words and hastily clamped his mouth shut.

Holly pushed her chair back, stood up and walked over to Emily's desk.

'The chipped-off flowers,' she breathed, stepping in closer. 'What are they doing in your handbag, Emily?'

Emily opened her mouth but seemed unable to enunciate any words. She looked up wild-eyed at Holly, Josh and Ben, who stood around silently in a semicircle.

'What's this, an impromptu staff meeting?' Mr Kellington called across in a jolly voice. 'I say, can anyone join in?'

'I think you need to take a look at this, boss,' Josh said gravely. 'Something's come to light.'

'I... I swear on my mother's life, I don't know how they got in there,' Emily stammered, wringing her hands. 'I mean, I'd hardly empty out my bag in front of everyone if I knew they were in there, now would I?'

'But you didn't do it in front of everyone! You emptied it out in a temper looking for your keys and we came to see,' Holly reminded her.

It was only natural that she'd enjoy paying her colleague back for her earlier aggression... wasn't it?

Mr Kellington didn't speak.

With pincered fingers, he gingerly picked out a flower and studied it in his palm. He did the same twice more until there were three tiny pink glass flowers nestling there, shining prettily under the lights.

'Most definitely the Lalique flowers,' he said sadly.

Holly found herself shaking her head. Earlier, Emily had enjoyed humiliating her in front of everyone, and now here she was, fighting for her own life.

Fat tears began to roll down Emily's cheeks, leaving pale tracks in the heavy blusher and powder. Holly couldn't help staring. She'd never seen the ice queen sobbing before.

'Someone's set me up,' she spluttered, suddenly a sad, soggy mess. 'Someone has made it look like *I* damaged that vase. And I didn't... I didn't!'

'Who?' Josh said, unconvinced. 'Who on earth would set you up?'

'*You* were the one who noticed the damage,' Holly added. 'You brought it to Josh's attention in the first place.'

Emily glared at her.

'And I saw you stow your handbag in your locker this morning,' Ben said. 'So the flowers must've already been in there when you got to work at the start of the day.'

'Sounds like the damage must have been done *after* I put the vase on display,' Holly added.

Emily's head snapped round, her face a mask of hatred. 'I don't know how you did this, but—'

'That's quite enough,' Mr Kellington interrupted. 'All this bickering is going to help precisely no one. Emily, Josh, I need you to come up to my office right away. Holly, Ben... have a good weekend.'

Holly walked out of the back of the store and into the fresh, bracing air.

'I'd like to be a fly on the wall up there. What a palaver.' Ben rolled his eyes.

'I'm glad the truth is out, though,' Holly said. 'I was beginning to think everyone thought *I'd* done the damage.'

Ben had the grace to look a little shamefaced as he wished her a good weekend.

As she walked past the glass kiosk, she looked in to see the young lad who did the afternoon car park shift painstakingly copying details onto a sheet of paper by hand.

'Night, miss,' he called after her as she walked out onto the street.

Holly smiled. Her first week had certainly been eventful, and rather stressful at times, but all had ended well and she now felt pleasantly vindicated after enduring sly and sometimes accusing looks from some of the others.

It had been a long, long time since she'd looked forward to the weekend, but right now, that was how she felt.

This new world of hers was real. Her job was grounded in a normal environment.

That had not been her experience working for Geraldine and Brendan.

CHAPTER 47

Holly

She'd been at Medlock Hall for two and a half weeks and still hadn't grown accustomed to the feeling of euphoria that washed over her when she opened her eyes each morning and found herself in that bedroom.

But this was no fairy-tale dream; this really was her new life.

She'd propped herself up against the mounds of duck-feather-filled pillows and looked out of the window. As with the apartment, she'd refused to close the curtains so that she could take in the view the second she opened her eyes.

The perfect landscaped gardens had seemed never to end, but of course Holly had known that beyond the far wall of neatly trimmed conifers lay the road.

Her job was basically to be best friend and confidante to Geraldine. Not a *real* best friend, however; there was an important difference.

She had very quickly realised that when Geraldine asked her something – *Does this colour suit me?* or *Does my hair look OK at the back?* – there was a right answer or opinion required. It was far more in her own interests to express the correct response than it was to speak the truth.

She had soon got the hang of it and it didn't really bother her at all. So far as she was concerned, she had the best job in the world. No complaints at all.

Every day, Geraldine seemed to approve and rely on her company more and more. They literally hung out together all the time.

Brendan hadn't spent much time at the house. He'd returned every day at some point and Holly would be expected to just disappear up to her bedroom for at least a couple of hours.

She'd welcomed that, looked forward to free time in which she could do what *she* wanted.

Geraldine asked her all the time would she like to do this or would she prefer to do that, but of course, as with other questions posed, there was a right answer. And that was for Holly to prefer to do whatever *Geraldine* wanted to do.

But Holly had hardly found it a hardship.

One thing still bothered her slightly, and that was the fact that she'd still not got her stuff back from the apartment after staying there the first night.

It had kept slipping Brendan's mind. Each time she'd asked, he'd hit the side of his head with the heel of his hand.

'Sorry! My mind has been like a sieve lately. I'll definitely sort it out later today.'

Each subsequent excuse had been a variation on this one. He seemed to have no trouble just plucking something out of the air. Eventually, she'd stopped asking.

Anyway, apart from a couple of bits – her mobile phone and a small, tatty photograph of her mother and a five-year-old Holly – there had been nothing she'd missed or needed.

The wall of mirrored wardrobes now concealed rails of clothes that fitted her perfectly, hanging neatly behind the doors.

The day after Holly accepted the job, Geraldine had taken her to the Trafford Centre, and they'd spent the day there selecting everything from underwear to a warm wool coat.

They'd taken time out in the middle of the day for a boozy lunch at a restaurant far beyond Holly's own financial capabilities. The waiter led them to a leather cushioned booth under glitzy lighting. They sat, enveloped in a discreet soundcloud of Ibiza chill-out tunes.

The menu had been amazing, packed with creamy, cheesy American-style dishes that made Holly's mouth water. But she'd known Geraldine would order a Caesar salad without dressing, and that she'd expect Holly to choose something similar.

'It makes me feel queasy to even look at that,' Geraldine had said the on the day of Holly's arrival and the first time they'd eaten out together. Holly had ordered a bowl of chilli con carne and rice with sides of sour cream and cheese. 'All that fat and cholesterol… I couldn't bear to touch it.'

She'd been quiet at the restaurant during dinner and a bit moody for the rest of the evening. Holly had got the message loud and clear and hadn't made the same mistake since.

Even though it felt a bit cheeky, once they'd relaxed into lunch, Holly had plucked up courage and mentioned the fact that she still had no mobile phone. Although Aunt Susan had her faults, she felt a quick call was in order, just to tell her she was OK and not to worry. She felt she owed her that much despite their final heated words.

She had already noted that there appeared to be no landline at the house; Geraldine had said there was only the one in Brendan's locked study, which was used purely for broadband purposes.

'I know it sounds completely paranoid, but we don't allow staff to keep personal mobile phones on the property,' she had explained in a regretful tone. 'We had a very bad experience once where Brendan's confidentiality was compromised by a disloyal staff member and it cost him nearly a hundred grand in a lost deal.'

Holly had widened her eyes.

'I know.' Geraldine had rolled her own eyes. 'He acted like a bear with a sore head for weeks after that. Sometimes you'll be party to business conversations or perhaps catch sight of confidential paperwork around the house, and it's just easier for us all if there are no mobile phones to take photographs or record conversations. That's why he asked you to sign the confidentiality agreement.'

Holly nodded and remembered that Brendan still hadn't provided a copy of her signed contract. She hadn't seen the confidentiality agreement yet and she'd hate to unwittingly breach it.

'I know you'd never do anything like that,' Geraldine had added quickly. 'But we have to treat everyone the same, you see. It's only fair.'

Holly had pondered on the fact that she was yet to see any other staff in the house apart from Patricia.

She had sipped her Bellini – Geraldine's favourite drink – and explained about her wish to contact her aunt.

'That's easily solved. I'll get you some pretty notelets and then you can write to her as and when you like. How's that?'

'Or I could use your phone just to make a quick call,' Holly had suggested. 'I wouldn't be on long, just so she knows I'm OK.'

Geraldine's lips had pressed together briefly before she relaxed them again into a smile.

'I'm sure your Aunt Susan would much prefer you to drop her a note. It's so much more personal, don't you think?'

Holly hadn't wanted to prolong the subject, but it seemed like a good opportunity to bring up the second thing she was missing.

'And… I wondered if there was a laptop in the house I could use at all?'

'Goodness! Whatever for?' Geraldine had run her fingers irritably through her perfect chestnut curls. 'Sorry, I didn't mean to snap. I'm just tired. Was there something in particular you wanted to do on the computer?'

'Just general browsing online and streaming movies and music.' Holly had shrugged. 'Nothing specific.'

'I'd have to ask Brendan, but the smart television in your bedroom streams everything, and you can play games on there, go on YouTube... everything you need, really.'

'Yes.' Holly had nodded, keen not to appear ungrateful. 'That's great, thanks, Geraldine.'

She'd hoped she might be able to track Markus down on Facebook or something. She'd heard nothing at all from him since he'd left, although when she'd asked Brendan, he'd told her Markus was loving his job at the Newcastle club.

She couldn't help feeling a bit miffed that he'd just left like that without saying goodbye.

'I'm sure he'll contact you at some point, but I think he's just having the time of his life right now.'

Subtext: he's probably forgotten all about you, Holly had thought.

CHAPTER 48

Holly

The next morning, David came round to the house to do some handyman bits for Cora.

Holly walked into the kitchen to find him glueing the handle onto a cream jug.

'Morning, Holly. How are you finding things at work?' he asked her hesitantly.

'It's turned out to be very good week in the end, thanks,' Holly replied. 'No doubt you'll hear all about it on Monday.'

'Hear about what?'

'Emily's in serious trouble. Pieces of a broken vase were found in her bag after she spent hours basically accusing *me* of damaging it in front of everyone.'

David didn't say anything, but she thought the ghost of a smile passed over his lips. Probably because he disliked Emily as much as she did.

'How about you?' she asked. 'I bet time drags stuck outside in that cramped little kiosk.'

'My office is really very comfortable,' David said, looking back down the jug. 'It's warm and dry in there and everything is organised. More space than that would be a waste, really.'

'Well, yes,' Holly said. 'I suppose when you put it like that…'

'And there's lots to do, of course,' David went on. 'Monitoring the car park, recording car registrations, issuing tickets and ensuring time restrictions don't lapse. Then there are the odd jobs I often do for Mr Kellington and sometimes Josh. Favours.'

'You must be very busy.' Holly nodded, eager to avoid further tedious details. 'I see that now. Well, I don't want to distract you from what you came here to do.'

She selected a glass from the cupboard and ran the cold tap.

'I have plenty of time,' David said behind her. 'I wondered...'

'Yes?' She turned.

'Well, it's fine if you aren't interested, but...'

She waited.

'It's just that you said about that book... the film... I thought, if you weren't busy... would you like to go to the cinema next weekend, to see *Rear Window*?'

Holly stared at him.

'It's fine! Don't worry. I thought you'd more than likely be busy, it was silly of me. I'm sorry, I shouldn't have...' His words tailed off and he coughed and turned back to his repair job.

'It's really nice of you to ask, David, and... thank you. I'd love to go to the cinema.'

He didn't look up and she suspected he was holding his breath, as his face seemed to become more flushed by the second.

'Were you thinking of going on Saturday, or Sunday?' she asked lightly.

He turned to look at her. His whole face was twitching, as if he'd just been given a slight electric shock. Not the most attractive look, she thought.

'Whichever you'd prefer,' he said, speaking quickly now. 'Saturday, Sunday... it's all the same to me. I'll find out the times, shall I?'

'Good idea.' She beamed. 'Thank you.'

'No,' he said quietly, clasping his hands together in front of him. She was reminded of a child standing in front of a present-laden tree on Christmas morning. 'Thank *you*, Holly.'

The house phone began ringing in the living room, so she left David to his mending and walked out of the kitchen.

Before she could get there, the ringing stopped and she heard Cora speaking.

'No, this is not she. *My* name is Mrs Cora Barrett... Yes. Yes, she does live here... Certainly. Who shall I say is calling?'

Holly froze just outside the door, her mouth dry.

'Very well. Hold the line, please.' Holly watched through the crack in the door as Cora put her hand over the receiver and called out, 'Holly!'

She held her breath and didn't move.

'Holly... Call for you, dear!'

To her horror, Cora shuffled forward and perched on the edge of the seat cushion before speaking into the telephone again.

'I'll have to go and get her,' she sighed. 'Can you hold the line a moment?... Hello? Hello?'

She replaced the receiver, muttering.

Holly pushed open the door and Cora looked up.

'Oh, there you are. Cheeky devil, just ringing off like that. Some people have no patience whatsoever.'

Holly swallowed, her mouth and lips suddenly parched.

'Who was it?' she croaked.

'A woman. Wouldn't tell me her name, can you believe it? Said it was confidential, about some kind of unpaid bill.' Cora narrowed her eyes. 'Are you managing all right? I know it's a while until payday.'

'Yes, of course,' Holly said briskly. 'Listen, Cora. Could I ask a massive favour of you?'

'Certainly.' Cora beamed, seemingly pleased to be helping out.

'Can I ask that if anyone else rings the house, you don't say that I'm living here?'

Cora's face dropped. 'Why would you want me to do that, dear?'

Mindful that David was still in the kitchen, Holly pulled the door to behind her and dropped her voice lower.

'I want to put my old life behind me, Cora. Some of the people I knew in Manchester weren't good for me and I like living here with you. I want to make a complete fresh start, that's all.'

It was the right thing to say. Cora smiled back at her.

'Consider it done.' She nodded. 'I shall make sure I don't drop you in it in future.'

'Thank you,' Holly said and blew out a long breath. 'I'll just dial 141 and see if it registered the number they called from.

A disconnected robotic voice informed her that the caller had withheld their number.

She replaced the receiver.

'Is your phone number ex-directory, Cora?' she asked, trying hard to keep her voice level.

'Oh no, I don't think so. I don't really see the point in keeping it private, otherwise why have a phone line in the first place?'

'Perhaps you ought to think about it. You'd get fewer nuisance sales calls that way,' Holly said, wondering how long she could keep the panic from her face. 'I'm just going to sort out some bits in my bedroom. I won't be long.'

Upstairs, she went straight to the bathroom, worried she was about to throw up. She hung over the toilet bowl but she wasn't sick, just had the feeling she might be.

She splashed water over her hot cheeks and stood for a moment until the feeling receded, then crossed the landing into the cool privacy of her bedroom.

When she lay on her bed, her insides felt as if they were turning to liquid.

Who had called Cora's landline? The words *unpaid bill* sounded like one of the debt collection agencies, which seemed feasible on the one hand; after all, there were about a dozen of them after her back in Manchester. She had all their ignored communications in the bag she'd stuffed under the bed.

On the other hand, it didn't make any sense for a debt collection agency to refuse to tell Cora their company name but then disclose that Holly had an unpaid bill. That didn't follow at all and didn't conform to strict data protection practices.

So then – she bit her lip – who was it who had called? Who knew she lived here? If they had this phone number, they probably had the address, too. She'd heard Cora give her own name, so it wouldn't be difficult to trace her through the electoral roll.

She had a sudden urge, and before she could talk herself out of it, she'd rummaged at the back of her underwear drawer and grabbed the bottle of wine hidden there. It was unchilled and cheap, but that didn't matter. It would help, and that was what counted.

She picked up a glass from the floor, glugged back the inch of water in there and half filled it with wine, which she gulped down in one. She refilled the glass, taking another few sips, then put it on the bedside table before lying back on the bed again.

She covered her face with her hands.

She felt like crying but was too tense to even try. It felt like every muscle in her body had pulled taut enough to snap.

CHAPTER 49

Holly

She'd drifted off a while, lying on the bed. The wine had helped to calm her down but the sick feeling in her stomach had got worse, if anything.

She sat up abruptly at the sound of a voice at the bottom of the stairs and baulked at the sting of reflux at the back of her throat.

'Goodbye, Holly,' David called up.

She sprang up off the bed and rushed to the door, calling to him far too brightly.

'Bye, David! Let me know about the cinema times.'

Sometimes he irritated her. He was odd – everybody thought so – and she still hadn't got to the bottom of what had happened to him, or indeed what was behind Nick Brown's rather vague warning.

But, as she'd discovered all those years ago at school with Markus, outsiders usually found and understood each other.

David had an air about him that tempted her to put her trust in him, in a similar way that she had trusted Markus in the early days.

Was it really too much to think that she might be able to confide in him about her fears?

A sinking feeling inside told her it would be a bit like letting the genie out of the bottle. If she told him she was afraid someone had tracked her down, she'd be forced to tell him why someone might be looking for her.

And David was probably clueless enough to mention it to Cora. She was trapped by her own secrets.

Still, it seemed like the best plan, even though she had another one simmering on the back burner. A contingency plan of sorts.

David seemed dependable, and she didn't really have that much choice in terms of finding someone trustworthy enough to talk to.

If she took things steady and didn't rush, he could prove to be a very useful friend indeed.

Holly had always been a low-energy person, but after six weeks at Geraldine and Brendan's, she barely recognised herself.

She'd adopted Geraldine's suggested schedule of gym training and swimming, utilising their basement fitness suite. She'd also, for the last week, been getting up an hour earlier than her usual seven-thirty daily rise and taking a twenty-minute run around the grounds.

She had dropped twenty pounds in weight. The puppy fat had melted away, her skin was clearer, her hair glossier, and she felt great.

'It's all thanks to you,' she'd told Geraldine as they enjoyed a fruit and vitamin juice breakfast on the patio.

'You're the one who's done all the work,' Geraldine had said generously, but Holly knew the routine too well to be fooled.

'But I'd never have thought of embarking on a fitness routine unless you'd suggested it,' she'd said dutifully. 'You've changed my life, Geraldine. Thank you.'

'Oh sweetie, stop.' Geraldine's face had glowed with something that resembled satisfaction more than humility. 'I just gave you a little encouragement is all. It's important to me that you be the best you can be. And I do care about you, I hope you know that.'

'It's really nice of you to say so.' Holly had smiled and touched Geraldine's hand. 'But I really am so grateful.'

It was true that Holly had to play the game, letting Geraldine get her own way and saying the right things all the time, but was it really such a high price to pay?

Everyone had complaints about their work, stuff that got on their nerves, stuff they wished they didn't have to do. Like working a twelve-hour shift on a boring production line, getting up at five in the morning for a two-hour commute, working August bank holiday weekend in a stifling, overcrowded call centre.

In Holly's opinion, these would have been things to complain about.

Complimenting Geraldine, ordering healthy food off the menu, following workout advice and shifting a bit of weight… these were duties that Holly felt able to fulfil.

Geraldine had talked a bit about her own past and had confided guiltily in Holly that she had come from a privileged background. She'd never been short of money or affection as a child or an adult; had gone from Daddy taking care of her to Brendan providing a very nice life.

Yes, Geraldine had been spoiled. Yes, she often complained relentlessly about things like running out of her favourite yoghurts, or Patricia not toasting her breakfast bagel quite long enough.

But Holly had believed her when she'd said she cared about her.

CHAPTER 50

David

I call it my *other life*, the one before I met Della Carter. The life before it happened.

Don't get me wrong, I've never been the sociable type, never been the sort to play footie with the lads on Saturday morning and pile into the pub to drink beer until teatime.

But I did have a life of sorts that suited me and wasn't based on fear.

Now, my days are a fine balance between routine and necessity.

Don't go out after dark, stay away from people (especially the ones you don't know), do the same things at the same time so there are no surprises, take your medication as advised, and most important of all: *don't get yourself into a fix again.*

I try to live by these rules every day, although I have to admit that recently I've once again felt the swell of uncertainty and disruption. There are still occasions when life catches me out and I have to try and avoid them to keep myself on the level.

And fixes are hard to avoid when you're not so good at recognising the warning signs.

Sometimes things get the better of me, like when Mother persuaded me, against my better judgement, to attend the local church's spring fayre last year.

I stood holding the cups while Mother went to the cake stall to find something sweet to have with our tea. The fayre was well attended and there were lots of people milling around.

The hum around me grew louder, the squeals, laughter, clattering… it all began to reverberate in my ears like I was back in the white room with no furniture.

A twisty feeling started up in my gut as I stood there frozen to the spot with sweat running down my face, the teacups starting to rattle in their saucers.

'Let me take those for you a moment,' a kind voice said. A man in a dog collar took the cups and put them on a table, and I said thank you and breathed out. 'They can be very taxing events, these fayres. Jolly noisy, too. Would you like me to get you a chair?'

'No. Thank you but I'm fine.' I was aware that people were already looking. 'I was just waiting for my mother, she's buying cake.'

'Ah, I see.' He nodded, smiling his understanding.

We stood for a moment without speaking. Him in his long black cassock, bouncing on the balls of his feet with his hands clasped behind his back, surveying his flock. And me frantically mopping my face with my handkerchief and trying to remember to breathe.

Then people – women mainly – started to gravitate towards us. *Oh yes, Father – no, Father – oh it's a marvellous event you've put on here, Father…*

On and on they droned. And when he eventually left to draw the raffle, they didn't go with him. They started talking to me instead.

It was a prime example of how I get lulled into a false sense of security where I start to trust strangers, and the same thing happens again and again no matter who I'm with or where I am.

Someone seems friendly enough and I start to talk and forget what I'm saying, and I don't know if it's the nerves or what, but soon I see their faces start to change.

I'm never really sure what it is I have or haven't done.

And that's what it's always felt like, being me.

But today, when I'm finished at Mrs Barrett's and I've said goodbye to Holly, I walk back round to the house and there's a light feeling in my heart.

Something's not right with Holly, I know that, like I knew it with Della. But this time, I feel sure it's nothing to do with me.

After the landline rang at the house, she was jumpy, nervous, and she wouldn't take the call. I couldn't hear what she was saying in the living room, but I know that tone. It's the same tone Mother has used all her life when she's talking about me, first to my father, now to Brian.

It's a tone that tries to conceal alarm and concern. It's a tone that can cover up lies very well, like a thick layer of butter might conceal mouldy bread.

I hesitate and look down towards number 11.

There's nobody on the street just now and no sign of life from the Browns', but I still rush straight back in through our front gate and down the short path.

Only then do I relax a little; linger down the side of my own house, press my back against the cool, rough brickwork.

There are only opaque windows overlooking me here, so I have plenty of time to stand and breathe and enjoy the light feeling that for once feels stronger than the panic.

I close my eyes and take in a deep breath of sharp, cool air. I hold it there a few seconds before releasing it again. I do it a few times more.

I look directly up at the side of Mrs Barrett's house, to the top floor.

Behind that wall is Holly's bedroom. It's where she sleeps at night. Directly opposite it, above where I'm standing now, is my bedroom.

At night-time, we are as close to each other as we can be. Just two slender walls between us.

There's a warm feeling in my chest.

Holly didn't make fun of me when I asked if she'd like to go to the cinema. She didn't disappear when I spoke a bit about my job. She seemed genuinely interested.

Holly is different in every way.

If she's in some kind of trouble, then perhaps I can be of assistance.

That's how it started with Della, too. I just wanted to help, that's all it was, and she told me she wanted me to be involved. She told me she *wanted* my help.

Otherwise I'd never have done something like that.

I haven't even looked at Della's photographs for a while. That's how good I feel.

I'm not going to get carried away this time, but I'm honestly beginning to think that Holly moving here was meant to be.

She's the first person I've met who I really do think I can trust.

CHAPTER 51

David

Holly decides that she'd like to see the film the following Sunday.

I text her the cinema times and then sit motionless in my bedroom, staring at the phone on my desk.

After ten long minutes of non-communication, I feel utterly convinced she has changed her mind, but then a pinging noise sounds and her name pops up on the screen.

Next Sunday at 2 sounds great. Look forward to it! H

I've had texts before, obviously, but just updates from the phone company I'm with or nuisance spam about prize draws. I've never had a text from a woman… a friend.

It feels special. Different.

I want to keep it all to myself, but of course, when I take my dirty pots downstairs, Mother knows instantly that something is up. She looks at me through narrowed eyes when I refuse a slice of her apple and coconut cake.

'David, I've been making your favourite cake for nigh on thirty years now, and in all that time I've never known you turn down a slice.'

'I… I'm just not that hungry, Mother,' I say.

'I've told you, love. A bit of graft on a building site would sort him out in no time.' Brian appears in the kitchen doorway. 'Sat on your arse day in, day out. That's your problem, Dave.'

'My name is David.'

'Touchy today, aren't we? Got a spot of that well-known ailment, single man's sexual frustration?'

My hand tightens on the handle of the mug I'm holding.

'Brian, please.' My mother closes her eyes with a pained expression.

'It's not healthy. He needs some proper graft and some fresh air in his—'

'I've already got a job, and it's one you need a brain to do.'

Two red spots appear on Brian's cheeks. He steps forward, clenching his fists.

'What are you trying to say, you little—'

'Just stop it, you two!' Mother cries out.

'I'm not going to stand here and listen to that twat talk about my job like that,' Brian says with quiet menace. 'He's no idea of the skill involved in bricklaying.'

We glare at each other wordlessly.

I am sick of Brian being in my space and on my back the entire time. Holly's face flashes into my mind – the way she looks at me, listens with interest to what I have to say – and instead of walking away from the situation, I say something.

'It's not your job any more, though, is it?' I hear my voice as though I am an onlooker. It is calm. 'You had to retire due to ill health… or something along those lines.'

'You'd better shut him up before I do it,' Brian growls, the two red spots exploding out into the rest of his podgy, sallow face.

'David, enough!'

He can say what he likes to *me*, but of course I'm never allowed to retaliate or to point out that I know they sacked him when he fell off his ladder drunk and crushed his leg.

'David, are you…' Mother lowers her voice as if to stop Brian hearing. 'Are you taking your tablets?'

'Yes.' I swallow hard and bite down on my tongue, thinking of yesterday's tablet, still nestling in its foil.

The pair of them stare at me, and it feels like I'm standing in fierce sunlight. 'I'm fine, Mother. Please don't worry.'

'Yeah. Keep taking the tablets, Dave.' Brian chuckles mirthlessly.

My arm pulls back, my fingers release, and I watch as the large, heavy mug sails through the air and glances against Brian's temple.

Mother screams as he staggers back, grabbing on to the corner of the table to support himself.

The mug shatters and lies in pieces on the floor. Mother runs to Brian, fussing needlessly when there's not a jot wrong with him.

I stand quietly and watch. It feels like one of those TV dramas is playing out in front of me.

Mother and Brian are whispering to each other, but I don't care. I'm not going to be the first to leave the room.

Interestingly, the anger that flared earlier has now drained from him, and, glaring at me as he passes, he limps back to the comfort of the television in the other room.

'David, I've never known you like this, not since… Perhaps you need to see the doctor.'

'I don't need to see the doctor. I just need *him* to leave our home.'

Mother sees a chance to make amends. 'He's out all day at the match next Sunday, so we can have a nice time at home together. I'll cook a roast dinner and we'll watch something on television. It'll be just like the old days. How does that sound?'

'I'm afraid I can't next Sunday,' I say quickly. 'I'm…' My voice drops to a whisper. 'I'm going out.'

Mother's mouth falls open and the cake knife clatters from her hand onto the worktop.

'Out? Out where? With whom?'

I slide this way and that on my stockinged feet and my hands start that habit they have of twisting in on themselves.

'I don't want to talk about it,' I say.

'It's that girl next door, isn't it?' Her voice hardens. 'Mrs Barrett's visitor?'

I don't look up.

'I knew it.' Mother grabs hold of my shoulders. 'Look at me, David.'

I look at her and her eyes burn into mine like glowing coals.

'It's too soon to be thinking of getting involved with another—'

'We're just friends,' I say curtly. 'We're going to the cinema. That's all it is, Mother.'

'That's how it starts, as well you know.' She snorts. 'You're playing with fire, David. Just think on that.'

I turn around and walk out of the kitchen.

As I step over Brian's muddy boots, I wonder where he's been to get them caked up like that, and then I remember. He's always down the bottom of the garden. I kick one on purpose as I head for the stairs.

Mother's bound to worry, I know that, but *I am fine*. I haven't felt so clear-headed and optimistic for ages.

Holly is different to… anyone else. I've already decided that I will confide in her at some point, if we become good friends.

I'm not dangerous, I'm not out of control, whatever others might think.

The last thing I want to do is scare Holly away.

CHAPTER 52

Holly

On Monday morning, all Kellington's staff convened as usual on the ground floor for the morning briefing. Emily's absence was glaring.

'As you'll see, no Emily this morning,' Josh said matter-of-factly. 'Sadly, she has now left the company. She handed in her notice late on Friday.'

There was a collective gasp as everyone glanced at each other and a second or two of awkward silence ensued. Josh didn't fill in the blanks; instead he simply launched into the day's new products overview.

After the briefing, everyone disbanded and Josh went straight upstairs to Mr Kellington's office.

Holly stood in her usual area of the showroom.

She realised that under Emily's ever-critical glare, she'd subconsciously defaulted to the rear of the space. Now she walked forward and stood in what had been Emily's hallowed spot.

The March sunlight that usually lit Emily up like an archangel flooded in through the enormous window and did the same to Holly. It felt so good that it was now she whose face was turned towards the rays.

She found she couldn't stand in the sun for long, though. She still had a dull headache from her drinking binge at the weekend.

She had quickly polished off the bottle of wine she'd brought with her from Manchester, and when Cora had run short of milk on Sunday morning, she'd taken the opportunity to pop to the local shop, where she'd invested in another two bottles.

She'd told Cora she felt under the weather and had spent most of the weekend in her bedroom, cowering from the sound of the telephone ringing or a loud knock at the front door.

But neither had happened. It seemed as if she'd done a good job of scaring herself senseless over nothing again.

Still, it was wonderful to feel so relaxed at the beginning of the day, instead of focusing on keeping out of Emily's way and trying to avoid annoying her in some inconsequential and unavoidable way.

Ben and Martyn were chatting at the top end of the showroom in their usual spots and the atmosphere felt so... well, *nice.*

'Hasn't taken you long to jump into Emily's shoes, I see!'

Holly spun round to see Josh approaching, a teasing grin plastered on his face.

'I wasn't... I mean, I'm not...'

'Hello? It was a *joke.*' He shook his head. 'If you hadn't been standing in her plum spot when I came down, I'd have asked you why not.'

'I'm shocked she isn't here,' Holly said. 'I didn't think she'd get *fired* for what happened.'

'What she did, it was pretty serious, considering.' Josh shrugged. 'Damaging an exclusive piece like the Lalique vase and then trying to pin the blame on a colleague. You're very generous, Holly. If she'd accused me, I would've demanded she get fired.'

He checked the price of a standard lamp next to him and ticked it off on a clipboard he held in the crook of his arm.

'Anyway, she wasn't fired. Mr Kellington was willing to issue her with a final written warning, but she took it upon herself to resign. Told him to stick his job where the sun don't shine... charming, eh?'

'Wow.' Holly took in this new information. 'She wouldn't want the stigma of it, I suppose. Colleagues and customers gossiping about her.'

Josh pulled the corners of his mouth down and shrugged his shoulders. 'Dunno. She said she had something far more important to do with her time, and that…' he affected a sinister tone, 'we'd all find out soon enough. Creepy!'

'What did she mean by that?' Holly asked faintly.

'Who knows what anything means with Emily?' He grinned. 'Good riddance is what I say. No place for that sort of underhanded business here at Kellington's.'

Holly stepped back and leaned against the heavy glass dining table behind her.

Emily's comments had sounded like some sort of veiled threat. And Holly had been on the receiving end of her threats before.

'What happened to the girl who had the job before I came?' she asked. 'Why did she leave?'

The grin slid from Josh's face. 'Why do you ask?'

She told him what Emily had said about her, and her subsequent warning in the staffroom.

'Oh God, I had no idea she'd been so bad with you.' He swallowed. 'You should've come to me, Holly, you should've—'

'So how did Emily get rid of the last girl?'

Josh was silent for a few seconds before clearing his throat.

'I'm sorry, I can't discuss private staff matters.' He took a step back from her. 'Confidentiality and all that. I know you'll understand.'

Holly's interest was immediately piqued. Whatever had happened to the last member of staff Emily hadn't liked might have well happened to her too. Irritation with Josh squirmed in her throat.

'Anyway, cheer up,' Josh said brightly. 'Mr Kellington's in no rush to take someone else on, so he wanted me to ask if you feel confident enough to look after Emily's regular customers.'

She wasn't sure she could follow Emily's Oscar-winning performances with Mr and Mrs Fenwick, but she felt delighted that Mr Kellington had displayed such faith in her.

'I'd love to, thanks.'

She pushed Emily's bitter words before leaving to the back of her mind. What could the woman do to her, really? Nothing. Unless she wanted to do time for it.

'Excellent.' Josh began to walk away. 'I'll tell him right now and you can thank me with a cream cake on payday… You've got to spend that enormous commission on something worthwhile, right?'

Commission! She reminded herself she'd be raking it in big-time now Emily had gone.

A pleasant place to work and a big fat pay packet… what was not to like?

It had been normal for Geraldine's mood to be on the low side.

Holly had quickly come to realise that although Brendan popped in and out of the house most days, he stayed away from home a lot. Consequently, there had been an ongoing expectation for Holly to think of suitable ways to cheer his wife up.

It didn't sound much, but Holly actually found it hard work to make suggestions and motivate Geraldine, particularly when she was feeling low. So it had made a pleasant change when Geraldine had approached her, upbeat, one morning.

'Brendan is home for dinner tonight and I'm cooking him something nice. Let's sit down over breakfast and discuss what needs to be done.'

Holly made skinny lattes at the coffee machine whilst Geraldine scribbled notes. She eventually decided on beef stroganoff with rice and a simple pavlova for dessert.

Holly had watched enviously as her employer scrolled through Google looking for suitable recipes. She'd almost forgotten what it was like to have your own phone to play with, swiping through the various screens.

She'd written Aunt Susan a short note as Geraldine had suggested, and the housekeeper, Patricia, had kindly posted it for her. But that had been a little while ago now and she'd had no reply.

It was at that point that Holly had realised that although she was out of the house a lot, shopping, at the cinema or restaurants, she was never out *alone*. Since she'd arrived, she had been constantly in Geraldine's company in *and* out of the house.

There was nothing wrong with it; just a funny little fact, she'd thought at the time. And when she'd mentioned it to Geraldine, she'd shrugged and asked Holly coolly if that was a problem for her. Holly hadn't mentioned it again.

'I'll help you get everything ready for the meal and then I'll disappear upstairs to my room before Brendan gets home,' she told Geraldine now.

'No way!' Geraldine had grabbed her hand. 'The three of us will eat together, I insist on it.'

Holly had smiled and successfully hidden the uncomfortable stirring in her stomach. She certainly didn't relish playing gooseberry to those two.

She had noticed that Geraldine was very touchy-feely with Brendan, on the few brief occasions he stayed at the house longer than ten minutes. It was as if she saw so little of him, she had to make it count when she did.

After an afternoon at Waitrose getting all the stuff, and then a couple of hours in the kitchen preparing the dishes, Holly had felt exhausted and sorely wished she'd got the night off.

In the last week or so, Geraldine had been proving to be very hard work.

On the face of it, Holly's job sounded like every young girl's dream. Lunching out in fabulous eateries, watching films, shopping, coffee and endless chats… but she had soon realised she could never be herself.

She hadn't thought she even liked herself that much, but now that 'new Holly' was the only one around, she'd started to mourn the more relaxed, authentic version of herself.

The one that wasn't always kowtowing to Geraldine, always down in the gym, always watching what she ate.

She could never complain that she was too tired for the next marathon shopping trip, or tell Geraldine that actually she didn't feel like watching yet another episode of *The Real Housewives of Orange County*. She couldn't decline Geraldine's offer to accompany her to the nail and hair salon and say that she'd much rather stay in her bedroom and read, or go for a nice relaxed walk around the grounds for a bit of space and fresh air.

It was also a job that had no set hours. Holly was on call twenty-four hours a day. One time Brendan was working away and Geraldine had suffered a stomach upset in the middle of the night and been unable to sleep. Holly had also been roused from her slumbers and summoned downstairs to look after her boss as you would do a sick child.

It was times like this that she had known she must swallow down the resentment that clotted in her chest.

She'd still felt lucky to have the job, but with no contract to refer to, she didn't know whether she'd actually signed up to such demands, so she couldn't begin to do anything about it.

Maybe, she'd thought, when she had Brendan and Geraldine together at last tonight, it would be a good chance to try broaching one or two uncomfortable subjects again.

It had seemed like a good idea at the time.

CHAPTER 53

Holly

Halfway through the first week at Kellington's without Emily on her tail, Holly felt like her life was truly coming together in ways she could never have envisaged.

Most of Emily's customers recognised her and made a beeline for her as they entered the store, and as a result, her month-end commission bonus was growing daily.

She felt delighted that she'd taken the trouble to introduce herself and say hello to the regular customers, even when Emily was the one who was benefiting from their spend. That decision was really paying dividends now.

They had all been terribly shocked when Holly enlightened them about Emily's sudden departure from the store. Josh had advised her not to discuss what had happened unless the customers themselves raised it, but actually, she'd taken great delight in instigating the conversations.

The Fenwicks' had been the best reaction. When she told them that Emily had left the store after damaging the Lalique vase, she thought Mrs Fenwick was going to need to be medically revived.

'But why? Why would Emily do that?' the woman had demanded, clutching her throat as if she couldn't get her breath. 'She was so conscientious.'

Holly had to be careful how she phrased what had happened, just in case one of the customers repeated something to Josh. She had to keep the pleasure off her face.

'I'm sure she had her reasons,' she said sadly. 'I was so shocked when she led everyone to believe *I* had damaged the vase, and then... well, I can't say too much, but when the flowers were found in her handbag, thank goodness I was cleared of suspicion.'

Mrs Fenwick gasped at Emily's treachery.

'You poor girl.' Mr Fenwick shook his head. 'What on earth must have got into Emily, to pull a stunt like that?'

'It's very sad.' Mrs Fenwick nodded. 'Emily always took such good care of us here, but...' she grasped Holly's hand and smiled at her husband, 'I just know that Holly is going to do an even better job. Am I right?'

'Of course.' Holly beamed. 'I'd be honoured to look after you from now on.'

And that had been the sum of it. Thanks to the Fenwicks' superficiality, Emily was swiftly forgotten and it was business as usual.

Half an hour after Holly's short conversation with them, the Fenwicks had spent another few hundred pounds in the store and Holly's commission pot had risen yet another notch.

After the couple had left, Holly made a cup of tea and took it to her desk so she could complete the paperwork from their purchases.

On her way back across the showroom, she spotted that Martyn was free. She walked over to him.

'How's things?'

He looked up from his phone and smiled at her. 'Good, thanks.'

She wasn't quite sure how to broach the subject so decided to just jump in with both feet. 'Listen, did you know the girl in the job before I joined?'

His smile faded. 'Lynette, yeah. Only as a colleague, but…
She was OK. Nice girl.' He tapped his fingertips on the table
next to him.

'She left the job quickly, as I understand it.' It was obvious
Martyn felt a bit awkward, but she had to know. 'What happened?'

Martyn looked at the stairs and back down to the floor.

'We were told never to speak about it or it'd be a disciplinary,'
he said. 'Sorry, Holly.'

'Come on, you know I won't say anything,' she pressed him.

He glanced at the stairs again.

'Look, you didn't hear it from me but basically, Josh was
shagging her.'

Holly's mouth fell open. Josh? She would never have had him
down as a sleazeball.

'Emily told me she got rid of her. How did she do that… and
why?'

'Let's just say things got complicated.' Martyn sighed.

'Complicated how?'

'You don't give up, do you?' He laughed but shuffled on his
feet. 'Josh was… well, he was also shagging Emily. Neither of them
knew about the other one.'

'Josh was… *with Emily*?' Holly also recalled that Josh was
married. 'What a rat!'

'Yeah, I know. She was less of a dragon then. We suspected
something was going on between them, but they were quite
discreet.' Martyn glanced around the showroom yet again,
obviously nervous of Josh somehow gathering that he was
gossiping. 'Then Lynette came to work here and he started his
double game.'

'And Emily found out?'

'She followed him after work, apparently. Watched as he met
Lynette in a bar in town and screamed the place down, we heard.'

'Did she make Lynette's life hell, then?' Holly shuddered, able to imagine just how miserable Emily Beech could make you if she set her mind to it.

'Well… Lynette left under a bit of a cloud. She was found to be stealing. Items from the shop-floor displays were found in her car.'

Holly could hardly believe her ears.

'Pretty much the same method Emily tried to use on me.' She frowned. 'Trying to convince everyone I'd broken the vase.'

'Yeah.' Martyn shrugged.

'Pity everybody seemed to believe her at the time,' Holly said acidly. 'Still, the truth shone through, thankfully.'

Martyn looked relieved when she moved away. She stood near the window and sipped her tea, watching as the traffic crawled by, still in shock that she'd been such a bad judge of character with Josh.

The previous day, after clearing it with Josh, she'd transferred the contents of her own drawers over to the larger desk that sat close to the window. Emily's old workstation. Josh had arranged for a couple of the warehouse men to relocate her computer there too.

It was a much nicer spot. From here she had an excellent view of the entrance doors, and it was easy to identify the genuinely interested window browsers and know what they had their eye on before they even entered the shop.

She had to hand it to Emily, she had been even cleverer than Holly had given her credit for. But now even Emily knew that things didn't always go her way. She hadn't been able to dispose of Holly quite as efficiently as poor Lynette.

Holly tapped at her calculator and happily added the day's sales figures to a piece of paper. She was just leafing through a product brochure to find a particular code when, for no apparent reason, the hairs on the back of her neck prickled.

She stopped working and looked up, just in time to see a woman in jeans and a hooded sweatshirt turn and walk briskly away from the window. Had she been watching Holly working?

As soon as the woman was out of sight, the creepy feeling left her. It had been impossible to see any identifying features from the back, but the woman had been around the same height and stature as Geraldine. Or even Emily, without her heels.

If only she'd glanced up a couple of seconds earlier.

Holly knew that David finished his shift at one, so at twelve thirty she slipped out of the back entrance to visit his office, as he seemed insistent on calling it.

'Holly,' he beamed, putting down his flask. 'How was your morning?'

'Have you seen anyone skulking around here at all?' She swallowed. 'I thought I saw Emily just now, at the front window.'

David frowned. 'Emily doesn't work here any more. Josh told me to revoke her staff parking rights.'

Holly shook her head in frustration. Why did he always have to take everything so damn *literally*?

'I'm fully aware she doesn't work here any more, David. That's my point. She shouldn't be anywhere around here.'

He reached for his jacket. 'I ought to tell Mr Kellington she's been seen trespassing.'

'No! I don't want you to do that because I'm not sure it was her; it might have been… Oh, never mind!'

'I'll be round later to do some jobs for Mrs Barrett,' she heard him call after her. 'Will you be in?'

That was all she needed, David and Cora rattling on all evening. She needed space to get her head straight.

The awful thoughts had started to come back with a vengeance. She could feel them.

CHAPTER 54

David

I lie in bed, turning this way and then that, but every muscle in my body feels stretched to its limit. My neck and shoulders tense and burn, my face and hands are sticky.

The glaring red digits on my clock inform me it is 1.30 a.m.

I wonder if Holly is sleeping soundly, just across the way. She was agitated when she came to speak to me at lunchtime. She even snapped at me a couple of times.

I know she didn't mean it. It will be the goings-on on the shop floor. I've heard all sorts of unsavoury rumours about who is getting up to what.

It feels like I haven't been in bed that long, but I came up at the normal time, I'm sure of it. My head feels full of fuzz, so I lie still for a few minutes in the hope it might dissipate.

It doesn't.

I get out of bed and crack the window open slightly, stand there a moment to enjoy the trickle of the cool breeze that filters through.

A cat walks nonchalantly across the grass and the outside sensors activate. It disappears into the hedge, and a few seconds later the lights go off again.

That's when I see that the Browns are still up.

As their house sits on the bend of the crescent, I can partially see the back of the property if I lean out of the window.

Their lounge is situated at the rear, unlike ours and the lights are still on… *at this hour*! Although the curtains are pulled to, they're of poor quality and don't quite meet in the middle.

With the aid of the binoculars, I see Mr Brown's feet and his striped-pyjama-clad legs. A light flickers within as the television bathes the room with its flashing images.

Upstairs, the curtains are closed and their bedroom is in darkness.

I've seen Mrs Brown drawing the curtains in there at bedtime, but I've never seen him. I wonder if they're sleeping in separate rooms. I ought to try and ascertain this, because if so, when put together with the other information I know about the Browns, it could be a sign that trouble is brewing again.

This time, I know I can do nothing about it. I won't get involved but I might call the police.

A slipper hangs off Mr Brown's foot, and as I watch, it falls to the floor, but his leg still doesn't move. He must have fallen asleep in front of the television again.

It's been proven that sleep quality is impaired when you're not properly relaxed in bed, and he does that regularly.

The image of him talking to Holly in Mrs Barrett's garden flashes into my mind again. What was he speaking to her about? I tried raising it with Holly, but she just batted the subject away.

She's naïve, and as I know only too well, he's the sort of man to take advantage, if there's any chance he can.

I switch on my lamp and flip the Rolodex until I get to the Browns' details. I turn on my mobile phone and tap in the landline number, switching off my lamp again before it starts to ring.

When the Neighbourhood Watch scheme was first launched in the area, members of the committee and residents – myself included – wrote down their contact details and a very useful list was circulated.

Holding the phone to my ear with one hand and waiting for the shrill ring to begin at the other end, I pick up the binoculars again with my other hand and watch as Mr Brown's leg jerks up in shock at the noise. Then he jumps up off the sofa.

His shadow darts across the room, magnified against the unlined curtains.

'Hello?' he breathes at the end of the line. 'Hello?'

I wait a second or two and then end the call. I put down my phone, still watching.

He sits back down on the edge of the sofa this time, the gap in the curtains revealing that his elbows are on his knees and his bowed head is in his hands.

Mr Brown looks to me like a man with considerable problems. Problems he's not entirely sure how to solve. I wonder if regrets over what happened lie heavy on his shoulders in the early hours, when the world around him is quiet.

I suppose if I'm honest, I like to think of myself as a fixer. I wonder what might happen if I went around there right now and surprised him, caught him totally off guard.

He might make a cup of tea and we could talk, man to man.

A wry smile plays on my lips. That could never happen now.

The morning after Della walked by me in the street, she visited Mr Brown again. This time I didn't bother calling into work, but I didn't go for my usual bus. I could hardly say I had another ailment that meant I'd be late in.

I waited at the end of the street again. This time, it was barely half an hour before I saw the front door open. Della rushed out and Mr Brown stood on the step, his hands laced on top of his head.

'Della... I'm sorry!' he called, but she didn't look back.

I waited in the shadows until he'd gone back into the house, and this time, when she drew level with me, I spoke to her.

'Are... are you all right?' I asked. I reached out and touched her arm, just very lightly, but it startled her all the same.

'Who are you? Get off me.' She pulled her arm away, her eyes wide.

Her skin was smooth, like porcelain. Pale curls framed eyes that were the colour of cornflowers. I'd never been as close to someone so beautiful.

'Sorry, I didn't mean any harm,' I said quickly. 'You just looked upset.'

'I'm fine.' She scowled and stomped past. When she reached the main road, she turned and glanced back at me, but she didn't smile.

I didn't go to work that day. I walked back to the house and for some reason stopped outside Mr Brown's gate. I walked up his path and found myself knocking at the door.

What am I doing? I remember thinking, but by that time it was too late. The door flew open and his hopeful, relieved smile turned into a frown.

'What do *you* want?'

'I... I just saw... I wondered if everything was OK.'

I watched as his expression moved from puzzled through realisation to pure annoyance. He leaned out of the door and looked up the crescent, but there was no sign of Della by this time.

'Your friend looked upset,' I said.

'Keep your nose out of my bloody business,' he snapped, his face puce.

The next thing, I was looking at a closed door again.

The following morning, Della didn't come. I didn't go to work. I watched Mr Brown in the garden. But he wasn't gardening as such; he was on more of a rampage.

He arbitrarily pulled out flowers and plants and tossed them aside to die in the sun. He lugged the mower out from the shed like a man possessed and tramped up and down one narrow piece of lawn repeatedly until not a blade of grass remained.

It occurred to me that he must really be very fond of Della. But Mr Brown was a married man and Della obviously wasn't that keen on him any more.

But she might want another man to take care of her. Someone who was available, I thought.

I suppose that was the point when my thinking changed. When I became very interested in Della. Some might say obsessed.

I've never had an apology from Mr Brown even after all this time, and it's hard to forgive that, but I feel so much better about my life since Holly appeared on the scene.

I'd like a chat with him; a conversation might clear the air, though only if he was prepared to listen, and I'm not all sure he would.

I look down at my phone and am considering whether to call his house again when his arm reaches over for the remote and the flickering light of the television ceases. A minute or two later, the lights in the living room go off.

I stand there a little longer, watching the upstairs window, but no faint hallway light enters the space as he opens the door. There is no sign that he has entered the main bedroom.

I fear my suspicions about the Browns sleeping in separate bedrooms may be proven right. My fears seem more real when I think about him whispering to Holly.

The seed of an idea begins to form in my mind, but it's late and I can think about that more tomorrow, I decide.

Back in bed, the restlessness returns to my body. I throw the quilt off and then pull it back on when my skin cools. I shove the pillows away and lie staring up at the ceiling, although I can see barely anything in the dark.

Holly is mere yards away from me in the next house. I wonder if she is feeling restless too.

Some people believe that if you focus on another person and send direct thoughts their way, they are received telepathically on some level.

I sit up in bed and stare at the faint shadow of the wall in front of me.

I've seen inside Mrs Barrett's back bedroom. I know that the bed is pushed up against the outside wall. Holly's headboard is directly in front of my outstretched legs.

I imagine for a moment beams of light leaving my eyes and travelling effortlessly through the brickwork into Holly's bedroom. The beams of light enter the top of her head and fill her with a reassuring warmth that I am here, looking out for her.

Even if she doesn't know the feeling comes from me, it doesn't matter. Maybe on one level she will feel it, know that I am thinking of her right now.

I blow out air, only realising now that I've been holding my breath, and then slip out of bed and walk to the wall opposite.

There is a chest of drawers there. I open the bottom drawer and place my hands flat on the clothes that Holly cast out to the bin on her first day at Mrs Barrett's. I pick up a T-shirt and hold it to my face, inhale the faint floral scent still lingering around the neckline and then sniff the acrid tang of sweat under the arms.

I close the drawer and squeeze in between the side of it and the edge of the wardrobe. I press my face and chest against the wall, spreading my arms wide. I splay my sticky fingers and push my palms against the cool plaster.

'Holly,' I whisper, closing my eyes and visualising her soft skin, her light breaths against my face.

I imagine, for a moment, that the wall is dissolving away so I find myself there in the room with her.

My breath catches in my throat and I let my hands fall, stepping away from the wall.

We are meant to be together. I can feel it.

CHAPTER 55

Holly

When Holly first heard the noise, she was still dreaming. In her dream, she was standing in the middle of woodland with nothing on but her nightdress.

There was a shuffling, scraping sound behind her... and then it flipped so it was somewhere in front of her.

Her dream self whirled around, bare-footed and frantic, trying to see into the dark spaces between the ghostly pale tree trunks.

When she snapped awake, the woodland had disappeared, replaced again by the four bedroom walls.

The dream had dissolved but she could still hear the noise.

Holly held her breath and listened for a few more moments. The glowing digits on the bedside table read 2.01.

She quickly identified that the noise was coming from down in the garden. Just under her window. She sat up and swung her feet down to the floor. Her head thumped dully from the drink she'd had before bed.

She knew that only a narrow stretch of unused land lay beyond the back hedge. There were no street lights, but tonight, her bedroom and the entire garden were bathed in moonlight. It should have been beautiful... if she'd been able to ignore the sick feeling already squirming in the pit of her stomach.

She padded over to the window and gently peeled back the edge of the curtain.

From this angle, she could only see the far end of the garden, the shrubs and hedges a dark, dense mass against the wooden fence.

She pressed up against the wall and tweaked the curtain again, pulling it a little further away this time so she could see immediately beneath her bedroom window, closer to the back door.

The breath caught in her throat as a long, thin shadow flitted across the yard, melting into nothing.

On a reflex, she yanked the curtains completely open and pressed her face to the glass, her eyes flashing around the garden to search out the trespasser – if that was what it was.

But there was no more movement. No fleeting shadows.

A puff of breath evaporated on the freezing window and obscured her view, so she unhooked the window and eased it open. Cold air funnelled onto her clammy face as she squinted down into the gloom. Her face grew watchful, fearful, as she waited on the slightest flicker of movement.

There! There it was again. The curious scraping noise that had visited her in her dream.

It emanated from the right-hand side of the yard, near the kitchen door. A small area that sat in complete shadow, untouched by the moonlight. The vague outline of old patio furniture and discarded building materials was only just discernible in the meagre light.

Holly made a sharp hissing noise, in the hope that any cat hiding there would show itself, but although the scraping stopped, there was no further movement.

It would probably turn out to be something quite harmless, she reasoned silently to herself. It could be a cat, or even a fox, crouching beneath the old patio table. Watching and waiting until she closed the window again.

She'd always had an overactive imagination. It had been responsible for her visualising an amazing future when she'd first moved to Manchester.

Now it was telling her that someone had caught up with her. That someone was watching her furtively from down in the shadows.

Yet nobody from her old life knew where she was, so that couldn't be the case, surely. But... *the person at the shop window*, a part of her whispered. *The phone call.*

Maybe it *had* been a debt collection company that had somehow managed to trace her. Was it feasible that Kellington's had registered her on some kind of system as an employee, some database that other companies had access to?

She shook her head in frustration.

It was time to knock her volatile imagination on the head. There really was no need to give herself a hard time like this. She should foster a common-sense approach.

She closed the window with a dull thud, praying it wouldn't disturb Cora. The last thing she wanted, at two in the morning, was a cup of tea and another raft of forty-year-old anecdotes to listen to.

She must learn to keep her fears in check and not panic at the first sign of something out of the ordinary.

If she'd reacted differently, a harmless noise in the yard could have been swiftly forgotten. With a pair of ear plugs and a pillow on her head, she could have drifted back to sleep, but instead she'd allowed herself to snap fully awake in an instant and conjure up a convincing batch of sinister explanations.

She'd basically written the beginnings of a pretty grim horror story in her head. And now she'd have to pay the price. She'd probably lie awake for hours, running over it all in her mind.

She'd arrive at work looking and acting like a zombie, and *that* was dangerous because she knew she needed to keep her wits about her. If Emily *was* lurking around, she needed to remain logical and watchful, and that wasn't easily done with sleep deprivation.

Maybe listening to some gentle music in her earphones might do the trick.

As she grabbed hold of the curtains to pull them closed again, a cry escaped her lips and her hands flew up to her mouth.

There was a figure at the bottom of the garden.

Square-shouldered. Just standing there, motionless.

She hadn't imagined it after all.

Someone was watching her. Someone knew she lived here.

She swallowed down the taste of sick in her mouth and looked over her shoulder at the bedroom door. Should she cry out for Cora to come… to witness that what Holly was seeing was real?

Clutching her pyjama top closed at her neck, she looked back at the garden, trying to decide the best action to take.

But the figure had disappeared. There was no trace of anyone having been there at all.

CHAPTER 56

Holly

At the shrill, unwelcome call of the alarm, Holly struggled to open her encrusted eyelids and pressed blindly at the snooze button until the dreadful noise finally stopped.

She tried to rub the sleep from her left eye but only succeeded in irritating her eyeball. She blinked a few times to dissipate the soreness but it still felt full of sand.

She'd lain awake for hours and then dropped into a restless light sleep in which she'd dreamed about what had happened to her back then. As could often happen with dreams, some things were mixed up, nonsensical, but unfortunately it had awakened the real, still vivid memory.

The day of the elaborately planned meal, Geraldine had continued to insist that Holly join her and her husband for dinner, despite Holly's polite protests.

She'd gone back to her bedroom for a rare half an hour's peace while Geraldine took a shower and got changed. Before she'd gone to her own room, her boss had told Holly what to wear and how to style her hair.

Sometimes Geraldine acted so weirdly, Holly had scowled to herself. What other woman would want a young girl hanging around like a spare part when she had the chance of a rare romantic night in with her husband? It didn't make much sense.

Holly had showered quickly, washed her hair and wrapped herself in a soft, fleecy robe. She'd dried her hair and then pulled the dressing table stool over to the window, where she'd sat, her elbows on the windowsill, staring longingly out at the greenery beyond, luxuriating in the few minutes she had alone,

Over the last week, she'd spotted a new gardener once or twice. A guy around her own age with crew-cut hair and muscled arms. In fact, he looked rather like a younger Brendan.

'What's the new gardener's name?' she'd asked Geraldine one day, keeping her tone level. Her boss didn't generally like Holly taking an interest in anything or anyone that didn't directly benefit Geraldine herself.

'What? I didn't even know we had a new gardener.' Geraldine had shrugged, uninterested. 'Brendan sorts all that sort of thing out.'

Holly had spotted him again yesterday morning. He had such a nice face, kind and trustworthy, she'd thought. It would be so nice to have someone else to chat to here.

But she hadn't seen him around today.

Movement caught her eye then and she saw a glint amongst the leaves as the metal gates swung back behind the trees. It looked like Brendan was home early.

That would no doubt panic Geraldine, Holly thought glumly. She'd already said she wanted to look perfect for when her husband arrived home.

The sleek black Ferrari glided up the driveway and parked outside the front entrance. Holly tracked it until it drew too close to the house for her to see.

Flicking the switch on the curling tongs, she began to style her hair the way Geraldine had suggested. She'd quickly learned that her boss's suggestions were actually clear instructions and were not generally up for debate.

It was always easiest to do exactly as Geraldine bade her.

She applied a bit of make-up, fluffed up her curls and sprayed them, then slipped on the silky kimono-style dress that she'd worn only once before but that Geraldine had deemed was a look that suited her.

Fifteen minutes later, she had headed downstairs.

'Wow, lucky me,' Brendan had grinned when she appeared at the lounge door. 'Two beautiful women to entertain me at dinner tonight.'

'Hi, Brendan.' Holly had smiled, but inside, she'd silently raged. Entertain him indeed! She'd much rather be watching tonight's episode of *Big Brother* in the peace of her own room than witness the two of them simpering at each other for hours down here.

'So, how're things going with my two favourite ladies?' Brendan had poured himself a generous whisky and Holly watched as he knocked it straight back before pouring another.

'Everything's good, thanks.' She'd nodded, sensing an opportunity. 'Brendan, I wondered if you'd had a chance to get a copy of my contract from Myra yet?'

'I am such a klutz!' He'd clapped his hand to his forehead. 'I'll get her to print it off on Monday when she's back in the office. Pinky promise.'

Holly was well past nodding and thanking him by now. It was the same old story time after time, and she didn't grace it with a response.

'Wit-woo!' Brendan had given a low whistle as Geraldine appeared. 'I'm the luckiest man on earth.'

Holly had to agree. Geraldine looked simply stunning, in a full-length powder-blue gown that set her glossy chestnut hair off perfectly. A simple diamond collar hugged the base of her throat and more jewels glistened on her fingers and wrist.

Her eye make-up was dark and sultry and her lips pouted in a shimmery pale apricot gloss. In contrast, Holly felt like a little kid dressed as a woman.

'You look really beautiful, Geraldine,' she'd said dutifully.

'Thank you, darling.' She'd gracefully accepted the glass of champagne that Brendan handed her. He'd picked up another glass and offered it to Holly.

'Thanks, but I was just going to have juice tonight,' she'd said.

'Ahem… nobody will be drinking orange juice on *my* watch.' Brendan had grinned, holding his own glass aloft. 'Cheers!'

They'd toasted and Holly took a sip of the fizz. She had to admit it did taste delicious.

After the food, which Holly had noticed they both barely touched, Brendan put on a George Michael album and the three of them retired to the big soft leather couches.

'I'll have another drink with you and then I'll take myself up to bed,' Holly had said. 'It's been a really lovely evening.'

'Nonsense,' Geraldine had replied. 'We hardly ever get the chance to chat together, the three of us. I don't want you to go up yet, Holly.'

Holly had forced a smile and wondered how many more of Brendan's business stories she could endure without falling asleep. They all ran along the same lines: an amazing business opportunity presented itself, somebody mucked the deal up, everyone thought all was lost, and then clever, resourceful Brendan saved the day. *Yawn.*

The worst part had been that he addressed everything he said directly to Holly, forcing her to pay attention and make all the right noises in all the right places.

Geraldine's initial brighter mood had seemed to desert her after dinner, and she'd sat staring into space as Brendan rattled through his stories, obviously bored out of her brains from hearing them all before.

Holly had thought the end of the evening was drawing near, that soon she'd be tucked up in bed savouring a little time alone before sleep. Precious moments when she could be herself again.

She couldn't have known that within the hour, she would lose 'Holly' altogether. That even years later, she would still be fighting to find herself.

CHAPTER 57

David

My eyes snap wide open.

For a second or two I don't know where I am, until I turn my head and see the reassuring square of the floral curtains filtering the early light at the window.

My heartbeat slows a touch but I still do the talking bit to soothe myself.

I'm at home, in my bed. I'm safe. Everything is fine.

It's the same voice that reassured the young lad in the playground when he had nobody to play with at break time and lunch. It's the same voice that calmed him down on the daunting walk home, wondering if Johnny Camps and his mates would be waiting for him round the next corner yet again.

It's all in the past now. I'm looking ahead to the future.

I do the breathing, in and out. Long, slow breaths that carry away the tightness in my face. I wiggle my jaw and get the satisfying crack that will release yet more tension.

In a rush, I remember that I forgot to take my tablets again yesterday. I'll need to remove them from the foil packets, flush them down the loo before Mother sees.

I kick off the covers, exposing my hot limbs to the cool air.

The dream… It was *so real.*

I was back there, on that very street. Della was screaming so loudly, but I couldn't stop myself… I couldn't stop punching and kicking, even when my knuckles were skinned. And then, when she collapsed on the floor, I still couldn't stop.

I did the only thing I *could* do in the dream… I ran. And when the police sirens came, I ran faster still.

That day, when they picked me up, I was still running.

Later, all the police wanted to know was why I'd tried to escape, and of course, I had no answer for that. I could hardly say I was so far gone in the red mist of rage that if I hadn't managed to get myself away, they'd be investigating a murder now.

I was sorry, I said. I was so sorry for Della and sorry, now, for what I'd done.

I shake my head to dispel the thoughts. This line of thinking is not remotely helpful.

Things are different now.

I have a good job and I have Holly's friendship.

I'm not a dangerous man. Despite everything that happened, things getting out of hand.

Everybody loses it at some point in their life; it's just that it had disastrous consequences for Della.

One day, I might even tell Holly about it, but not now. Probably not for a very long time.

The last thing I want to do is scare her off.

CHAPTER 58

Holly

Holly sat up in bed and swung her legs out from under the covers until her feet touched the scratchy threadbare carpet.

She stared at the window, the spot where she'd stood in the early hours.

As predicted, she'd lain awake for ages after hearing the noises outside and then spotting the staring figure at the end of the garden.

Finally forcing herself back to bed, she'd had to fight the urge to keep getting up to peer out of the window, terrified that the figure had returned. A paralysing fear had kept her motionless and cowering under the duvet.

Hour after hour, the glowing red digits had marched relentlessly onwards, and ironically, the more she fretted over getting up for work, the more sleep completely evaded her.

As she'd watched from the window, clouds had drifted across the moon like a cliché, and the figure had seemed to disappear before her very eyes. Yes, she'd looked away, but only for a second or two.

Now, in the cold light of day, she knew she'd managed to get herself in such a state, she really couldn't be certain that she hadn't imagined the whole thing.

Maybe nobody had *ever* been out there watching… except in her head.

Logic told Holly that it was very early days for someone to have found out where she worked, where she lived. It wasn't as if Manchester was on the doorstep; it was over eighty miles further north.

At work, she'd been careful to study every customer's face as they'd entered the shop, and no one had ever looked remotely familiar to her, apart from some of the regulars she was now getting to know.

Why did this have to happen? Things at work were going better than she could ever have imagined. Since Emily had left, Holly had been undisputed top dog in terms of sales.

Emily.

Holly shuddered at the thought of her previous threat, and then it hit her... She'd assumed the figure watching her last night had been a man, but what if it wasn't? What if it had been Emily, come to seek revenge for having resigned from Kellington's – something she'd made clear she considered Holly's fault.

Thanks to Martyn spilling the beans yesterday, Holly knew that Emily was quite capable of scheming someone else's demise. She'd certainly had no trouble getting rid of poor Lynette.

Holly had been telling herself that the woman she'd seen walking away from the shop window yesterday and the mystery phone call to the house both had perfectly logical explanations.

But what if her instincts had been spot on, and it was in fact Emily Beech who'd been watching her as she worked? She could have obtained Holly's address from Kellington's records and traced Cora's landline from that.

Likewise, the figure could easily have been Geraldine. Or someone sent by her. Geraldine had more than enough financial clout to pay some violent numbskull to track Holly down.

But if that was the case, why hadn't something awful already happened to her? Perhaps Geraldine was just waiting for the right moment.

Holly didn't know how long she could cope living constantly on her nerves, waiting for something to happen.

Last night she'd had a few glasses of wine again to help her sleep. She knew that if she didn't watch it, she could find herself with a drink problem like before. But it seemed at the moment that booze was the only thing that could keep her frayed nerves at bay.

On the surface, most of the people around her seemed supportive and kind. But Holly knew only too well that under their benign everyday masks, people could turn out to be truly monstrous.

The night of their family dinner, as Geraldine had insisted on referring to it, Brendan had got up time and time again to refresh their glasses.

Holly's head had felt woozy, but she knew there was no point in protesting that she'd rather have a coffee. She'd learned a while ago that what *she* wanted simply didn't count at Medlock Hall.

Brendan had brought her yet another glass of champagne.

'Now, this is the Pol Roger 2008 and it's not cheap, so don't spill a drop,' he'd instructed her with mock sternness before breaking into a grin. 'Go on then, taste it.'

She'd taken a tentative sip while he watched. 'It's good,' she said, feeling a little queasy.

'*It's good!*' he had mimicked, then turned to Geraldine, laughing loudly. 'Well, that's reassuring to know, at nearly seventy quid a bottle.'

His wife had managed a weak smile but didn't chortle back as she usually might. Holly noticed through bleary eyes that Geraldine's previously perfectly made-up face had become a little smudged and her earlier soft expression had now turned brittle.

Brendan had sat down with his own glass and quietened down at last. Thank God, she'd thought, the stories had finally stopped.

Geraldine and Brendan had looked at each other and then back at her.

Holly clamped her hand across her mouth... had she actually said that out loud?

As her employers watched her, they seemed to be moving very slowly away from her. Further and further they slid, until Holly had barely been able to distinguish their individual features any more.

Her fingers had still been wrapped around the delicate stem of the crystal champagne flute, but now she seemed completely incapable of lifting it to her mouth. It had felt like she was no longer sitting, but floating in mid-air.

She'd smiled, finding the incapacity quite funny, until a sick dizziness hit and her head lolled back against the soft, buttery leather.

George Michael's 'Careless Whisper' sounded like a distant echo. The whole room softened like melting wax around her, and then the walls began to spin closer and closer, pulling her around with them.

Holly had fought the extreme tiredness but simply could not stop her eyelids from closing.

Looking back, she realised that must have been the moment she finally passed out.

She'd known something wasn't right that night, felt it in her bones, but she'd ignored her gut feeling.

Standing here in Cora Barrett's house ten years on, she still couldn't trust herself to decide whether or not someone was watching her every move.

All she could do was try and be vigilant without becoming paranoid. Not an easy balance to strike with the growing sense of panic that seemed to be rising from her core.

Maybe it was time to do something about it, to put her plans into action.

Maybe it was time for her to finally take control.

CHAPTER 59

Holly

After her shower, Holly tried to steel herself for the day at work that lay ahead.

But first, she sat at the dressing table, stared into the mirror and waited for the little girl to come.

She could feel her stirring from her place of slumber, restless with her eternal nightmares. It took a while, but then there she was, staring back at Holly.

Holly lifted a hand and gently traced her smooth, creamy skin.

'You're beautiful,' she told her. 'They told you the opposite, but you are, you know. You *are* beautiful.'

A warm glow broke through the cold, empty feeling in her chest. Just briefly, but it helped.

'You made it through. You're strong, clever and kind.' Holly caressed the child's dark wavy hair. The hair she had hated, that they had cut short because it was *wild*. 'You're safe now. They can't ever hurt you again.'

The warm feeling returned, flooding Holly's chest and remaining there for a second or two longer. She breathed in and out, long spaces that let the relief expand within her.

The tiny flame within that they had tried to stifle, to snuff out… she felt it flickering, growing in strength, deep in her core. They hadn't tried to kill her; it was worse than that.

Over the years, they had tried to dim her glow, to silence her, to make her disappear. Nobody had really wanted her.

Yet despite the cruel words, the rejection, the loss, that little flame survived and burned bright still.

From the mirror, the little girl smiled at Holly.

It felt like the noose around her slender neck had finally loosened. The rope was still there; it probably always would be. But at least *she* controlled it now.

Nobody else could pull it tight again, and because of that, the fear would slowly begin to dissipate.

No more strange men in the house, brought back by her mother. No more waking to a dark shape above her in the middle of the night. No more lying awake until the early hours, listening for a creaking step or a light on the landing.

'You're perfect, little girl,' Holly whispered, cupping her own chin gently and smiling into the glass. 'You always were. Nothing they said or did can ever change that.'

The little girl cried. Holly allowed her glistening teardrops to fall unhindered onto the pale wood veneer of the dressing table.

Perhaps, she thought, this was what people felt when they cut themselves. A pure relief, a sense of creating space within.

The old ravine had opened again inside, and Holly felt herself slipping down into its comforting grip.

She wouldn't let Geraldine ruin her life again.

CHAPTER 60

Holly

'You've been quiet this morning,' Josh remarked when he came over to her desk mid-morning. 'Is everything OK?'

She couldn't bring herself to look at him.

'Everything's fine,' she said in a thin voice. 'I just didn't sleep very well.'

'Ah, I see. You're living in... Wollaton, aren't you?'

'That's right,' she said, wondering how he knew.

'I overheard you telling the other sales staff when you first started,' he said, reading her mind. 'It's nice and quiet in that neck of the woods. Me and the wife would like to move there ready for us to start a family, hopefully in the next year or so, but we haven't a hope in hell of paying those prices.'

How refreshing to hear him mention his wife. Holly couldn't help wondering what sort of a life the poor woman had with him.

'I'm just lodging... well, visiting there, I suppose.' She hesitated. 'Josh, have you seen anything of Emily since she resigned?'

If Josh knew where Holly lived, maybe Emily did too. Worse still, they might be in touch.

He frowned but showed no sign of discomfort. 'Nope. Don't really expect to see her again. Why?'

Holly had no intention of explaining to Josh that she thought Emily might have been outside the window watching her; it would make her sound totally paranoid. And now she knew about their affair, she could never trust him again.

'I… I just wondered if she lived in the city… whether we'd see her around.'

'She does live in the city, in an apartment near Weekday Cross, if I recall. Don't think you'll see her around this end of town again, though. Knowing Emily, she'll have invented a whole new life for herself already.'

Weekday Cross was central, nowhere near Wollaton. If Emily *had* been lurking around at the bottom of Cora's garden, it would be quite a way for her to come at such an unsociable hour.

Josh went on his way and Holly sat staring out of the window, scanning each passer-by. She couldn't do this all day long or it would draw attention. She'd have to tear herself away from her desk at some point.

It was interesting that Josh had said Emily would invent a new life for herself.

Perhaps she and Holly were more alike than Holly had first thought.

She had no way of telling how long she'd been unconscious after the dinner that night.

She remembered resting her head back on soft leather and closing her eyes. The next thing she knew, she'd snapped awake, sat bolt upright, now in her own bed, and promptly vomited all over the quilt.

When she'd stopped being sick, she had a compulsion to shield her eyes from the daylight with a shaking forearm.

'Let's get you out of bed,' a voice had said. It sounded far away at first, and then too close and too loud in her ears. 'Patricia, could you change the bed, please, while I sponge Holly down?'

Holly had squinted at Geraldine and registered Patricia's unimpressed scowl as the housekeeper began to unceremoniously pull the soiled sheet from under her.

'She had far too much to drink last night, I'm afraid, Patricia,' Geraldine had said in a disapproving tone. 'Won't listen to advice, will they, young people? They don't know when to stop.'

Had she been drinking last night?

Holly sensed powerful negative memories and had a strong sense of foreboding. Yet she couldn't quite grasp the pictures that floated around inside her head like strings of fog. She couldn't remember any detail at all.

Foolishly, she'd tried to stand up briefly and immediately swooned, before Geraldine caught her and helped Patricia to lower her onto the dressing table stool.

'Holly. Tell me, sweetie, how are you feeling?' Geraldine had gripped her shoulders and spoken very softly and slowly, pressing her face too close for comfort.

Holly had retched again and Geraldine had grabbed some kind of container, held it under her chin.

More yellowish-looking bile had spewed out, burning her mouth and throat.

Geraldine had mopped her mouth with tissues.

'Better out than in,' she had said pleasantly.

The bus journey home from work had quickly become Holly's thinking time.

Not that thinking was always useful. Particularly the awful memories she'd dredged up lately, reliving the horror that had happened at Medlock Hall.

She supposed it was inevitable that her old life would take the opportunity to creep up when it could and cosh her with the memories she'd tried so hard to bury alive. They were always going to push back until Holly had put things right.

Most days, she looked forward to getting back home. While Cora prepared tea, Holly often took a relaxing bath to help prepare her for the ear-aching hour or so during which the older woman, having been alone for most of the day, would regale her with any gossip she'd overheard at the local shop or, more likely, more endless anecdotes from her past.

Holly had managed to dodge the last few sessions, but she knew that she'd do well to remind herself that she felt safe living with Cora. And that meant doing what was required to cement her place there.

CHAPTER 61

Holly

'Cora has gone to the spring fayre at the village hall and is going to be a little while,' Holly said when David popped round to finish off a few DIY jobs on Sunday.

She handed him a mug of tea. 'I've been thinking about what I can do to show my appreciation to her for letting me stay here.'

'That's nice of you,' David said blandly. In the time since she'd seen him last, he seemed to have developed a tic in his left eye, and it occurred to her he seemed rather distracted.

'This house is lovely, but in my opinion, it's well overdue for a little TLC,' Holly said, looking around the room.

'TLC?'

'Tender loving care?' She stared at him. How did he get to be so consistently clueless?

'Oh yes. I see now.' David sipped his tea and his bony knuckles shone white with the force of his grip. He seemed to be making a great effort to act normally, but it was clearly proving a challenge. Holly wasn't at all sure David really knew what *acting normally* actually was.

Still, she pretended not to notice and carried on chatting, thereby avoiding any difficult silences.

'Cora's bedroom is a little tired now, and I thought it would be nice to pep it up a bit without changing anything major. I think she'd like that.'

David nodded.

'I wondered if you'd just help me measure a couple of things while she's out?'

'Of course,' David said, putting down his mug. 'I'd be happy to help.'

Holly grabbed the tape measure from the kitchen drawer and David followed her upstairs. He lingered awkwardly at the door of Cora's bedroom.

'I do hope Mrs Barrett won't mind us coming in here without her permission,' he said doubtfully. 'It feels a bit... underhanded.'

'Don't be silly.' Holly rolled her eyes, pulling the curtains back as far as they'd go. 'It's for her benefit, and I know you think a lot of her.' She pressed her index finger to her chin and looked around. 'I'm thinking some new bedding and soft furnishings and... a new headboard.' She tossed him the tape measure. 'Can you do the honours and measure that, please, David? I'll record the figures.'

They worked amicably together. David read out the measurements in a very precise manner and Holly duly wrote them down.

'Some pretty new curtains and perhaps a velvet padded headboard instead of that hard old thing,' Holly murmured, looking around again. 'Then I'll get some sparkly cushions and things to pretty the rest of the room up.'

'I think you'll find that *hard old thing* is a solid walnut headboard,' David said doubtfully. 'I'd imagine it would cost a fortune these days to get one of comparable quality.'

'But it's so ugly.' Holly pulled a face. 'And old-fashioned. I'm afraid it'll have to go.'

'Well I'm sure she'll appreciate your efforts,' David said uncertainly. Holly suspected he wondered why she was making changes to a perfectly functional room.

She'd like to explain, but David would never understand.

In the afternoon, they went to the cinema as planned.

David seemed to fancy himself rather an authority on the Hitchcockian style. He chirped constantly about how the famed director had used the camera to mimic a person's gaze, so you watched the film like a voyeur. He went on and on about Hitchcock's use of metaphors and his ability to foster anxiety and fear in the viewer.

He also complained tirelessly that the wheelchair-bound photographer in the movie simply wouldn't be able to see as much as he did of his neighbours from his spying vantage point. How he knew that sort of thing, Holly couldn't imagine.

She had to stop herself yawning several times. She felt glad she'd already seen the film, as she'd missed a good third of it listening to David's ramblings in her ear.

David's anxiety levels had seemed to peak once they got inside the cinema. Holly couldn't help noticing how he scratched constantly at the inside of his wrist, leaving great red welts that stood proud from his pale skin.

He had approached the ticket clerk first and asked for one seat for himself, which he'd paid for in cash. Holly had been slightly taken aback but had said nothing. She'd bought her own ticket after his transaction was completed, and that was when he'd seemed to realise his error.

'I'm so sorry… I should have got yours too. I'm an idiot. I wasn't thinking, I—'

'David,' she'd said. 'It really doesn't matter. Please, forget about it.'

They hadn't bothered with snacks or drinks. The option didn't really come up, for as soon as he had his ticket, David rushed towards Screen 5, where the film was to be shown.

It was clear to Holly that he found even the most cursory decisions difficult, and his social skills were bordering on non-existent.

Holly had chosen their seats and had made a bit of harmless conversation while the lights were still on, asking David about his job. As usual, he seemed more than happy to speak at length about Kellington's.

'You seem to be getting on very well too,' he'd said finally, as though belatedly realising that she might have something to say herself.

'I think I am,' she'd said, pleased. 'Everything is going nicely, considering.'

'I'm glad Emily Beech has gone,' he'd said suddenly. 'She deserved to be thrown out. I couldn't stand her.'

His outburst had surprised Holly enough that she stayed silent.

Throughout the film, she managed to cast a few glances his way. He barely moved, she noted with some amusement, sitting for the full one hundred and eighty-six minutes bolt upright with a hand on each knee.

Periodically he'd lean sideways and enlighten her with some learned observation about Hitchcock's directing methods.

He wouldn't take off his anorak, and frankly, Holly wondered how on earth he could feel comfortable so togged up and rigid.

Nick Brown had been right. David was an odd one.

But Holly didn't mind that. In fact, now that she was clear in her mind about her plans, it suited her just fine.

CHAPTER 62

Cora

Cora had been to the bank, her third visit this week. And she had sorted everything out to her satisfaction upstairs. Everything was in order.

Still, she couldn't shake the uncomfortable feeling that had been gnawing at her insides for the best part of a week.

Something wasn't quite right, but infuriatingly, she couldn't put her finger on exactly what it was. She just knew these things.

As a little girl, her mother used to say she had a sixth sense. Young Cora had liked that; it had always made her feel special. She'd nearly always know someone was coming before a visitor knocked. And she could sense, on waking, whether it was going to rain.

Not the most useful sixth sense to have, she supposed, but still, even now she'd get a feeling about something and be proved correct more often than not.

The frisson of discomfort she'd been experiencing was to do with the two people around her: David and Holly. She'd been gratified when Holly told her they were going to the cinema together this afternoon.

'Just as friends, obviously,' she had said flippantly that morning, as if no one in their right mind could possibly want anything more from poor David.

Cora often worried about him. Despite his age, there was something vulnerable about him that clutched at her heartstrings.

When she looked at him, she still saw that awkward young lad dashing round to sit with her in the kitchen whilst Harold's back was turned in the vegetable patch.

David had always been protective of her. Loyal. Since Harold had died, he'd been so kind, popping round to do odd jobs for her despite his phobia of doing anything outside of his tried-and-tested routine.

That was why she'd joined Pat in protecting him. That was why she kept Nick Brown on side.

Cora had often thought that David was the closest thing she had to a son.

So a new friendship with Holly was a good thing, in Cora's opinion, and she would encourage it.

But aside from this, she'd been sensing something out of kilter in the air. Holly had been very quiet of late. She hadn't sat and chewed the fat with Cora for a while, and every time Cora had attempted to carry on with her life story, Holly always seemed to remember that she had some job to do that couldn't wait, upstairs in her bedroom.

Cora suspected that her visitor wasn't sleeping too well. She'd heard bumps and shuffles from across the landing on a number of nights. But in the morning, when Cora had asked if she'd had a restful night, Holly had simply nodded.

David also seemed to have what Cora could only describe as a strange energy about him. Pat had once explained that the medication he took kept him stable and calm.

'The doctor said the worst thing he can do is get himself excitable,' she'd told Cora over tea and a slice of carrot cake in the café after David had been discharged from the hospital. 'It's very important he finds himself a suitable routine so he can manage everyday life.'

Very recently, Cora had noticed that David seemed a little jumpy, as if the acute nervousness might be returning.

This could well be because that clod Brian Buckley had moved in with them. What on earth was Pat was thinking, allowing that to happen? It was bound to be disruptive to David's routines.

There was no accounting for some people's taste, she thought disapprovingly.

Brian could be quite cutting with David, and Cora had spotted him coming out of that disreputable betting shop on the high street. It had been packed full of men old enough to know better, she recalled. All of them frittering valuable bill money, no doubt, Brian included.

It was difficult to explain even to herself, but Cora was also finding it hard to relax in her own bedroom.

Goodness, she'd lived in this house nigh on forty years so there shouldn't be an inch of it she didn't know. Certainly nothing to make the hairs on the back of her neck prickle.

Yet the past couple of nights when she'd gone up to retire for the night and slipped into her nightgown, she'd felt uncomfortable to the point of convincing herself someone had been in there, even though nothing had been disturbed.

As she thought about it now, she felt a little foolish. She was certain that Holly would never take it upon herself to nose around in her things.

Besides, Cora seriously doubted that any young woman would ever see past the bottles of lavender water, the heated lower back pad and the collection of support pillows arranged just the way she liked them on the bed.

There wasn't a scrap of evidence Cora could find to support her feelings of discomfort. But if it was all in her imagination, why couldn't she shake the feeling she was somehow being watched?

CHAPTER 63

Holly

'Oh, there you are,' Cora called from the living room the second Holly walked through the back door. Holly hung her jacket up in the hallway and slipped off her shoes. 'You're late tonight, dear. Did work ask you to stay a bit longer?'

Holly glanced at the clock on the mantelpiece. It was nearly six o'clock, which was the exact same time she usually got back from work.

'I'm not late.' She forced a smile. 'I left at the usual time.'

Cora frowned and stared at the clock as if she were trying to make sense of it.

'Should I make tea?' Holly suggested, hoping to get her off the subject.

Cora's face brightened and Holly headed into the kitchen. She filled the kettle and took the biscuit barrel out of the cupboard, laying a few of Cora's favourite custard creams on a small decorative china plate.

While she waited for the water to boil, she stood by the window and stared down the long garden. The bushes and trees at the end that had looked so terrifying in the early hours seemed completely harmless now.

The garden was surrounded by a fence, too, of a reasonable height. It wasn't as if someone could just walk in off the street; they'd have to make a concerted effort to gain entry.

Sometimes the memories could seem so real, it was like everything had just happened yesterday.

Holly couldn't help wondering if the stress at work over coping with Emily's initial belligerent attitude and then all the trouble with the vase had caused her imagination to run riot, convincing her that Emily was out for revenge. Maybe she'd also been dreaming up things that weren't really there.

She reached for clean cups and the tea caddy and made the tea on automatic pilot while her thoughts jumped back to Cora's obvious confusion.

During the short time she'd been here, Holly had realised that some days Cora seemed to be more confused than others. She'd get something irrational in her head and run with it. Today, for instance, she'd convinced herself that Holly was late back from work when she wasn't at all.

Holly knew she'd keep hold of it like a terrier, going on and on, constantly turning it over in her mind. Even hours afterwards.

It was most unsettling. Holly thought it couldn't be normal, but it wasn't her place to suggest Cora visit her doctor, and besides, the last thing she wanted to do was upset her.

She took the tea and biscuits through on a tray. When she got back into the living room, Cora was smiling and holding a white envelope in her hand.

'I quite forgot, dear. This came for you earlier.' She waved the letter in the air. 'Somebody pushed it through the letter box, didn't knock or anything. And curiously, when I opened the door and looked up and down the crescent, there was no one to be seen.'

CHAPTER 64

David

I'm about to begin my evening monitoring duties at my bedroom window when my phone buzzes.

I set aside the tray of food I've just carried upstairs and stare at the screen. It's a text, from Holly.

Can you come over asap? Need some advice. H

A warm swell fills my chest. Holly needs some advice and *I'm* the person she has chosen to ask to provide it.

All I've ever wanted, really, is to help.

That was the sole reason I followed Della on the final morning she visited Mr Brown. I tracked her to a coffee shop on the high street. When I walked in a few minutes later, she was crying, mopping at her face with a tissue.

I sat down opposite her, expecting her to tell me to get lost, but when I explained I was Nick Brown's neighbour and had seen what he'd been up to, stuff just came tumbling out of her pretty rosebud mouth.

She told me everything. How they'd met, how she loved him… which had stung. Imagine loving a buffoon like that!

We met up several times a week after that. There was nothing in it romantically – for her, anyway. But I loved her with all my heart.

I used to sit staring out of my bedroom window, imagining what life might be like, married to Della. Making her happy enough that she might start love me back.

But Nicholas Brown put paid to it all. He had her like a puppet on a string.

One minute it was over between them, the next he'd charmed her back again.

It was very hard to see him giving Della the runaround like that, promising her that he'd leave his wife but clearly having not the slightest intention of doing so.

It all seemed so hopeless. Her emotions were up and down; she didn't know which way to turn.

So I asked her if she'd like me to try and help her, and she said in what way, and I said I'd have a think about it and let her know.

In the summer, I'd see him fetching and carrying for Mrs Brown, who'd sit morosely in the garden for hours on end. He was so good at assuming the role of the perfect husband.

My rage blossomed like a cherry tree, and over the weeks, it eventually bore fruit.

Mrs Brown was astonished when I turned up at the dental surgery. She stood behind reception, mouth open and eyes wide as I told her everything.

'They're at it right now in *your* bedroom,' I told her. 'While you're here, working your socks off.'

In my fervour to get the facts over to her, I'd quite forgotten about the people in reception and the other staff behind the desk.

Mrs Brown burst into tears, grabbed her coat and bag and ran out there and then.

I sat around for a bit in the reception area like a patient, everyone staring. I didn't really know what else to do. I felt quite dazed.

Then the practice manager came over and said, 'I think you'd better leave, sir.'

By the time I caught up with Mrs Brown, she'd already got to Della and they were out on the street with Mr Brown trying to get in between them.

Della was screaming loudly as Mrs Brown attacked her; she was a mere wisp of a thing compared to the older woman. And then Della slapped Mr Brown across the face, calling him a liar and a love rat and he thumped her back. Right in her beautiful face.

And that's when I couldn't stop myself... I waded in amongst them, I couldn't stop punching and kicking, and even when my knuckles were skinned and he collapsed on the floor, I still couldn't stop hitting him.

The police were called and I ran and it was just a big fat mess.

A couple of days later, Della jumped from the seventh-floor balcony of her new apartment block by the canal. They found a letter to Nick Brown on the kitchen table telling him she couldn't live without him.

I didn't go to the funeral. Mother said it would be too unsettling.

I lean forward now in my chair and peer down into Mrs Barrett's yard, but no one is out there.

People are starting to arrive home from work, using the back door like we do. This is usually my busiest time, recording and monitoring that nothing is amiss, that nobody is acting strangely or out of the ordinary.

But Holly needs me and I decide that this must take priority.

I go back downstairs, plucking my jacket from the hook in the hallway on the way out.

'David?' Mother looks up, startled, from stirring a pan as I walk through the kitchen. 'What's wrong? Where are you going?'

'I'm just popping out for a bit,' I say calmly. 'I won't be long.'

'But...' She puts down her wooden spoon and turns, her eyes wide. 'Is everything all right? I mean, you're not in any trouble, are you?'

'No. I'm not in any trouble.' My stomach contracts. 'Why do you always assume the worst, Mother?'

'Because you've been acting very oddly recently. You keep going out and… Are you going to see that girl next door?' She spits out the words as if they're responsible for a nasty taste in her mouth.

If I am, it's nothing to do with her. I've let her control my life for far too long.

'Your mother asked you where you're going.' Brian swaggers towards me as if he's still a fit thirty-year-old builder instead of a fat mess. 'You live off your mother like you're still a ten-year-old, so you'll be treated like one.'

As I turn to him, the air around me explodes into colours of the rainbow.

I register that Mother is wailing, but that's fine. I am focused.

I grab Brian by the shoulders and push him as hard as I can. He slips on the kitchen tiles in his sock feet and keels over like a great hog. His head smashes into the wall and I watch, fascinated, as his cracked skull leaves a trail of red down the paintwork.

He doesn't move. His coarse dirty mouth stays closed and silent. But Mother is screeching in the background like Maria Callas.

I don't look at her. I just say, 'I'll be back soon.'

I step outside into the cool, cleansing air and close the door behind me.

I might be acting fairly calm but my heart is racing and I feel a bit nauseous. But Holly needs my help.

I walk up the side path between the two houses and look directly up at her room. She has the wrong idea about me, thinking I can help her.

I feel disingenuous. Pretending to be something I'm not.

I knock, and Holly comes to the door.

'Thanks for popping over, David,' she says, her face pale.

'Who is it, dear?' I hear Mrs Barrett call.

Holly rolls her eyes and speaks in a low voice. 'She's been a bit confused today. I need to talk to you, in private. Shall we go for a walk or something?'

My chest suddenly feels tight. Perhaps the incident with Brian has unnerved me more than I thought.

'It's quite cool out here, and there are a lot of people out and about, so...'

She nods slowly. 'OK, well you'd better come upstairs then.'

'Upstairs?'

'We can't talk down here. Cora will be interrupting us every few seconds.' She hesitates and her eyes glisten. 'And I really need to speak to you, David.'

'Fine.' I step inside. 'Lead the way.'

En route, I pop my head round the living room door.

'Hello, Mrs Barrett.'

'David! Come in, sit down, dear. I wanted to ask you if—'

'David is just going up to measure my room for some shelves, Cora,' Holly says kindly. 'We'll be down soon and then you two can chat.'

Mrs Barrett begins to object, but Holly pulls my arm and guides me towards the stairs.

CHAPTER 65

David

In Holly's bedroom, the heat channels up the middle of my body and into my face and neck with a vengeance.

'I'm sorry,' she says, noticing my high colour. 'The last thing I want is to make you feel uncomfortable.'

'It's fine,' I say quickly. 'What seems to be the problem?'

She walks into the room and snatches something up from her bedside table.

'This.' She holds up a white envelope. '*This* is the problem, David.'

She hands me the envelope. On the front, written in neat block capitals and underlined, is her name: <u>HOLLY NEWMAN.</u>

I turn it over and look at the unsealed flap.

'Go ahead,' she says. 'Open it.'

I slip out a single sheet of folded paper.

'Read it out loud,' Holly directs. She sits on the bed and fixes her gaze on me.

I clear my throat.

'"I am watching you. And when you least expect it, I will come for you."'

The words aren't particularly threatening or violent in themselves, but together they add up to something more. A very sinister intention.

I read through the message silently again. Something about it sounds familiar, and I push thoughts of Mr Brown from my mind.

Silence descends on the room for a few moments, and then a rushing noise starts in my ears. Holly shifts and a bed spring creaks, and the sounds inside my head fade.

I turn over the paper to check that it's blank on the other side. 'Do you know who sent this?'

'No,' she says. 'But I've got a good idea. There's someone in Manchester who hates me. She'd do anything to hurt me. I think… I think she might even send someone after me.'

I look at her tense face. 'Is this the first note you've had?'

She sighs. 'Yes, but I think someone was in the garden the other night. I woke up because there was a strange noise. I looked out of the window and there was a man… I think it was a man. Standing at the bottom of the garden, staring up here.'

The CCTV image of Brian at the bottom of our garden, staring towards the houses, flashes into my mind, and I shiver.

Holly's narrow chest rises and falls like a small, dazed bird that has flown into glass and is trying to recover before next door's cat comes along. She looks very afraid, vulnerable. Just like Della did.

I wonder if she wishes I could protect her somehow. Perhaps she'd like us to be more than friends.

'David… are you feeling OK?'

'I think I might have killed Brian,' I tell her.

She laughs without mirth. 'This is no time for jokes. I'm scared that someone is watching me.'

'I have a good view of your garden from my bedroom window,' I say faintly, thinking about Brian's blood running down the kitchen wall. 'I could keep an eye on things if you wanted me to.'

'But what if someone comes in the middle of the night again?' Her breath catches in her throat and she coughs. 'You can't help me then, can you?'

I can't tell her about my monitoring equipment, the cameras. Without a lengthy explanation, it could make me look a little odd.

'I don't mind getting up a few times during the night for the next couple of days,' I tell her. 'To make sure nobody is out there messing about, I mean.'

'Would you honestly do that for me?' She shakes her head slightly as if she can't believe my offer. It makes me wonder how much actual kindness she's had in her life.

'It's no trouble.'

She makes me feel strong, capable.

'Thank you, David.' She stands up and walks over to me, taking the letter and brushing my hand as she does so. 'I really am grateful. With you around I don't feel nearly so alone.'

I feel a rushing sensation in my chest, like someone just opened the floodgates to a great backlog of pent-up emotion.

I grasp her hand and squeeze but I don't say anything. There seems to be no need for words. There's a sort of knowing between us.

Holly squeezes my hand back, then begins to retract, but I hold onto her fingers. I don't want to let go of this feeling.

'David,' she says softly. 'We'd better go downstairs. Cora will be waiting.'

I come to my senses and release her hand.

'I'm sorry,' I say. 'I didn't mean to…'

'It's fine.' She smiles. 'Honestly, it is.'

I feel hot all over. I wipe both hands on the sides of my trousers.

Holly clears her throat. 'What will you do? I mean, if you catch someone in the garden?'

I think for a moment and realise I don't know what I'll do.

'I'll ring the police,' I say.

'The police?'

A trickle of sweat runs down from my temple. I wipe it away quickly, but I think she sees it anyway. I'd better not ring the police.

'I'll chase him away,' I say.

'I thought you didn't like going outside after dark?'

I stare at her.

'David?' I focus again and see that Holly is looking at me with concern. 'I'm not sure you're feeling quite yourself. You look… confused.'

Who's been telling her things… embarrassing things?

'Are you coming down soon?'

As soon as I hear Mrs Barrett's voice call up, I know it's her. She's been blabbing about what happened to me in the past.

The anger backs up in my throat but I swallow it down. If I let it out, it might never stop.

I must start taking my tablets again tomorrow. The world is too dark a place without them.

CHAPTER 66

Holly

Thinking back to Manchester, to waking up feeling so ill, Holly couldn't begin to hazard a guess at how long she'd been in the bedroom.

She'd been too ill to question what had happened or to think logically about the situation.

'You got drunk and acted like a slut,' Geraldine had told her repeatedly. 'Brendan is a hot-blooded man, not a saint. I went to bed early and you threw yourself at him, wouldn't take no for an answer. He told me you threatened to tell me he'd raped you.'

'I'm sorry... I can't remember.' Holly had hated herself, had shaken her head and repeated the same line again and again.

And then Geraldine had suggested she carry out a pregnancy test.

When the blue line appeared, Holly couldn't believe that Geraldine didn't throw her out of the house.

'We'll help you look after the child,' she had said. 'And when you're completely well, we'll set you up in your own place.'

There was a doctor who came to the house several times a week. One day, Holly peered through the crack in her door to see Brendan paying him in cash before he left the house.

When Brendan was home, Holly now stayed upstairs. Geraldine seemed to be interacting with her husband perfectly normally.

One day, she'd crept onto the landing and listened to them talking at the bottom of the stairs.

'Why has it taken her so long to recover?' Geraldine had hissed.

'The doctor said some people have a particularly adverse reaction to Rohypnol,' Brendan had replied. 'I told him someone spiked her drink when she was out. Good job we never gave her any Ecstasy as we'd planned.'

When Patricia came into her bedroom to vacuum, Holly closed the door behind her. Patricia eyed her suspiciously.

'Am I the first girl to come here?' Holly asked, keeping her voice as level as she could. 'Or have there been others?'

'There have been two others like you.' Patricia shrugged. 'They also got themselves into a state like this and had to leave. Now it is you.'

Holly could see that the housekeeper viewed her as just another inconvenience to clean up after.

'I'm having a baby,' she whispered.

Patricia shrugged. 'So were the others, but they both miscarried. Miss Geraldine, she is always disappointed.'

Everything had fallen into place then like a sinister jigsaw. Right back to Brendan's interview, him so interested in Holly's life story, her parents and heritage… the pressure for her to get into shape, keep healthy… The whole thing had been planned.

Brendan and Geraldine had done this before.

She had pushed past Patricia and run downstairs, confronting the two of them.

'You drugged me… raped me!' she spat at Brendan, and then turned to Geraldine. 'And you knew all along what would happen. All because you're desperate for a child.'

'Calm down!' Geraldine had slapped her face and Holly had been stunned into silence. 'You're talking nonsense… you're losing your mind. We're offering you support, that's all. Nobody wants to take your child.'

Holly had cried and Geraldine had held her like a baby, soothing her with words. She felt so confused, so alone… Was it true? Was she losing her mind?

These two people were all she had.

Holly grew stronger, became well, and the whole incident was ring-fenced as a no-go area.

Geraldine treated her like glass.

'I've told Brendan I want a divorce,' she said one day when they were out for lunch. 'You're like a sister to me now, Holly. He's going to move out and I'll help you look after the baby.'

Holly had felt as if she was playing a lead role in some kind of sick play. Without Geraldine, she had literally nothing; she was penniless, alone and pregnant.

But despite Geraldine's assertions that she was furious with her husband, Holly felt she wasn't quite as innocent as she claimed. After all, Patricia had told her there had been two others.

Holly had tried speaking about the other girls, but Geraldine had shut her down.

They shopped for baby clothes, a cot, a car seat… and the nursery was currently being decorated in lemon.

Geraldine accompanied Holly to her hospital appointment, playing the role of the baby's father almost. Geraldine paid privately for Holly to have an early ultrasound scan which included photographs.

'We'd like to know the sex of the baby if possible,' she said.

'Sorry,' the medic had said. 'You'll need to wait until your daughter is a minimum of sixteen weeks.'

Holly watched as Geraldine's jaw set in irritation at his mistake but she said nothing.

*

Holly went into labour two days before the expected delivery date.

'I'll stay with you the whole time,' Geraldine had said, clasping her hand in a caring manner. 'Don't be afraid, we'll get through this together.'

A doctor and a foreign nurse who couldn't speak any English came to the house, but Holly didn't feel sad or lonely or afraid. She simply felt dead inside.

She had an epidural and the birth was straightforward. But before she could hold her baby, Geraldine had taken him from the nurse and spoken quietly with the doctor.

When she returned to Holly's bedside, her cheeks had been flushed and her eyes bright.

'Evan is doing fine,' she told Holly. 'He's the perfect weight and the doctor says he's strong and healthy.'

'Evan?' Holly had frowned.

'That's the baby's name,' Geraldine had told her.

CHAPTER 67

Holly

Holly had been watching Cora for a long time.

It had soon become apparent that every time Cora visited the bank, she shot straight upstairs, closing her bedroom curtains.

She had complained several times to Holly about mistrusting banks and how disgusting it was that people got no interest at all on their savings in the current economic climate.

She sometimes talked about her late husband's set ways and strong opinions, but as far as Holly could tell, she had seemed to perpetuate these needlessly, long after his death. Holly had often wondered who Cora used to be before a controlling marriage had slowly stripped her of her true self.

Then there had been all the shuffling and scraping that day Holly had stood listening outside the bedroom door. The high colour and heated sheen on Cora's face indicated that she'd been over-exerting herself, perhaps lifting… and suddenly, pairing this knowledge with the contents of the letter Holly had found, all the pieces had come together and Holly knew.

She'd waited until Cora went out again and then crept upstairs to her bedroom. She'd tucked both hands under one corner of the mattress and pushed up with all her might… and there it was.

She'd stared at it, her eyes filling up with the realisation that she had at last uncovered the key to finding her son again.

Now all she had to do was to work out the best way of getting her hands on it.

CHAPTER 68

Holly

On the way into work the next day, Holly stopped at David's kiosk.

'I need to speak to you tonight,' she said urgently. 'Can you come around to the house?'

He tore his eyes away from the top of the car park. 'Yes, of course. I…'

'Are you listening to me?' She stood in front of him to make him look at her.

'Yes, it's just that…' He did a double-take. 'Are you feeling all right, Holly? You look so pale, and your eyes are bloodshot.'

'If you must know, I feel *terrible*.'

David stood up and shrugged on his high-vis jacket with urgency. 'I'm so sorry, Holly. I have to deal with this. Give me a second.' He pushed open the kiosk door and shouted, 'Excuse me, can I have a word?'

The man who'd just got out of a silver BMW looked back at them.

'Just a word, *sir*.' David spat the word out as if it offended him to say it.

Holly watched as the driver checked his watch, openly sighed and then walked slowly towards them.

She felt woozy, like her centre of balance was off.

'Are you aware, sir, that this is a private car park?' David said pompously, pushing his shoulders back as he consulted his clipboard. 'My records show that in the last two weeks, you have parked here illegally on a number of occasions…'

Holly gripped the side of the kiosk to stay standing. She tried to gulp in air, but her chest was burning. David's voice faded out until there was nothing but a furious rushing noise in her head.

She stared at the driver and he stared back.

David's mouth stopped moving. His head flipped from Holly to the driver and back again.

'Markus,' she whispered before she fainted.

CHAPTER 69

David

The driver springs forward to help, and together we manage to get Holly inside the foyer, laying her down on the visitor seats.

While he stays with her, I rush to the kiosk and summon Cath, the nominated first-aider, from her office.

Within minutes, Cath and Josh are attending to Holly, helping her inside the shop and the driver and I step back outside.

'I'm Markus,' he introduces himself. 'I'm sorry that I've taken liberties with the parking here. I didn't know... I mean, it was such a shock to see Holly standing there.'

'You two know each other... *how*?'

For a few seconds he looks dazed, stands there like he's altogether forgotten what day it is. I think about inviting him to sit in my chair for a moment but I can't bring myself to do it. Not with how he's blatantly flouted the rules here.

'We went to school together and then we met up by accident...' the driver says vaguely.

'Holly called you Markus, is that your name?'

He nods and it occurs to me that this man could be a useful source of information. I've long suspected there's more to Holly's than she's been letting on.

'Come and sit inside for a moment, you look as if you've had a shock.'

I steer him into the foyer and he willingly sits down on one of the comfy chairs that Holly had been laid on only minutes earlier.

I get him a beaker of water from the cooler.

'Thank you,' he says.

'You were saying that you met up with Holly again by accident,' I prompted.

'Yes, a year after leaving school. I told her about my life in Manchester and she jumped at the chance to...' He shakes his head and looks at the floor. 'She was in a bad time in her life. I wasn't such a good friend.'

'Why's that?'

He shrugs. 'My boss, Brendan, he'd been looking for a young woman suitable to be a companion to his wife. I knew there was something not quite right about it, with all the weird questions he got me to ask the girls, but I didn't know exactly what. Then, when I got talking to Holly, I realised she'd be perfect.' He bites his lip. 'I swear I would never have taken Holly to him if I'd known what he had planned...' His words trail off.

'What happened?' I shake my head. 'Holly has been scared of something, of someone. She thinks perhaps somebody is following her... watching her, even. What happened to her that was so bad?'

And then Markus tells me Holly's story.

He tells me *everything*.

CHAPTER 70

Holly

'Come in,' a raspy voice called when Holly held her breath and tapped on Mr Kellington's door.

David opened the door for her.

'Good luck,' he whispered, before returning downstairs.

Inside, both Mr Kellington and Josh waited with concerned faces. Mr Kellington sat bolt upright behind his desk, and Josh had perched stiffly on the edge of one of the visitor seats.

'Thanks for coming up, Holly. I understand from David that you've had a bit of a shock.' Josh patted the chair next to him. 'Come and take a seat.'

Her hands shook and so she tucked them under her thighs.

'Are you feeling quite well now?' Mr Kellington said kindly. 'You were lucky that David caught you as you fell; you could have sustained a nasty head injury from hitting the edge of the kiosk.'

'Yes, thank you. I'm fine now,' she replied, shifting in her seat.

'David said that you recognised someone who came into the car park… that it was quite upsetting for you.'

'I thought I knew him, but I didn't after all,' she said quickly.

'This is a pastoral chat only, Holly,' Mr Kellington confirmed. 'We are concerned only for your welfare; your private life is your own. You're not in any trouble… as such.'

She stared at him, her heart pulsing in the top of her throat. *Private life…* What had Markus told David while she'd been out of it?

'However, you've been acting a bit odd over the last few days,' Josh said softly. 'I've noticed, and so have some of your colleagues.'

Her eyes narrowed. She remembered seeing Ben and Martyn whispering and looking her way last night before she left.

'I don't know what you mean,' she said, grateful that the shaking in her hands hadn't yet transferred to her voice.

Josh sighed.

'I'll spell it out for you, Holly. You've been distracted to the point of neglecting the customers. Sitting staring out of the window for long periods of time and scribbling constantly in that notebook of yours, which I believe has nothing to do with work.'

Holly shrugged. She'd glanced out of the window a few times, making sure Emily wasn't watching her every move, but she hadn't been writing in any notebook. Had she?

'They're lying,' she said simply. 'Whoever told you that is jealous of my sales. They're trying to get rid of me like happened to *Lynette*.'

She said the name meaningfully and fixed Josh with a look.

He coughed and glanced at Mr Kellington, who showed no sign of understanding the meaning behind it.

'Also, I'm afraid I received a concerned call from our long-standing customer Mr Fenwick this morning,' Mr Kellington added.

Holly remembered that the Fenwicks had popped into the shop yesterday… or had it been the day before? She seemed to be losing track of the days. Her head was only full of the chance to find Evan and take him far away, where they could make a new start together as mother and son…

'Holly?'

Mr Kellington had been talking and she'd missed it.

'Sorry,' she said. 'Can you say that again?'

'You sold him the panther sculpture for more than double the list price,' Mr Kellington repeated, a little more sharply. 'Embarrassingly they discovered the guide price sticker still on the bottom when they got the piece home.'

'So what? They've got more money than they know what to do with,' Holly snapped. 'Nothing better to do every day than come in here, buying more and more trinkets for their already overstuffed home. Why don't they do something good with their money for once?'

'Well! I hardly think that's your concern,' Mr Kellington blustered, pulling at his green-striped bow tie. 'Lucky for us that they choose to spend their money here.'

'You talk about this shop and the furniture in it as though it's something important,' Holly said slowly, shaking her head. 'But it's all just a load of overpriced crap that doesn't mean anything. Don't you see? It's not real, it's not what's important in life. There are far more precious things than fancy lamps and feather-filled cushions.'

Mr Kellington's mouth fell open.

'That's enough, Holly,' Josh said. 'I think you need to go home and rest for a few days.'

Someone rapped sharply on the door. Josh rose, but it opened before he could take a step towards it, and a figure appeared in the doorway.

Holly swallowed and closed her eyes.

'Emily! What are *you* doing here?' Josh said with a start.

Holly opened her eyes and looked wildly at the two men. They said nothing.

Emily wore jeans, boots and a black fleece hoody. With minimal make-up and her hair pulled back into a messy knot, she looked so different. As if all her power had evaporated.

But when she began to speak, Holly realised she'd be a fool to underestimate her.

'I might not work here now, but it doesn't mean I've been idle. On the contrary, I've been very busy since I resigned.' She smiled and closed the door behind her.

Without invitation, she sat on the chair opposite Holly.

Mr Kellington pressed his lips together. He didn't look happy with the situation, but he didn't tell Emily to leave either.

'Why are you here, Emily?' he asked calmly.

Emily slowly folded her hands in her lap, seemingly intent on enjoying every second of whatever she was about to say.

'I decided to look into your life before Kellington's, Holly,' she said. 'Your life in *Manchester*, to be specific.'

Holly gasped, the air locking in her throat.

'Yes, I thought you might be surprised,' Emily told her. 'It didn't take me very long, actually, to uncover what went on there. Once I found out you'd been hired by Brendan Godson.'

Holly felt a trickle of sweat edge its way down her spine.

'How did you…'

'I lived in Manchester myself for five years. Worked in the clubs there as a student and knew the scene very well. In fact, I knew a lot of people back then, some of who I'm still in touch with online.' She tapped her lacquered nails on her thigh. 'I drew a blank until I bumped into a guy called Jay, an old acquaintance of Brendan Godson. He told me the awful news… that Brendan had died under a truck. A terrible accident, apparently. Must've just stepped out into the road, they said at the time.'

Holly felt the blood draining from her face.

'That didn't really mean anything to me until Jay got into his stride and asked whether I wanted to hear the rest of the story about Brendan and his family… it featured, he said, a psycho woman they'd employed, called Holly. He couldn't remember her surname but he thought I might be interested as she too was from Nottingham.'

Holly closed her eyes. She'd retained her first name but changed her surname when she returned to Nottingham. She'd paid a lot of money for new documentation and ID.

'How is this relevant to us?' Mr Kellington said curtly.

'Because she isn't who she says she is,' Emily snapped at him. 'She has a very chequered past that I think will interest you. *She's* the one who damaged that vase and set me up very cleverly. When I tell you the story, you'll understand what she's capable of.'

Holly stood up, trancelike.

'I have to go,' she said in a vague manner. 'I have things to do at home.'

Josh stood and placed his hand gently on her shoulder. 'I could ring your landlady if you like…'

She shrugged him off.

'I'm not a *lodger*. I'm a visitor there.' She paused and spoke softly. 'I'm always just a visitor in everyone's life… I come and go, but nothing ever changes.'

CHAPTER 71

Holly

Holly rushed past David in the kiosk. He called out to her, but she didn't look back.

She couldn't face the bus but managed to hail a cab on Huntingdon Street. She sat slumped in the back, staring sightlessly out of the window, her head full of unwanted images.

Markus… Emily… There wasn't much time. She had to put her plan in place now. She had to get back to Manchester to find Evan.

'You OK, love?' the driver asked, looking at her in his rear-view mirror.

She said nothing but knew she looked a state. Unbrushed hair, pale, drawn face… but what did it matter? What did anyone understand about it all?

When she got home, Cora was out. She felt like crying with gratitude.

She dropped her handbag at the bottom of the stairs and rushed upstairs. In Cora's bedroom, she pulled off the quilt and pillows and heaved the mattress half off the bed, then began piling the cash on the floor.

When that half was empty, she hauled the mattress the other way and began doing the same on that side.

'Holly? Are you feeling quite well?'

She let out a small scream at the voice behind her. Cora stood in the doorway with a strange, calm look on her face.

'David rang me to tell me what happened at work. He's on his way over here now.'

'You won the lottery,' Holly said accusingly. 'I found the letter.'

'If you'd just asked me, I would have helped you, you know,' Cora said, stepping towards her. 'I could have given you some money.'

'I need all of it!' Holly spat. 'Your life is virtually finished; you've no need for all this cash. My child's life is at stake. I have to find him.'

She turned back to the bed and carried on taking out wads of cash, stuffing them into a black bin bag she'd grabbed from the stairs.

Cora stood, watching her, saying nothing. Holly was unnerved.

'Why are you staring at me like that?' she snapped at the older woman. 'Just go – leave me alone.'

'You know, when I was a young woman of your age,' Cora began, 'I too thought that—'

'I don't want to hear any more of your stupid stories!' Holly glared up at her, wide-eyed. 'You talk too much, that's how I found you in the first place.'

'Found me?' Cora's voice faltered. 'But I met you in the post office. I found you.'

Holly stopped stuffing money in the bag and wiped her brow with her forearm and shook her head in irritation.

'I'd been in a few shops you used. It was just lucky that day that things went wrong and you came to my rescue. But I watched you… before that. In the café, with Pat.'

Cora's composure began to wobble.

'You knew me before… but how… why were you—'

'It was obvious you had money by the way you talked,' Holly said. 'Telling Pat you didn't trust the banks and you'd got plans underway to draw it all out. I thought it was just savings and then I found the letter about your lottery winnings.'

They both started at the sound of footsteps bounding upstairs.

'David!' Cora gasped in relief.

He stood in the doorway, his expression incredulous as he took in the wads of cash scattered everywhere.

Holly looked from David to Cora. She felt trapped, like a rat in a cage. Her head swam with faces, past conversations. It drummed a beat of fear into her chest. She stood up, still, closed her eyes against it. She heard their voices far, far away.

Then Cora's hand touched her shoulder. Holly swung around and pushed with all her might. She watched as the old woman staggered back, slipping on the cash underfoot.

David cried out, tried to reach her, but he was too far away.

As Cora toppled backwards – it seemed like slow motion to Holly – her head hit the edge of the black iron fireplace with a dull thud.

Holly stood over her and watched the thick pool of red trace its way neatly around the edge of the stone hearth.

She stiffened as David grasped her arm.

'What… have… you… done?' His words sounded like an old record, slowed right down.

They both looked at Cora on the floor, her eyes wide and staring, her body bent at an unnatural angle.

'Holly, what have you done?' David repeated.

'I have to get some fresh air… I have to get out of here.' Holly's legs felt as if they didn't belong to her. She took long strides out of the room.

Holly watched as David bent over Cora's body, feeling for a non-existent pulse.

'Please.' He looked at her as she left the room. 'Call an ambulance.'

She ran downstairs, through the kitchen and burst out of the back door, gulping in air.

How did it get to this? What could she do now… she had to get the money and go. It was her only chance to find Evan again.

She made the call and stepped back inside. There wasn't much time now.

Holly half-filled a glass with water from the tap and drank it. Then she took a deep breath and slowly climbed the stairs again.

David sat next to Cora's body, his head bowed in sadness.

When he saw her he slowly rose to his feet.

She thought he looked queasy, as if he might be sick at any moment. He opened his mouth to speak but closed it again.

'Just say what you want to say,' she told him. 'For once in your life have some bloody courage.'

'It's time,' he said. 'To tell me the truth about what happened back in Manchester.'

CHAPTER 72

Holly

'We'll keep Evan at ours, look after him while you get your strength back,' Geraldine had told her.

'No!' Holly had squared up to her. 'I want him with me.'

'You can't live here any more, Holly, for obvious reasons. You had sex with my husband behind my back.'

'I didn't! He—'

'Save it. I don't want to hear it.'

'But you said… I thought Brendan was leaving. You said we'd live together like sisters.'

'Fortunately, Brendan and I have settled our differences. Take Evan if that's what you want. If you have the money and experience to care for him then go.'

Holly had stared at her, an icy hopelessness sweeping up from her feet into her chest.

Geraldine had touched her arm.

'Look, I'm just saying we all need some space, that's all. You can visit every day, of course; he's your baby. But you can't live here.'

Holly couldn't speak.

'If you want to take me up on the offer, we'll find you a nice apartment and give you an allowance. Just until you get back on your feet, and then you can take Evan back. I promise.'

What could she say? She had nothing, *nothing* without them. She *was* nothing. She knew Geraldine's preferences better than she knew her own.

They had put her back in the apartment she'd shared with Markus for one night, overlooking the River Irwell.

'Back where it all started,' she'd whispered to herself as she pressed her forehead to the cool glass.

The once sparkling river looked flat and black now, and the animated people who walked by on the bank seemed stooped and broken, like Lowry figures.

Holly phoned Geraldine constantly, asking to visit Evan, but she was always either unavailable or busy or Brendan was home.

She used her allowance to buy alcohol. Bottles of cheap white wine, which she'd drink before staggering around the streets searching for her baby, unsure in her addled mind of his whereabouts.

Then the allowance ran out. Stopped.

Holly took to her bed. For days she didn't eat, didn't sleep.

She'd hear the door open and bags rustling. Then footsteps, and the door would close. When she went into the kitchen, there was food in the cupboards, the fridge.

The doctor visited her a couple of times, but then that stopped too. She wasn't ill, he told her; she just needed to get out, get some fresh air.

'You need to start living your life again.' He'd said it like it would be an easy thing to do.

One day she'd heard someone in the kitchen, opening and closing cupboard doors. She'd crept out of her bedroom and peeked around the door.

'Patricia!'

'Missus says I shouldn't talk to you.' The housekeeper had emptied the carrier bags out hastily. 'Go back to your bedroom.'

'Do you know what they did to me that night?' Holly had whimpered, her feet pressing into the cold laminate floor as she stepped closer. 'They've taken my baby. Geraldine said I can see him any time, but there's always some excuse. They've *stolen* him.'

'I only know what missus tells me,' Patricia had said firmly, placing the last two tins on the shelf. 'If you go to police, I have to tell them you asked for baby to stay with them.'

'Is that what they've told you to say?' Holly raked at her arm, her crawling skin. 'Have you heard of DNA?' she had shrieked, picking up a bottle of orange juice and throwing it against the wall. 'I can prove that Evan is mine!'

Patricia was unmoved by the act.

'Mister and missus, they want a baby for long time. Your boy, he has good home now,' Patricia had said calmly, squeezing past Holly to get to the door. She looked back at her with pity. 'You cannot win, miss. Best to let things lie.'

'Patricia, please don't go,' Holly had cried, and reached out to her, but the housekeeper hadn't looked back and the door clicked shut behind her.

Holly had looked around the sparse, quiet apartment and realised that everything around her belonged to *them*. She had to take back control of her life, otherwise Evan would be a distant memory.

She started to eat a little, to take a few steps outside and breathe in fresh air.

She'd wrap up in layers of mismatched clothes and spend hours looking at the undulating black swell of the river. Slowly, over a few days, her health improved a little.

One day, she'd caught three separate buses and finally, after a ten-minute walk, reached the gates to Medlock Hall. When they had eventually opened to allow a delivery van through, she had walked up the driveway.

She looked up and saw the bedroom where she'd sat for all those weeks, unaware that she'd been little more than a prisoner from the moment she'd arrived.

She rang the bell. Patricia opened the door and called to Geraldine.

She came to the door with a small boy of about eight months on her hip. He had soft brown hair and he looked like Brendan, but his eyes... his eyes were mirror images of Holly's own.

'Evan,' Holly had whispered.

'You need to arrange a proper visit.' Geraldine had looked pale and nervous. 'You can't just turn up like this.'

'But it's never a good time!' Holly had shrieked. 'He's mine. Evan is *mine*!'

She'd reached to touch him and Geraldine had jumped back. Evan began to cry.

Geraldine had shouted at Patricia to close the door, but Holly had put her foot inside.

'I want to see my baby,' she'd screamed. 'He's mine!'

'Look, Brendan got sole custody through the court as his biological father,' Geraldine told her. 'You're an unfit mother.'

'That's impossible,' Holly gasped. 'I can prove I'm his mother. I'll—'

'It was *proven*, on doctor's evidence, that you are a drug addict. We have witnesses, photographs of you passed out drunk on the street. Take it to court... see how far you get. The judge will laugh in your face. Brendan is Evan's father and we'll always fight for him. You'll save yourself a lot of heartache if you just accept that.'

Holly had staggered back as the door slammed in her face.

She'd stood there on the step for a minute or two as reality hit.

The job that Brendan had offered her was never as a companion to his wife. It had one duty only: to produce a baby who'd possess Brendan's own DNA.

After that, they'd engineered Holly's demise in order for Brendan to win sole custody.

Evan lived with his millionaire father.

She'd never have the money to fight Brendan and win her son back.

But that was only so long as she played their game…

Two weeks later, Holly was evicted from the apartment.

One day she was lying in bed with a broken heart; the next, the bailiffs were knocking on the door.

One of the thuggish-looking men had pointed to a pile of unopened mail on the carpet.

'You'll find numerous communications giving you notice in that lot. Then there's this…' He'd pointed to a notice stuck to the apartment door. 'That says you were to be out of here yesterday.'

She'd gathered up a few meagre belongings and walked out onto the street. It was a drab day. The roads were busy but there weren't many pedestrians around.

She'd walked into town. Her feet had recognised the vehicle before her brain caught up. It was a distinctive black G-Wagen.

Brendan had parked, just like that time outside Costa, half on the road, half on the pavement, on double yellow lines. She'd looked around but couldn't see him anywhere, although there were lots of office buildings nearby.

She'd crouched down by the jeep, pretending to tie her shoe-lace. When there was a lull in the flow of traffic, she dumped her rucksack next to a large litter bin and lay flat, shuffling under the vehicle until she was directly underneath the driver's side.

At least there was one benefit to being skeletal, she'd thought wryly.

You could get flattened… he could drive over you… you'll get caught…

'I don't care,' she'd told the voice in her head. 'I don't want to live.'

She'd lain there for just five or six minutes when she heard shoes scuffing on the asphalt. She heard Brendan talking on his phone and the beep as he unlocked the car. Next, she heard the heavy rumble of an approaching HGV.

Then suddenly, his boot-clad feet were next to her face, and as the rumble of the truck grew closer, she reached out and grabbed his ankles, pulling hard and sending him careering off balance and into the road.

The screech of brakes, Brendan's scream... She didn't wait to see the glorious result of her impulsive gamble.

She'd crawled to the edge of the chassis, squeezed out from under the jeep, picked up her rucksack and walked away.

She just walked away and she didn't look back.

CHAPTER 73

David

'I don't know how long I was in the clinic, but it seemed a long time,' Holly says softly. 'Nobody believed me about what happened, about Evan. I told the nurses, the doctors, and they just thought I was deluded.'

'What about Brendan?' I ask her. 'Did they find out what you did?'

'No. Incredibly, I got away with it. They thought he'd been distracted by his phone and stumbled into the road. The caller on the end of the line heard the truck and the long beep… It was classed as a tragic accident. But you see then *she* had my son. Still has. I have to find him, David.'

'We haven't got long. The ambulance will be here, and then…' I look at poor Mrs Barrett's prone, lifeless body and feel a catch in my throat. But I have to press on. 'You told me you were scared of someone from your past trying to find you… that someone was watching you.'

'I got… confused,' she whimpers. 'Some of it I did so you'd protect me, so you'd get closer to me. I sent the letter to myself; I imagined someone at the end of the garden… I mean, I *convinced* myself it was true.'

'But now you think there was nobody there?'

Holly shrugs and squeezes her eyes closed. 'It's like a house of cards has collapsed around me. All this time I've believed Geraldine would look for me, that she'd suspect I was the one who killed Brendan. I've felt Evan's presence in my head... as if he's missing me too.' Her voice drops and becomes faint. 'But none of it was real.'

'But why hurt Mrs Barrett? After everything she did for you... and you pretended to be my friend. This is how you repay us?'

'I liked you, David. I really did.' She says it in such a regretful tone, I almost believe her. 'You know what it's like to be an outsider. Perhaps we could have been true friends under different circumstances.'

I stand up. 'I have to call the police now, you know that, don't you, Holly?'

She smiles at me.

'You still don't understand the final part of my plan, do you, David?'

I look at her.

'I didn't hurt Cora. *You* did. You pushed her so hard she cracked her head on that fireplace.'

I shake my head and scowl at her. She sounds just like Mr Brown – blaming everything on me, trying to wriggle out of what he'd done.

'No, Holly.' I swallow hard and stare at her stretched mouth. 'The truth is, you got mad and pushed her. I followed you just to try and help, that's all.'

'*You* pushed her, David. Your fingerprints are all over the headboard. There's a copy of the lottery letter addressed to Cora in your crummy kiosk at work. I put it there, you see. There's a recorded conversation between your mother and Cora, both worrying about your erratic behaviour and the possibility that you haven't been taking your medication.'

She holds her phone up above her head.

'When I went outside for air, I rang the police, not the ambulance. And they'll be here any moment.'

I stare at her, lost for words. Eventually I say, 'Why? Why betray *me*, your one true friend?'

'I wanted to find Evan, and for that I needed money, lots of it. I'd been watching Cora for a while; I knew she'd be in the post office queue that day. I'd got to know her routines, but only with a view to finding a place to stay. I thought she was probably well off but never actually knew she'd had a lottery win until I found the letter, and then it all dropped into place. And you... you were a gift. An oddball next door who everyone knew was strange.'

I pause, unsure whether to tell her. Nothing around here seems certain any more. Holly doesn't seem like Holly any more. Perhaps she's just like all the others.

'What is it?' She narrows her eyes at me.

'Markus told me what happened. When you were in the hospital.'

She stares.

'Geraldine couldn't cope without Brendan. She became terribly depressed, and...'

'Go on.'

'Holly, she went into the garage with Evan and killed them both. Carbon monoxide poisoning.'

Her face crumples in on itself. I cover my ears as she roars in pain like a wild animal.

I want to put my arm around her shoulders but I can't quite manage it.

She jumps away from me and starts stuffing money in the bag again.

'It's a lie. Not true. Not true.'

'Holly. Markus told me they're all dead... Brendan, Geraldine and Evan. You're the one who's inadvertently been living a lie all this time.'

There's no reaction; it's as if I haven't spoken. Her eyes aren't flashing any more, they're empty. Dead.

'I'll get away with this just like I got away with killing Brendan.' She's so self-assured, I could almost believe her.

'You don't get away with everything, Holly. I saw you break that vase at work; I was watching from the top of the stairs when you snapped the flowers off.'

Shock flits over her face, but just as quickly it is gone.

'I'm sorry it had to be you, David,' she continues. 'You were a gift to me, the final piece of the jigsaw. I don't believe what you're saying about Geraldine and Evan. Markus lied to me all those years ago and he's lying again now.'

She looks to the window, craning her head in anticipation of the police arriving.

'But that's not the final piece of the jigsaw, Holly,' I say carefully. 'I'm afraid the puzzle isn't that simple.'

'I've got about twenty-five grand here and as soon as they arrest you, I'm out of here. I'm going to find Evan.' Hope flickers in her eyes. 'You should have carried on taking your medication, David. You made it too easy for me. Now your own mother will have to give evidence about how worried she was about your strange behaviour.'

'That's just it, though, Holly,' I say softly. 'Mrs Barrett... she didn't want to make things too easy for *you*.'

She stares at me.

'A couple of weeks ago she told me she had a bad feeling about you. She was big on feelings, Mrs Barrett.'

'Don't lie! She really liked me. She told me I could stay here as long as I wanted.'

'She did like you, but nevertheless, she had a bad feeling. She told me she didn't trust you. That's why she asked me to do a few extra bits for her in the house.'

She looks unsure. I'm feeling a little more powerful now.

'You're making no sense.'

'It's quite straightforward, Holly. Mrs Barrett had a bad feeling and that's why she asked me to install the covert cameras. In her bedroom and in the lounge.'

'What?' Holly's eyes scan the room. 'There are no cameras in here.'

'Look at the shelf, at Mrs Barrett's lovely figurines. The lady in the middle… she's not Capodimonte; she's just a cheap ornament off the market. Go and look closely at her.'

I hear car doors slamming outside, but Holly seems not to notice. She is entranced by the figurine.

'Oh my God… there's a hole…'

'And inside the hole is a covert camera. They're everywhere, Holly, and they feed straight back to my computer. The footage is captured in the Cloud. For the last two weeks, everything has been recorded.'

'You…' She flies at me just as the room fills with officers.

CHAPTER 74

David

Mrs Barrett left everything to me. The money, the house… every stick of furniture in it.

They found the will buried underneath paperwork.

It all seems a long time ago now. Here I am, almost two years later, the master of this house.

It's handy having Mother still next door. She likes to make my meals, but sometimes I cook for her around here. She likes time away from Brian these days.

I refuse to see him now. I'm done with tiptoeing around and spending time with people I don't like.

I've apologised to him, though, for losing my temper that day. Apart from a headache and a couple of stitches, he was OK in the end.

I still work at Kellington's, and they took Emily back when she asked if they'd give her another chance.

We never mention Holly, and I never did tell them I'd seen her break the vase.

Good friends don't desert people, and that's why I'm still in touch with Holly.

Sometimes, really bad things happen to good people and they're not always strong enough to bounce back to the person they were.

I, for one, am not about to write my friend off, as others have done.

The way Holly created that twilight world in her head taught me something. She lived in a place halfway between the truth and illusion, and I realised I'd been guilty of exactly the same thing myself.

I'd built Nick Brown up into some sort of superman who was hell-bent on avenging my interference. Yet in reality, he didn't give a toss about me, his wife or Della. He cared only for himself.

I've been round there to apologise, and we shook hands. I don't think we'll ever be best buddies, but I'm not scared to walk down the street any more.

I'm spending my time getting the house shipshape. I take swatches and pictures in to Holly and we choose stuff together. She says she lives for my visits.

It's a nice feeling, knowing that someone is reliant on you, couldn't manage without you.

The clinic staff tell me she's doing well, and although there's no release date yet, we both live in hope that one will come. It's a pleasant establishment as these sorts of places go; I pay the fees from Mrs Barrett's lottery winnings. The money Holly dreamed of finally getting her hands on.

When she recovers, she's going to come here and live with me. Just as friends, of course. We've both got our hang-ups, thanks to our colourful pasts.

I take a stack of new lilac-coloured towels upstairs. I bought them yesterday, when Holly told me she'd like a lilac and cream bathroom.

Before I get to the bathroom, I open the door on the left and look inside. Holly's old bedroom.

Her face smiles out at me from the thousands of pictures that cover the walls and even the ceiling. My secret photographs paid off in the end.

I spot the ones taken from the bottom of the garden with my zoom lens… Holly in her bra and pants, lit up at her bedroom window like an angel.

I thought my cover was blown that night she spotted me out there in the bushes. I was only there to watch out for her, keep her safe, but I've never told her it was me.

I don't want to worry her or disrupt her plans to live here.

I'm taking it easy, not rushing anything. I have all the time in the world.

But once she gets here, I'll make sure she never wants to leave.

A LETTER FROM KIM

Dear Reader

I do hope you have enjoyed reading *The Visitor*, my fifth psychological thriller. If you did enjoy it, and want to keep up to date with all my latest releases, just sign up at the following link. Your email address will never be shared and you can unsubscribe at any time.

www.bookouture.com/kl-slater

The seed of the idea for this book initially came from a newspaper article about a woman who successfully hid a troublesome past from all the people closest to her. It set me thinking about the different masks we wear: at work, at home, socially… We all naturally have many different facets to our personality. But what if we made a concerted effort to hide a sinister side? To appear one thing whilst secretly scheming to be another? It could have disastrous consequences for ourselves and the people around us.

I also began to explore, through the character of David, what it might feel like to be labelled as 'odd' by society when inside one feels perfectly normal. To be told to just 'be yourself' when actually that's the last thing people want to see.

Who are we, really? And how are we shaped by our past? These are the questions that prompted me to write *The Visitor*.

The book is set in Nottingham, the place I was born and have lived all my life. Local readers should be aware that I sometimes take the liberty of changing street names or geographical details to suit the story.

Reviews are so massively important to authors. If you've enjoyed *The Visitor* and could spare just a few minutes to write a short review to say so, I would really appreciate that. You can also connect with me via Facebook, Twitter or my website.

I've loved getting to know Holly, David and Cora whilst writing this book, but the voices of my next cast are already demanding keyboard time! Until Book 6, then...

Best wishes,
Kim x

 KimLSlaterAuthor/

 KimLSlater

 www.KLSlaterAuthor.com

ACKNOWLEDGEMENTS

I'd like to give especially huge thanks to my editor, Jenny Geras, who for the last year has looked after me so wonderfully while my original editor, Lydia Vassar-Smith, has been on maternity leave. Although I am, of course, very excited for Lydia's return, I will miss working with Jenny and would like to thank her for her guidance, insight and tireless enthusiasm for my work.

Special thanks also to Lauren Finger and Kim Nash and indeed ALL the Bookouture team for everything they do!

Thanks to my writing buddy and fellow Bookouture author Angela Marsons, who is there any time day or night to offer advice, listen to a moan or share a giggle… and to give Netflix recommendations, of course!

Thanks must go to my agent, Clare Wallace, who continues to give valuable support and advice in my writing career. Thanks also to the rest of the hard-working team at Darley Anderson Literary, TV and Film Agency.

Massive thanks as always go to my husband, Mac, and to my family, for their love and support.

Special thanks must also go to Henry Steadman, who has designed the most fantastic cover for *The Visitor*.

Thank you to the bloggers and reviewers who do so much to help make my books a success. Thank you to everyone who has taken the time to post a positive review online or has taken part in my blog tour. It is always noticed and much appreciated.

Last, but not least, thank you SO much to my wonderful readers. I love receiving all the wonderful comments and messages and I am truly grateful, from the bottom of my heart, to each and every one of you for your support.